T3-BPD-352

KNIGHT'S LEGACY

TRENAE SUMTER

Jewel Imprint: Amethyst
Medallion Press, Inc.
Florida, USA

Dedication:

For Carmetta Jean Adamson, my best friend.

Published 2005 by Medallion Press, Inc.
225 Seabreeze Ave.
Palm Beach, FL 33480

The MEDALLION PRESS LOGO
is a registered tradmark of Medallion Press, Inc.

If you purchased this book without a cover, you should be aware that this book is stolen property. It was reported as "unsold and destroyed" to the publisher, and neither the author nor the publisher has received any payment from this "stripped book."

Copyright © 2005 by Trenae Sumter
Cover Illustration by Adam Mock

All rights reserved. No part of this book may be reproduced or transmitted in any form or by any electronic or mechanical means, including photocopying, recording, or by any information storage and retrieval system, without written permission of the publisher, except where permitted by law.

Printed in the United States of America

Library of Congress Cataloging-in-Publication Data

Sumter, Trenae.
  Knight's legacy / Trenae Sumter.
    p. cm.
  ISBN 1-932815-00-7
  1. Women stunt performers--Fiction. 2. Knights and knighthood--Fiction.
  3. Americans--Scotland--Fiction. 4. Time travel--Fiction. 5. Scotland--
Fiction. I. Title.
  PS3619.U48K58 2005
  813'.6--dc22

                              2005020730

ACKNOWLEDGEMENTS:

To the Father of celestial lights for "every good gift and
every perfect present" for writing is a "good gift."
To my dearest husband of twenty-nine years, Joe. It's
still fun to have coffee with you every morning.
To Winona Sumter Cole who believed in
me and my dreams before I did.
To Leslie Metcalf Burbank,
my literary fairy godmother.

Chapter One

He that is slow to wrath is of great understanding,
but he that is hasty of spirit exalteth folly.

~Proverbs 14:29

Scotland, 1230

The warrior knight wanted to kill a man. He looked forward to it. His righteous rage at what he had seen demanded retribution. The village had been laid waste. Women and children were ill and starving. His loyalty to his King was the only thing that stayed his hand.

Sir Roderic de Montwain had been sent to appraise the conditions of the small clan of Mackay in the Scottish Highlands. He was to bring back a report to the King. More and more his mind screamed at the injustice of it. The outlaw Scot responsible for this was going to be rewarded, and King Alexander tolerated this travesty for one reason only. A woman. He wanted an alliance, a marriage.

Roderic was to marry the daughter of this renegade who had literally sacrificed his child for his own freedom.

King Alexander would bargain with a demon to fulfill

1

a promise made long ago to Elizabeth Mackay. As Roderic viewed the handiwork of Calum Mackay, he concluded that dealing with Lucifer would be preferable.

The outlaw Scotsman was a nuisance to the King. Alexander wanted him banished, or dead. Roderic would prefer dead. Yet, he held in his possession the very document that would free the man; a decree of clemency signed by the King. He was to present it to Mackay the very day his marriage took place.

Roderic had sworn his allegiance to the Scottish King, so he would marry. These lands would be his and these people of the clan, so skinned and tossed about, his responsibility, but he had no longing to marry, even at his age of eight and twenty.

The King wanted peace in this land and an agreeable marriage for Brianna Mackay, although his affection for the daughter of the outlaw was a puzzle to Roderic. King Alexander had not seen the girl since she was a child when her mother held a special place in the King's heart, and he had given her a promise to see her daughter wed properly, in spite of her father.

Roderic's loyalty was tested by the request. He had spoken freely of his feelings to the King.

"The daughter of such a man could indeed share her father's character, sire."

"No. I disagree. She was a sweet-tempered child, like her mother. I must hope that this marriage will be the saving

2

grace for all concerned, Roderic. I hate with a passion the very thought of the pardon. Mackay deserves to be hung a thousand times for his sins, but I must think of the clan, and the girl. You are needed there, and the marriage is necessary. The clan willnae accept you without it, for you are English. You must wed one of their own. Who better than the daughter of the Laird?"

So, it was done. Roderic stood ready to meet his bride.

Gavin MacLaurin approached, and Roderic turned to his friend. "Still no message?"

Gavin's handsome face glowered in rage. "None. Tell me the insult is enough to attack the scurvy dog and be done with it!" His tone was contemptuous, despite the soft burr of his speech.

"I struggle with my own self-control, Gavin. Do not tempt me to override it. The insult to me is of little consequence when we see the pain these people have suffered. Mackay feeds his band of thieves and leaves the women and children to survive alone!"

"Yet, he escapes again. I only hope your bride is worthy of such a mercy," Gavin said.

"Aye," Roderic agreed.

"She must be fair indeed, if she favors her mother. The King has spoken of her beauty, has he not?"

Roderic smiled and inclined his head. "Gavin, trust you to turn our discussion of battle to that of a woman's beauty. You are entirely too enticed by the subject of wenching."

3

Gavin chuckled. "I agree, 'tis true. Yet, it is a subject on your mind, my friend. Why not speak of it? You stand ready to marry a woman you have never seen. How can you not be curious, or concerned with the prospect you may be enchained to a homely shrew, or a goddess?"

Roderic gave an impatient shrug. "I will be content should she prove to be somewhere between. It matters not. I will not expect the lass to swoon with pleasure at our first meeting."

Gavin stared at his friend and silently disagreed. Roderic was a massive, self-confident presence. His profile was rugged and somber, and his strong features held a certain sensuality that never failed to attract the ladies. His hair was a shade between black and brown, silky straight, and fell past his shoulders. Gavin had witnessed many a lass strive to catch his friend's eye. He even used it to his own advantage by consoling their hurt feelings.

"This marriage is something I will endure, no more. It is for the land and the good of these people. My wife will not change my goals. It is her duty to obey her husband," Roderic said.

Gavin smiled indulgently. "In my judgment, few women understand the concept of duty and honor. A wife will be no exception. Perhaps you can instruct her on the responsibilities of a capable wife, but dinnae be misled. A woman will allow many things, but being ignored is not one of them."

"I have no intention of mistreating my wife in such a

way, Gavin. I do not share your jaded opinion. Women are fascinating creatures. I love their scent, their softness, the way they move. I find them capable of honor and courage. If treated tenderly, with the right amount of firmness, they can, and do display loyalty."

There was a sparkle in Gavin's green eyes as he raised a brow. "The same can be said of a good horse," he drawled.

Roderic smiled, brown eyes warm with amusement. "I thought nothing could make me smile today. I understand they have killed some of their horses for food?"

"Aye, though I thank all that's holy they had them."

The two men turned to the sound of voices suddenly raised in argument. A thin woman with pale, sallow skin and brown hair was trying to struggle past one of Roderic's men.

"Leave her, Alec," Roderic ordered.

She pushed the man's grip from her forearm and faced Roderic, standing proudly, defiantly, her blue eyes snapping to his. She took a deep, unsteady breath and looked at him intently.

"Ye be Montwain?" Her voice was brittle.

"I am," Roderic said.

He was unprepared for the sight of the woman dropping to her knees before him. She took his hand and kissed it, her hot tears bathing his wrist, and he felt her body shudder with emotion.

"I be grateful to ye." She looked up into his eyes. "My name is Mary. Ye have saved my bairn by giving us food.

I'll not forget it. I will pledge my fealty to ye this day, do ye want it."

Roderic's brown eyes were warm with compassion as he gently reached down to help her stand. "I do, milady."

She inclined her head in a respectful nod. "Ye be a mon of honor. Ye have shown kindness to this clan, so I will beg of you to extend your mercy to another."

"If you ask for Mackay . . ."

"Ach! May that devil die in hell," she hissed. "The mon raped my sister when she was little more than a wee lass, and died birthin' the babe, Kenneth." Her expression softened with the name. "He be a lad now of only four and ten summers, with bright red hair, but he is mute, never spoken a word. Mackay doesnae claim him as his own, but he willnae banish him from the keep. When you attack and breach the walls, I beg ye to spare him. Although fey, he wouldnae hurt another, for he is a gentle lad, and he dinnae rate a sword in his belly because his father is wicked."

"It is my hope that it will not come to that, milady. I cannot speak to you of matters of war. Yet, no one here save the warriors of Mackay will be put to death. If I see the boy, I will look to his safety," Roderic said.

"Bless ye, sir. I now at least have hope." She turned to leave them, her steps proud and strong when she walked away.

Roderic muttered furiously to Gavin. "God, give me the strength not to kill him."

Wanting to be alone with his anger, he turned on his heel

and marched away from the camp, Gavin in step beside him.

"Do we charge now?" Gavin asked.

Roderic soon spoke to him over his shoulder. "Nay, we will not attack the keep at this time. We will give him two more days. Have all the children been fed and looked after?"

"Aye, we have fed them from our own stores. Some are ill. We have done our best to make them comfortable. None are beyond recovery," Gavin said.

" 'Tis a blessing," he sighed. "I would dread the prospect of presenting the King with word of yet another death at Mackay's hand."

The thin old woman took another cruel blow to her cheek. Her stubborn resolve alone saved her from crying out, but a groan escaped her lips when she fell to the stone floor.

"You lied to me, you old witch," the burly Scot bellowed as he stood over her. Calum Mackay kicked the woman viciously, and she curled up before him in agony.

"You helped her escape! I should kill ye now, ye worthless bitch!"

Angus Mackay ran to shield the woman, his powerful body moving with an easy grace. He shook his head with defiance.

"Nay! Leave her be, Father."

Angus stepped in front of Edna. The kindly lady with

the long gray hair had saved him many a beating as a child by keeping him out of the way of his father's wrath, and he would do the same. Angus would fight the man, kin or no, for he respected the woman's courage. She had stood up to Calum Mackay in spite of his rage.

Angus felt Edna's hands wrap around his ankle as she placed her face gently on the back of his calf. His leg was bare, for he wore a kilt, and could feel the blood streaming down her face.

"You dinnae know what she's done! The little whore is gone! My own daughter has defied me! She's run off to rut with that Kincaid whelp!"

"Dinnae call Brianna a whore! How can ye speak in such a way of your own kin?"

The older man had a cold-eyed smile when he snarled his answer.

"She's no kin a mine! From this day she is dead to me! If I ever see her again I'll kill her myself. What do you ken we tell the English bastard waitin' at our gates to marry? I will have that clemency and be gone, or we will all be put to the sword!"

Angus shook his head in disbelief. "Brianna is truly gone?"

"Aye, every inch of the keep has been searched and there's no sign of her! Her horse is missing too, and I be more heart-sore for the animal than the girl."

"If it be true, she could not have gone far," Angus replied. He reached down to help Edna stand, and spoke to the

8

woman in a whisper. "Go, now!"

Edna walked away as quickly as her trembling legs could carry her, and Angus continued.

"I'll find her. If not, we shall do something else to appease the King."

Calum grasped his son's shoulder in a punishing grip. "All else be lost! There is nothing that will satisfy Alexander now except to see the lass wed. You find the little bitch and bring her back. If I don't see the pardon promised by the King, I'll burn this keep to the ground a'fore I allow the Englishmon a hold here! We must stall for time! I'll send a message to Montwain that his bride will be prepared to wed him in a week's time. Take Graham with you! I don't care what ye must do, but find her!"

Angus nodded curtly, and walked briskly from the keep to the training field. Spying Graham in the distance, he put his fingers to his lips and let out a shrill whistle. Graham came his way at a trot, and Angus studied the old warrior. Barrel chested and short, he had white hair and beard, arms with the strength of some one half his age, and a perpetual frown. Angus did not trust the old thief with his horse or his coins in any wager, but the man was more skilled at tracking than any other in the clan.

"Brianna has run off. We must go and fetch her, or there will be hell to pay."

"Aye. Calum willnae come with us?"

"Nay, he must try to bargain for time." They were silent

as they gathered provisions and packed them on the sturdy mounts. One horse was chestnut in color, a stallion that belonged to Angus. He frowned at the old brown horse Graham mounted. "Ye won't keep up on that animal."

"Aye, I will, for though he be not as swift as your red, he is agile on the cliffs, and willnae be dumping me from the saddle. What possessed the lass to leave us?"

"She wants to wed Kincaid," Angus grumbled.

"The Laird?"

"Nay, she cares for Alistair, the Laird's younger brother. Although I pity her going to the Englishmon, I dinnae believe she would defy Father, and I curse her folly."

They rode on for an hour until the tracks bore witness of another rider. Graham was on one knee as he studied the signs in the ground, and shook his head. "Laird or brother, it matters not."

"Aye." Angus knew the young man well; he was of the Kincaid clan to the north. Apparently, he had come for Brianna and stolen her away.

By nightfall Angus knew it was useless. They were too close to Kincaid lands, and he would accomplish nothing save their own capture if they crossed the border. Kincaid had Brianna now. They would be married, and she would become part of a clan in the Highlands that was both strong and formidable.

Alastair Kincaid was younger brother to the Laird, and he would call hundreds of his warriors to fight before they would give up one of their own. Calum Mackay faced enough tribulation with the King and Montwain ready to make war on him. He dare not attempt a rescue that would start another war with a rival clan. Brianna was lost.

The holding and all the land would go to the Englishman, and they would do well to escape with their lives. There was no way out.

Finally, their horses bone weary, they stopped near a waterfall, bedding down in the forest. Neither he nor Graham wished to think of the fight to come with Montwain. It would be the death of them all.

Chapter Two

…but time and chance happeneth to them all. For man also knoweth not his time.

~Ecclesiastes 9:11-12

SCOTLAND, OCTOBER 2000

"*ollow the lavender mist*? You can't be serious! You're daydreaming of mythical fairies again."

The tall man with the sandy blond hair laughed as he parried the sword thrust of his opponent.

Catherine Terril turned with the grace of a ballerina and made a wide swing to counter with five lightening-quick thrusts of her own. She knew all of David's tricks. He used mundane conversation to distract her, but she didn't allow it.

Cat worked very hard at her job as a stuntwoman on the film crew. They were choreographing a scene of sword fighting, and it had to be perfectly timed before they could present it to the actors.

"Don't play innocent with me, David. I know you're behind the joke. I didn't recognize the actor, but I know you talked him into it. The old man had a thin face, long, white hair, his eyes were bright blue, and he wore a long, black monk's robe. He pulled the cloak off his head, stepped in front of me, and said, 'Follow the lavender mist.' "

Cat whirled and drop-kicked David in the back of the calf just as he came close to disarming her. It was one of the more difficult parts of the scene, and she executed it well.

Cat was dressed as a medieval squire in black tights and a leather tunic. David was her boss, the stunt coordinator of the film, and he, too, was in costume. She continued to elude him while he used the familiar strategy of rapid, continuous blows designed to weaken her wrists.

For her size, Cat was extremely strong. Lifting weights and kickboxing had honed her muscles and increased her endurance. She was small-boned, however, and delicate in her build, and even the weight of her small sword eventually was a strain on her wrists. It was becoming difficult to catch her breath as she worked to keep him at bay. Bending down, she threw some imagined dirt into his eyes. This would be the actress' next move.

"Never fight fair when you're fightin' for your life, girl. You're learning, lass," said David. He did his best to speak in a rolling Scottish brogue.

"You're better than the actors with that accent! Stop! Time out! I've had enough!" She raised her sword to signal she needed a rest, then turned from David and wiped the sweat from her brow. She worked at dragging the air into her lungs.

"I don't want to be an actor," said David, breathing just as heavily. "Besides, you're the one the director is after! I know he offered you a part. Don't deny it."

Cat paced to walk out her fatigue. Her bright green eyes flashed when she grinned. "I won't. He did offer me a small part in his next film. He also asked if I would have dinner with him." She shook her head. "Not interested."

"Your first experience with the infamous casting couch?"

She nodded. David walked up behind her and took hold of her long red hair. It was in a braid which fell to her hips. "It's this dark auburn flame that's so thick and beautiful. Men love long hair."

"It doesn't matter. As you said, I don't want to be an actor. The only part I would ever want to play is Errol Flynn." She smiled, displaying straight, white teeth.

"Let's get back to your mysterious monk. Maybe he was a method actor? They become the character they portray for the duration of the film. He was probably using you to test your reaction."

She lifted her brow. "It's no mystery, even though you won't admit it! I'm a sucker for the legend of Excalibur, so you told him to be Merlin. You still want to pay me back for the loss of your tights. I told you Jim thought of that gag! We couldn't resist the idea of you dressed only in tunic and boots in that scene."

"Carter knew the shot would be cut off at the waist so he went along with it. Jim is too good a stuntman to lose, or I'd fire the blackguard. Plus, he can pinch-hit as a key grip when we need him. Directors love people who are multi-talented. It saves them money. You're a perfect example. A stunt-woman who's an expert on antique swords and cutlasses is invaluable on this production, although I think Carter would have given you the job on your choreography alone. He was thrilled with your experience. Also, it's obvious he finds you drop-dead gorgeous. He made a similar remark when he watched you work yesterday. Ready for another go?"

He took his stance and held up his sword.

Cat nodded. "In a second."

She stretched forward in a practice lunge.

"You shouldn't have turned him down, Cat. You've dreamed of coming to Scotland, and I happen to know you haven't taken the time to see any of the sights. Have dinner with the man. You needn't be afraid of sexual harassment. Carter Welles is a decent man, and that's not his style. He's divorced, but he doesn't have a steady stream of starlets in his bed, and we both know he could. I've spoken with him. He talks about his children a lot. I think he was very hurt by the divorce."

"Just what I need," she huffed derisively. 'My ex is a witch, but I can't stop loving her', or talking about her! I gave up on that type of man a long time ago." Cat shook her head.

"So cynical at twenty-four. You're too independent for your own good."

"Maybe. But most men I meet are interested in a

temporary sexual relationship with no commitment. I want . . . the fairy tale." She fluttered her lashes and bowed.

"I have a strong suspicion that you're just as innocent sexually as the princess in a fairy tale. True?" She favored him with a look that would strip the hide off at ten paces.

"What makes you think I'll answer such a question?"

David gave her a wink. "Don't be angry, Cat. I think you just did. I find your discretion not only admirable, but wise in this day and age. If you want true love with all the trimmings, you should have it. I wish you luck in finding it."

Cat resumed working on the routine for another hour, and was fatigued when she made her way through the castle. The director wasn't going to film the scene until sunset, so she wanted to find a secluded corner and rest.

As she had done often since arriving, Cat took a wrong turn down the corridor. The castle was like a maze, and she walked for about twenty minutes. Finally, becoming frustrated, she gave up and decided to re-trace her steps.

It was then she caught sight of the mist. It was lavender, but unlike any she had ever seen. Cat shook her head, convinced David had persuaded someone from special effects to be in on the joke.

She was intrigued and instantly determined to find out how they created such a pretty mist. It wasn't just lavender; there were tiny particles in the air that flashed like diamond dust. It swirled up from a narrow staircase.

Cat was so fascinated she was caught off guard when

someone appeared behind her. She took a deep breath as a startled scream fought its way from her throat.

"All right. That's it! I've had it with you!" She stared up at the actor in the black monk's robe. He pulled his hood back.

"Tell David it worked. You've had your fun! You frightened the life out of me, so he's paid me back in spades! It almost worked too well. My first instinct was to attack you with this!" She brought her sword down in a sweep to bring home her point. "Although it's not sharp and meant to do you no damage, it would make an excellent club." The old man smiled, his blue eyes shining.

"You needn't fear me, Catherine. Trust your heart. Follow the lavender mist. Use the keys. You never could resist a challenge, and you will enjoy the quest."

"Well, that's a new one. What keys? What are you talking about?"

He walked backward slowly, blue eyes piercing the distance between them.

"Trust your heart."

She ignored the melodramatic line and shook her head. "Wait! Didn't David tell you no one calls me Catherine?" She spoke the words as if amused. She wanted him to know she intended to be a sport about it. His black robe billowed out when he turned.

"None, save your mother when you were a child. She would sweep your hair behind your ears and sing to you

17

before you slept."

He watched her silently.

Cat felt a shiver as a wave of apprehension swept through her. She floundered under the brilliance of his gaze.

"How do you know that? David doesn't know about that. No one here knows my mother sang to me. She would sing that little song . . ."

Cat searched her mind for a plausible explanation, and glanced uneasily over her shoulder, looking for a way out. She was suddenly anxious to escape his disturbing presence.

"She loved you. Very much. As the song said, 'a bushel and a peck, and . . .'"

Cat stepped back and instinctively took a defensive stance as she finished the song for him in a frightened whisper.

"'. . . a hug around the neck.' Oh God! You can't know that! How do you know that? Wait!"

"Trust your heart, Catherine." Her feet were at once unable to move. This was no coincidence.

Her thoughts raced to her childhood. Her mother had died when Cat was twelve years old. Barbara Terril had tucked her in every night and performed the little ritual the old man had described. She remembered the softness of her mother's touch when she pushed her hair behind her ears, kissed both cheeks and sang the little song. It was their own private time. Cat was not at all sure even her father knew of it. As a teenager, there were many times she had heard

door was wooden, ornately carved, and polished to a brilliant shine. The mist flowed from beneath it. Green ivy framed the edges, and a heavy black iron gate covered the door. One padlock hung on the iron chain wrapped around the gate. The doorknob was golden with two key slots, one above the other. In the very center of the wrought iron gate was a black velvet pouch tied to the iron by its drawstring.

Cat crouched down before the door for several minutes, and touched the mist that flowed like water from under it. It circled and wafted around her hands when she untied the pouch.

Her fingers trembled as she opened the soft velvet bag to find three skeleton keys. Each key was unique and delicately carved. Curiosity tugged at her. What was behind the door?

Was it magic? The source intrigued her, but she wasn't afraid.

She studied the keys. One was longer than the other two. The two smaller keys appeared to be identical in shape and size.

Cat took the larger key and worked it inside the old padlock that held the chain to the gate. It opened easily. The chain was small, but heavy, as she unwound it from the iron gate and pulled it open.

Cat took a deep, shuddering breath and examined the doorknob.

"Trust your heart," she spoke to herself aloud.

There were two keyholes, one above the other. She tried one key and turned it, then the other. She turned the knob only to find it still locked. Cat began to get frustrated as she worked to open the door. She turned the bottom key first. Nothing. She turned them slowly in the opposite direction. Nothing. Finally she removed both keys, inserted them simultaneously, and turned them one at a time. She turned the knob and pulled.

The door came open, and she was pulled violently through the doorway in a powerful vacuum of cold air, rendered as helpless as a rag doll. The centrifugal force pinned her arms tightly to her body. The lavender mist enveloped her in a whirling vortex.

All she could do was scream.

Chapter Three

*For they sleep not, except they have done mischief
. . . for they eat the bread of wickedness, and drink
the wine of violence.*

~Proverbs 4:16-17

Angus heard the lass screaming before he saw her.
He and Graham bounded up from their plaids and
grabbed their swords.

The sound of the waterfall muffled her cries before she
slipped beneath the surface of the water. Angus handed his
weapon to Graham and plunged into the cold lake. He swam
to her side, grasped her leather tunic, and pulled her head up
to the surface. She had swallowed a great deal of water, and
coughed to force it from her lungs. The lass was doing her
best to drown.

Angus reached around her waist and felt the sword in
the leather scabbard. She didn't have the breath to fight him
when he dragged her to the bank. He took the sword and
deposited her face down in the grass. She was dressed as a
lad, but a mane of long auburn hair had come loose from its

braid and lay in a tangle down her back. She coughed up more water.

He unsheathed the sword and held it up to Graham.

"Would ye look at this? 'Tis light enough to be a child's toy."

"A pretty toy at that. Think ye she means to wield it?"

Angus shrugged. " 'Tis so blunt it will do little damage."

Cat was on her hands and knees. "Of course it is, it's a stage combat weapon. A choreographed fight isn't meant to cause injury."

They stared at her in confusion, then Angus spoke. "And what is a korrea fight, lady?"

"This is not funny. I don't care who's in on the joke. Give it back. The sword is mine, you idiot," Cat complained.

She turned over and faced them. Angus looked into a visage so fair that, were it not for her bedraggled state, he would think her a vision, an elfin beauty. Her eyes were the color of spring grass in the Highlands. Her eyelashes were black, long, and spiky wet. Her skin was creamy and her cheeks pink from her efforts to save herself from the deep water.

"Who are ye, lass?" His voice was soft, and his thoughts turned lustful as he gazed down at her curves beneath the tunic. The belt at her waist defined its smallness. Her body was slender; her hips slim.

"Who are you? You two don't work for the production company." She looked around, fear and confusion in her eyes.

"Befuddled, are ye? Ye saucy wench! Hit your head on a rock? Ye be daft. Ungrateful too! Angus, ye should have let her drown," Graham grumbled.

"No. She's too beautiful for that fate. Better she warm my bed."

"In your dreams, cowboy! If you don't work for Carter Welles, then you must be part of the Castle tour. Either way, I am not amused."

They both stared at her as if she had two heads. The older man enjoyed a hearty belly laugh.

"Now, ye are part boy, part cow!"

She stood up and reached for her sword. He wouldn't give it to her, but laid a heavy hand on the back of her neck.

"Your weapon belongs to me, wench, as do you."

It was the arrogant way he said it. Cat's temper got the better of her, and she caught him by surprise with a round-house kick. Her foot made brief contact with his groin in a sharp jab. Angus buckled to his knees from the unexpected attack, and let out a roar of anger.

Graham stepped up when Cat moved to take her sword. He grasped her arm and backhanded her across the face. The blow would have knocked her to the ground had he not been holding her arm.

"No! Dinnae beat her!" Angus spoke the words in a strangled gasp. It was difficult to speak through the pain. "If she pays, it will be at my hand!"

The girl stared up at Graham as if suddenly terrified.

She gingerly touched the blood at the corner of her mouth where her teeth had cut her cheek.

"Dear God, where am I? You would not have done that unless . . ."

"She's mine!" Angus said.

Cat scrambled to run from them, but Graham held her. He was kicked so much as they struggled, he roared his complaint to Angus.

"Ye want me to keep this demon from leavin', ye best help me. Or there will be a lot more damage to the body ye be lustin' after!"

Angus recovered enough to help Graham tie the girl, using leather strips to bind her wrists behind her back. Angus grabbed a handful of the auburn hair and pressed his knee into the small of her back. He pulled her head back until she winced.

"Ye fight me any more, lass, and I'll beat ye black myself. Ye be a scrapper, I'll say that."

She was having a hard time breathing as he pushed his weight down on her back.

"Give her another lick or two, Angus. She has earned it. She come near to puttin' an end to your wenching for all time." Graham let out a lusty laugh.

"Cease your jesting, old goat! I have a plan. If it's to be, she's not to be beaten! We must not mark her if she is to be given to the Englishmon as a wife. She can be Brianna!"

Graham narrowed his eyes. He glanced down at the lass,

now still and subdued as Angus sat astride her. He looked back at Angus and shook his head in disbelief.

"Nay . . . 'tis foolish. It willnae do."

"You think naught? She be as redheaded as Brianna. She's close to the same size. If we be crafty enough Montwain will never know she is not Brianna until they be wed, and we be gone! Even the King hasnae seen Brianna since she was a wee lass."

"And if the lass screams her plight to Montwain?"

"We don't give her the chance! She willnae be alone with him until they be wed!"

Angus stood up in a fluid motion and pulled Cat's hair, wrapping it around his meaty wrist. She cried out when she looked at him, wincing in pain when he forced her to stand. He tugged her hair to yank her to him, and placed his lips a hair's breadth from her ear.

"You willnae say a word to Montwain, lass," he warned. "If I say ye be Princess Joan, sister of King Henry of England, ye be it! Or I'll slit your throat here and now. Do ye ken?"

Angus could see he frightened her. It was his intention. She did not answer. Her eyes narrowed in anger, but she looked away from him and nodded.

Angus enjoyed the scent and the softness of the lass, and kept her before him on his mount during the ride back to the castle. She was weak and confused, did not speak, but he didn't miss senseless chatter from a wench who could be mad. He wanted her, but he fought down the desire. She was his captive, and she would marry Montwain.

Cat caught sight of the first clump of trees that looked familiar, and her heart pounded with excitement. The landscape was the same as she remembered around the castle used by Carter's crew.

"Merlin did it!" she whispered in awe.

She glanced around and twisted in the saddle, trying desperately to make sense of it.

"Keep still," Angus said. He tightened his hold around her waist.

Cat held back her anger. There were a number of things she could do to defend herself, but not while they were on a horse. Reluctantly, she held her tongue. Although it was not in Cat's nature to bide her time and wait, it wasn't long until they reached their destination.

Cat stared at the castle and felt a profound sense of relief. It was the same stone fortress, but none of the beauty that had been restored in her time was evident. They dismounted swiftly, and Angus took her arm somewhat roughly. She was dragged to a passageway that led to the great hall.

There were none of the rich paintings and tapestries that had hung on the sloping walls of the castle the film crew used. Cat felt a thrill of excitement. What would it be like to live in another time? Would she be able to return to her own time? She remembered only the cold vortex of air before she fell into the water. If it were still a portal of time travel, how would she find it again?

The outer walls of the castle had only high slit windows suitable for resisting attack. Angus took her up a flight of steps to a tower room, and Cat noticed the rest of the castle was neglected, somewhat bare.

But the room where the Laird received her was luxurious, crowded with furniture and with soft skins of fur on the floor. There were heavy leather pieces thrown back from the windows to let in the light.

Cat took an instant dislike to Calum Mackay. He was a huge man with thick, muddy gray hair and beard. The first time she looked into his eyes she felt a sense of evil, as if a rat had crawled down her spinal chord. He and his son wore kilts with the same colors of blue and green plaid. His chest was covered with more of the same.

It didn't take Angus long to inform his father of his plot. "Marry Montwain!"

The older man looked her over, glancing disdainfully at her clothes.

"Father, it be the only way. Look at her! She could stir any mon's blood! I want her for my own, do ye not agree?"

Calum brought his hand up in a dismissive, silencing gesture. He measured Cat up and down with his gaze as if she were for sale and the price was too high.

"I won't do this! My name is Catherine Terril! Help me

find the strange dude that brought me here, and I'll leave. You don't understand. I'm from another time and place!"

"Another time?" Calum laughed derisively. "Do ye fly with the fairies too?"

Angus smiled at his father. "She must have wandered off from her clan. Graham thinks her bewitched, or mad."

"Mad . . . but she be fair enough to stir the bastard's lust! Aye, she will do. You leave her be! It will be my joy to dupe the King and his English lap dog! Lock her up! She's to get no food or drink until she agrees!"

The older man dismissed them with a sweep of his hand.

Angus took Cat to a small, cold room that was bare of furniture. There was one tiny window covered with a leather skin. When he bolted the door behind him, she went to the window to pull back the skin and let a small bit of light flood the room. She was still damp and uncomfortable, cold and thirsty, but at least her confusion and fear had been alleviated somewhat since they reached the castle.

There was no sign of the twenty-first century. She was a time traveler.

Cat had a strong sense of adventure. The experience could be invaluable, and she was intrigued. But still, she had to be cautious. She was also a woman they all thought mad. That could be a problem.

Cat heard footsteps and a few moments later the tall brute with the red hair returned. He had a thin adolescent boy with him.

"This be Kenneth. He will guard ye. He is a mute, so don't think he can go anywhere for help. He hears us, but we dinnae ken he understands. He is fey. Touched. So ye should get along well." His voice dropped to a seductive whisper. "I will sharpen your wee weapon, lass. I'll use it to slice my bread from the kitchens. If ye ask me sweetly and give me a kiss, mayhap I will return it to ye. The sooner ye agree, the sooner we can be together. We have a bit of time before your marriage." He gazed at her mouth.

"Don't hold your breath! I'd rather crawl over broken glass!"

Angus leaned forward with a look of icy resentment. "So be it! Let the Norman bastard tame ye! He's welcome to ye!"

He shoved the boy into the room and bolted the door behind him. Cat was alone with the young lad who could not have been more than sixteen, with bright red hair. He sat down by the wall and watched her silently.

"So, it's true? You can't speak?"

The boy's blue eyes were expressive, bright, and shining. Cat sniffed and shook her head. She rubbed her arms up and down as she paced.

"I can't say I blame you, son. No one here would listen if you could. It's freezing in here. I take it they don't intend to feed me, either. Food I don't miss right now, but oh . . . what I wouldn't give for a drink of water."

She worked her hands through her hair in an attempt to dry it. She touched her swollen cheek cautiously and continued to pace.

"Old Graham packs quite a wallop, but then, you probably know that from experience. Pardon me while I pace."

She took a deep breath and was silent for a time. The boy watched her as though she were an animal he had never seen.

"A swollen cheek is the least of my problems, Kenneth. You see, I'm having a really rotten day. This morning I'm working at my job, minding my own business in Scotland and then like that!" she snapped her fingers, "my own personal magician slash travel agent appears! Merlin the Monk. Sounds like a bad rock group. Of course, you don't know what a rock group is. Too bad. You would think they were cool, just like everyone else your age. Anyway, Merlin the Monk tells me to follow the mist. I open the door and land in another century. Not only do I almost drown, I lose my sword to Mister Personality in the kilt!"

She stopped pacing and smiled at Kenneth.

"Wish you could have seen it, Kenneth. He took my sword, and I nailed him with a roundhouse kick right in the nuts! I'm sure that old boy felt like singing soprano for a couple of minutes. It wasn't enough! Damn, I loved that sword! It was custom-built to fit my hand. If I had been able to breathe, I'd have had a chance at fighting them. I'm not certain, though. It's not like I have a director to yell 'cut' when I've had enough. You notice, I'm avoiding the only subject I should be worrying about. Like, what the hell am I going to do?"

She turned to him and shook her head. "I don't know. I don't know, Kenneth."

The young man smiled brightly when she spoke his name.

"I suppose it's my persistent curiosity. I wanted adventure. Let's think for a moment. What was it Angus said? What was it he said? Who was the King of England? If he told me to be Princess Joan, sister of King Henry of England, I would be it or he would kill me. Princess Joan?" She put her hands to her temples.

"Think, Cat, think! Princess Joan married King Alexander the second. She's Henry's sister. He married her in an effort to make peace with England. Alexander the second died in 1249. That means I'm here in Scotland somewhere between 1200 and 1249." She leaned her head against the stone wall and heaved a sigh.

"Medieval Scotland. I always wanted to live in the time of chivalry, but let's think about it. No cars. No hot showers, no room service, which believe me, I could use right now. No carry-out pizza. No modern medicine. Now, that's a good one. No phones, no fax, no computers. Be careful what you wish for, Kenneth. You may get it. I'm going to miss my job."

She turned to glance at the boy. "I was exceptionally good at it. I trained and worked hard physically to do those stunts. Anything they came up with, I tried. I broke my collarbone once on a covered wagon stunt. David pushed me to do the fencing work after that happened. The work with the swords . . . now, that was fun."

She stretched and put a hand to the small of her back.

"Angus has an adequate weapon in that knee he put in my back. I feel kind of rough. As my daddy used to say, 'like I've been rode hard and put up wet.' "

She sat down wearily on the cold stone floor, and watched the shadows of the sun going down for a long while, then moved carefully to the only patch of sunlight on the floor. It did little to warm her.

Cat barely slept the long night, and was grateful for a crude iron pot with a lid in the corner of the room. She relieved herself discreetly after the boy dozed off to sleep.

The following day, just as the sun came up, they heard sounds of a battle. Kenneth became agitated and frightened, and Cat was concerned herself. She heard the horrible sounds of men screaming.

Eventually, she was left alone when someone came to fetch Kenneth. Late that evening, he returned with a small wooden cup of water. She drank it and thought it the most heavenly thing she had ever tasted.

"Bless you, Kenneth."

She sat in silence for a while, then, grateful that at least the sounds of the battle had ceased when the sun had gone down, she spoke again.

"I wonder how long I have before they kill me. I'll wager it won't be long. I don't plan to be their surrogate daughter and marry anyone! Can you imagine what kind of man they want to pawn me off on? If he's their enemy, it means there's a distinct possibility he's even more 'charming' than they are. It boggles the mind, Kenneth."

She tossed some of the thick curls of her hair behind her shoulder, and she smiled at the boy who watched her intently.

"It's funny, what you think of when you may face your own death. No one I know and love exists now, so I can't even say good-bye. My dad . . ."

She took a ragged breath and exhaled. She did her best to clamp down on her emotions, and she put her head on her knees. It would serve no purpose to give in to tears or fear, and she needed her wits about her.

Cat felt a slight pat on her shoulder, and looked up at the boy. He stroked her hair, his eyes troubled. He looked at her with such deep empathy and caring, Cat wanted to hug him.

"You're a good boy, Kenneth."

They both turned at the sound of the key working the lock on the door. The heavy bolt slid back, and an old woman in a dark-brown woolen shift came into the room.

Cat stood up and moved back defensively while she studied the older woman. Kenneth shook his head and smiled at Cat reassuringly.

He reached up and touched her face with the back of his fingers in a motion down from her cheek. He also beckoned to the older woman to approach them.

Her long gray hair was tied back and neatly plaited. There were bruises on her face. Her eyes were a lovely hazel color.

"He be tryin' to tell ye to have no fear of me, lass. Kenneth has his own way. He watches people. He must like ye fine if he reaches out to touch ye. He fears most, an willnae let them close. I've raised the boy. My name is Edna. So, tell me, should I fear ye? Be ye truly mad?"

Cat smiled at the woman's forthright question. She shook her head. "No. I'm not mad."

The old woman stepped forward and took Cat's hand.

"Listen to me, lass. I want to save your life. He will kill ye do ye not agree to pretend to be my Brianna. I heard him talking. The Norman at our gates be verra favored by our King. He's given him the lands to keep Brianna safe and punish the Mackay, who be a murderin' thief. He's robbed and killed so many, the clans to the north and south have gone to the King to demand justice. They've all tried to kill him and avenge their own, but he is crafty and has the power of a ghost for gettin' away. The Englishmon has five hundred warriors with him, and he has Mackay now like a rat in a hole. The pardon spared their lives, but the warriors be condemned to life as renegades. Thus, some were determined to fight. All but twenty of Mackay's men are dead. They did number to a hundred. Montwain has nothin' to lose or go back to, for the Saxons killed his family. He wants this marriage for the lands. The King is indebted to him. He be a fightin' mon of honor.

"Calum Mackay cares naught for the women and children of our clan. They have been starvin' of late. Montwain's men fed them before the battle. He wanted a marriage celebration, not a bloodbath. Now that Mackay's army is crippled, he sent another message. He wants an end to the fightin' and is still willing to wed. He must be a kind mon. Dinnae be afraid to agree to marry him. Ye shall come to less harm than being a prisoner of the Mackay."

Cat pulled away and crossed her arms. "Where is the real Brianna?"

Edna dropped her gaze as if ashamed.

"This be on my head. I helped my little lamb, my Brianna . . . get away to be with young Alastair. Angus wouldnae ha' taken ye if he had a choice. Tell me, lass. Do ye have family that will come for ye?"

Cat sighed heavily, and shook her head. "No. There is no one."

"How did ye come to be on our land?"

Cat's mind raced for a plausible lie. "I had to leave my . . . clan. I hit my head in the water. It addled me. I don't remember much before Angus dragged me out of the stream."

Edna nodded in sympathy. "They are pardoned by the King if Brianna marries the Norman. Mayhap in time I can sneak ye away. Ye have no choice. Montwain gives Mackay only one more night. I dinnae want your blood on my hands. Make no mistake, he has no fear of God's vengeance for killin' a woman. Ye will die do ye not agree to wed on the morn."

Cat's thoughts turned to the immediate hope of finding the time portal. It was not just the hope of possibly going home. She faced the fact that she might never find it, might be forever trapped in this time. It didn't matter. She still wanted to live. Desperately.

"I agree."

The older lady sighed in relief. "Good, lass. I now have an hour or two. We will spend them together, you and I. I will tell ye all I know of Brianna. Ye must pretend for only a bit. We will hope to steal ye away any way we can after we see the last of Calum and his band of thieves. Come, I will get ye some food. You need dry things and a bath."

Cat slept surprisingly well that night. She was given a comfortable room, and a light meal of bread, cheese, and fruit. The next morning her ordeal began, and she spent the first part of the day being primped until she was weary of it. Her hair was washed, combed, and curled.

Edna sent for a woman named Mary, who was told of the plot to deceive Montwain.

Marry scoffed as she glanced about before she spoke. "That devil Mackay will slip away again. 'Tis forever his way. Don't fret, lass. I have met Montwain. He is handsome, and kind. Ye may decide to stay once your eye rests on him. I never seen such a tall, wide-shouldered mon. I begged him for mercy for Kenneth. He told me, Edna, that he willnae kill women and children, and I vow he dinnae lie. I pledged him my loyalty. I pray he kills Mackay."

Edna quieted Mary in a hushed, frightened tone. Mackay always had his spies about the castle.

Cat was given a long silk undergarment that fell to her feet. It was a white chainse. Over it she wore a gown that Edna called a bliaut. It was deep green with a golden belt to hold a dagger. Ladies carried them to use as their eating utensils. Still, she was a prisoner and was given no knife that could be a used as a weapon.

"The gown is lovely," Cat said.

"Calum sent me to fetch it. It was one of Elizabeth's gowns. He wants you to look your best for the Norman."

Mary sat carefully fashioning a garland of flowers for Cat's hair, which fell in a glorious mass down her back.

"I have never seen such a pretty color. 'Tis not dark brown, or fire red, but a mix of the two."

"Thank you, Mary," Cat said.

" 'Tis time to go downstairs. He's waiting. Remember, child, to answer only to Brianna," Edna cautioned.

Cat nodded solemnly and picked up her long skirts. She hoped she could grow accustomed to such clothing. She glanced at herself in a mirror they held for her, and thought she really did look pretty. The gown could have been one from the wardrobe department on the film.

I suppose, Carter, I'll see what kind of actress I can be, she thought as she stared at her reflection.

They walked downstairs, and within minutes she was presented to the man she was to marry. Suddenly, she knew what Merlin meant when he had told her to trust her heart.

She knew why this had happened to her. It was a strange,

disturbing feeling as she met Sir Roderic de Montwain.

The first time she looked into his liquid brown eyes, she felt profoundly touched, as if he reached down inside her to blend with her soul.

She felt as if she had come home.

her friends complain about their mother's interference, and Cat found it ironic that she longed for the same, for just one more day with her mother; her sense of humor, warmth, and wisdom.

Merlin. *Mama, how did he know?* Was he the man of magic and legend? Time traveler? It was too outrageous to believe.

Her skin was clammy and cold, and she stood still for a long while. The mist was now sweeping around her boots, and she turned to watch the narrow stairs from which it came. She had been frightened, but now felt a profound curiosity. It settled over her shoulders like a warm blanket.

As if hearing her own voice would bring her back to reality, she spoke aloud. "Face it, girl. You're too inquisitive to retreat."

It was colder, and the air was musty when she followed the steps down to a long passageway. The mist came from the left, and her steps slowed while she pondered the wisdom of her actions. Nervously, she ran a hand through her hair and continued on to another staircase. This one went straight down, the narrow steps banked by the castle walls.

"This is a nightmare of claustrophobia," she said as she sheathed her sword in the scabbard at her waist. She put her hands on either side of the walls and made her way gingerly down the ascent. When she saw the door, Cat gasped out loud at the beauty of it.

It was very low, suitable for a child's playhouse. The

Chapter Four

Be ye therefore merciful, as your Father is merciful.
~Luke 6:36

"Tell me again ye dinnae care if she be comely," Gavin whispered.

Roderic turned to give Gavin a silencing frown. *He jests because he knows I am unnerved.* Roderic stared at the beautiful young woman and, for a moment, could not catch his breath. Brianna Mackay was exquisite. She was a goddess, indeed, with dark red hair and green eyes. Her skin was flawless and her mouth, dear heaven, her mouth could lead an archbishop to sinful thoughts.

He was grateful she had taken his mind from the desire to do murder. Calum Mackay stood smirking, his hatred for Roderic and his men evident.

"Ye must fetch a priest!" Mackay said.

"We need not. Father MacNair has traveled with us. He stands ready to perform the ceremony."

Roderic did not trust Mackay to provide the priest. He meant to take care that the man who married them was truly a man of the church.

"Be on with it. Think ye I am pleased to lose all that is mine? The stench of ye English will fill my home, and I have no wish for it in my nostrils!"

Gavin moved to draw his sword, and Roderic reached out to stop him.

"No! By the King's order! We will not!" Roderic said. "Cease, Mackay, or 'twill be your blood that stains these filthy rushes, in spite of your daughter." His voice hardened ruthlessly as he addressed his enemy.

"Another word and you will have the King's clemency wrapped around your own bloody tongue, cut from your head!"

Angus Mackay stepped forward and glared warningly at his father. He took Cat by the arm, and though his touch was gentle, Roderic had an urge to step forward and fling off his hand.

"Gentle sister. Go to him," Angus said. Roderic perceived the look given by the brother to be a veiled threat. His suspicions were many, and his inner voice called out a warning. Those in league with Mackay were plotting; he would watch his back. The great hall was filled with his armed men, and if Mackay attacked, he would be dead in an instant.

Roderic turned to Cat as she came to stand before him. She made a brief, awkward curtsy, then leaned her head back to look at him. Raw hurt glittered in her dark green eyes. She was afraid of him, and it didn't set well. He was immediately struck with the desire to take her in his arms, to comfort her, and convince her she need not fear him. He noticed the fullness of her mouth had a swollen cut on the corner. Had she been beaten? Was cruelty necessary for her to agree to this marriage? Her father despised him and the King. No doubt she had been told many lies about him. Mackay cared no more for his own daughter's needs than he did for the rest of the women and children of the clan. Roderic felt a hot, boiling anger at the idea of the huge Scot beating this lovely creature.

"Leave us," he ordered. "I wish to speak to the lass alone."

"Nay! If ye have the priest here, get it done!" Roderic ignored Mackay and turned to Gavin.

"Take the Mackay and his men to the next room. The two women may stay."

"Aye," Gavin said.

They were escorted from the hall at the point of a sword, and Cat sighed as she watched them stomp out of the room. Roderic read a wealth of meaning into her expression of amusement, seeing her father and brother in such a position. Her green eyes sparkled with it, and the beginning of a smile tipped the corners of her mouth. He offered her his hand.

Her fingers trembled when she placed her small hand in his. He bent down and kissed the back of her knuckles. He didn't imagine it. A soft trembling gasp escaped her when his lips touched her skin. She enjoyed his touch.

"Did they hurt you?" His voice was tender. Cat hastily glanced at the older woman standing near before she answered.

"No, no more than I am accustomed." There was a gentle softness in her voice, yet it was lyrical. He enjoyed the sound of it. But, her answer did little to quiet his discontent.

"Do not fear me, Brianna. I will never hurt you." He could see in the depths of her green eyes that although she wanted to trust him, she did not. He would give her time. He squeezed her hand gently. Far from being soft as a lady's should be, her hand was ridged with calluses. Roderic found even more evidence that condemned the Mackay men. She had worked very hard.

"Tell me if you do not want this marriage," he said.

Her expression was cynical as she raised a brow.

"Does it really matter what I want?"

Roderic knew the question was not all bluster. A woman had little say in these matters. "The King wants your happiness, as do I," Roderic said.

She sighed sharply and glanced away from him. "It would make me very happy to have my sword back!"

Roderic frowned inquiringly, shocked by her request. "Your sword?"

The older woman Edna, shook her head and made warning gestures from where she stood. Cat ignored her.

"Yes! My brother took it from me. I would like to have it back."

Roderic read the challenge in her gaze.

"And do you know how to use your sword?" A gentle amusement lurked in the depths of his brown eyes. He made her angry, and her voice was clipped when she answered.

"I do, sir."

He brought her hand up and kissed her fingertips.

"Then you shall have it. It will be returned to you."

She pulled her hand back abruptly, and Roderic smiled. He could see it was not her anger that rattled her composure; it was the shiver of pleasure she felt. She was unaccustomed to the passion that had flared between them from their first glance, and Roderic found himself pleased.

He wanted her. He wanted to kiss her until she begged him to take her, and longed to taste and suck her soft breasts so full under the green gown. Roderic could imagine the feel of her silken thighs around his waist as he plunged inside her. All this she stirred in him, all because of a simple kiss of her hand. Never having been so aroused at once by a woman, he was intrigued. All the favors she could have asked of him, and she asked for a weapon.

"So, you will marry me?"

She glanced about briefly as if the keep were on fire and she was trying to decide which way to flee.

"Brianna." His voice was compelling.

"I . . . will," she said.

Roderic had a hearty dislike for the reluctance with which she answered, but he overruled his bruised vanity as unworthy of his concern. It was crucial to see to her safety, and the way to do so was to get the marriage over and done. She would then be under his own protection and no longer subject to her cruel family. Roderic called to Gavin.

Mackay's men were brought back into the great hall. Father MacNair came forward and spoke to Cat.

Roderic took note of the small sword in the unusual leather scabbard that hung from Angus Mackay's waist.

"Brianna has told me the sword is hers. Return it to your sister," Roderic commanded.

"It be easy to stand so tall and preening with a hundred daggers at my back. Think ye the courage to take it, English? Justly, with no help?"

Roderic smiled and drew his sword, excited by the prospect.

"Aye. If you are determined to die, in spite of the King's clemency, I will oblige you."

The men from both sides stepped back to give them room, pushing the women aside. The Scots were anxious to see Angus spill the Englishman's blood. It would be salve to their wounded pride, being driven from the keep in disgrace. Gavin stood near the women, smiling as if he were beginning a game.

"You don't seem worried." Cat spoke softly to Gavin.

"Dinnae fash yourself, lass. Roderic could best four of your brother and not be weary."

Roderic and Angus crossed swords, and soon it was

apparent to all Angus was unmatched. He was unsurpassed in brute strength, but Roderic had more skill. He avoided most of his opponent's thrusts by his grace and speed.

Roderic was agile and strong, and Angus began to let his anger overwhelm him. It was a fatal mistake. Roderic caught the muscle of his upper arm with the first wound. It was not deep, but blood streamed down through his shirt. Angus countered with several blows hoping to weaken his enemy, but Roderic parried them and forced him off balance. There was a disgusted sigh from the Mackay's soldiers when Angus stepped back and left himself vulnerable. Roderic caught his upper thigh with the tip of his sword. The men were aware Angus had been given quarter. Roderic did not press his advantage.

It ended abruptly. Roderic disarmed Angus with one sweeping stroke that sent his sword flying through the air. Angus dropped to one knee as Roderic held his sword's point at his throat.

"No!" Cat cried. "Please . . . no more." She appeared ashamed as she stared at the older woman, who was now weeping. She turned to Roderic. "Just let him go. I merely wanted my sword."

Angus favored her with an angry glance. He reached down, untied the sword and flung the weapon at Roderic's feet.

Calum Mackay was ashamed of his son's defeat, and his voice held an undertone of cold contempt when he roared out his complaint. "Finish it!"

Roderic lowered his sword while Angus stood up before him. He glared at Roderic with burning, reproachful eyes.

"My father is right. Ye should have finished me. Ye will regret it, English. I'll follow ye to hell to kill ye, now."

Gavin came forward and grabbed Angus by the scruff of the neck and hauled him to stand with the others. They were heavily guarded by the soldiers.

Roderic picked up the small sword and turned to Cat. "Consider it a bride's gift," he drawled.

She was married with it strapped to her belt.

The priest began the ceremony, and Roderic watched his bride as the priest spoke. Her voice faltered only once when she made her vows to him. When it was done, Roderic turned to Cat and bent down to kiss her.

He planned a quick gentle kiss, and was quite unprepared for the passion that instantly fired his blood when his mouth covered her own. She gave a little whimper, and he found the sound incredibly enticing. She opened her mouth to him, and he tasted her, rubbing his tongue against hers. They heard cheers and laughter from his men, and he pulled away and smiled at her bemused expression. He kissed her again quickly, seeming unable to get enough of her.

Mackay demanded his clemency, and was given the King's decree. Edna tended Mackay's wounds, and when the task was done, Roderic's men escorted him, his father, and twenty of their men out of the keep. Cat did not so much as glance at her father and brother when they were driven out.

Roderic left Alec, his second in command, with Brianna, and began giving orders. The keep was to be cleaned, and Edna went to fetch women from the clan to help. When she began working and ordering his soldiers about, her boldness amused Roderic, and he spoke to the old woman briefly.

"Is there a chamber in this castle that is not in filth and disarray?"

"Aye. That be the tower room, the one Mackay himself used."

"Have it cleaned from bed to floor and make haste. Take my wife there and make her comfortable," Roderic said. He turned and succeeded in knocking a young lad flat on his back.

"Kenneth, watch where ye be puttin' yourself! Dinnae be angry, milord."

Roderic looked chagrined, and apologized. "You are the boy that does not speak. I hope I didn't hurt you." He put out his arm to the lad.

Kenneth got a mischievous sparkle in his eye and threw his body into Roderic as if wrestling in jest. Roderic's voice was deep and warm when he chuckled. He easily countered the boy's attack by hauling him up around the waist, and held him dangling like a sack of grain. Kenneth smiled, enjoying the game, hanging limp as cloth.

"He is a gentle lad, milord. He does love to play. Forgive him," said Edna.

"Be easy, old woman. He's done no wrong." Roderic set the boy on his feet and tousled his hair. "We will follow the Mackay to see them off the clan's border. You want to go on a short ride with us?"

The boy's face filled with joy. "Milord, Kenneth needn't pester ye so," Edna pleaded.

"Be at ease, he will come to no harm. Come, Kenneth, let's fetch you a horse."

Cat sat in a chair in the kitchens while Mary worked to prepare food to take to others who needed it.

"So, do ye tell him the truth? Tell him ye willnae answer to 'Brianna'?"

"I can't. He wouldn't believe me. No one will come for me from my clan. It wouldn't matter if I answered to Brianna Mackay or not."

"Edna tells me ye are not mad, but were knocked senseless in the water. Your speech be strange, but Kenneth favors ye. That boy . . . he has a gift of love in his heart. If ye be trustworthy to him, there be good in ye. I knew that by ye sparin' Angus just to save Edna's grief. I seen it in your eyes. Ye dinnae want to cause her pain."

"I don't wish to cause trouble. Edna was good to me, and even Angus didn't deserve to die for taking my sword."

"Sir Montwain be quite smitten with ye. Could it be ye

fancy him just a bit?"

Cat was astounded by the transformation, for when Mary smiled with a beaming sparkle in her eyes, she was pretty. No doubt the many hardships she had suffered induced the pinched, hard expression of fear which was so often present. Cat's attraction to Roderic had not gone unnoticed by Mary, yet she found no humor in her plight. Cat put her head in her hands, leaned on the table, and sighed.

"May I speak freely with you, Mary? You will keep my confidence?"

"Aye, milady."

"I don't know what to do. Edna said she would help me get away, yet . . ."

"Get away?" Mary was shocked. "And how did she think to do this with hundreds of Montwain's soldiers about? Think ye the man willnae see his wife is not in his chamber?"

Cat was suddenly running her hand through her hair in apprehension.

"That's just it. The marriage bed. I can't do this. How am I going to tell him I've never . . ."

"If ye think tellin' your husband ye be innocent will cool his blood, ye be wrong! Men love bein' the first to lay with a lass. I saw the way he kissed ye. The mon willnae wait to bed ye. Is it the lies wearin' on your heart?"

"In part," Cat admitted. She shook her head. "I had no choice but to marry him. Yet, I should try to make him understand that I'm not Brianna. Mary, someday I'll have to go

50

back where I came from."

"But not now?"

Cat had searched the castle when she was alone after Roderic left with the others. She had found no clue, no hint of where the portal could be.

"No, not now. I can't."

"Ye never did answer me. Ye do fancy him?" Mary asked.

"I'm confused. I can't describe it. My friends back home would call it 'falling in lust.' But, it's more than that. It's frightening, Mary. The first time I looked into his eyes, I felt he owned me. Even Samuel never made me feel this way, and I thought I loved him."

"Samuel?" Mary said.

Cat nodded. "He's someone I knew long ago."

"Will he try to come for ye?"

"No, that isn't possible," Cat said.

"Understanding ye, lass, be like walkin' through a fog. Did the mon have your father's promise for your hand?"

"No, he didn't want me. I'm sorry, Mary, I know this is confusing. I won't speak of my home. There's no point, because I don't know if I can ever go back there."

"Thereupon ye best be Brianna, until the day ye leave us. If Sir Montwain has his way, ye will be a wife to him. If ye fight him, it will change nothing. Men live to fight. I don't think he would be cruel to ye as many a mon would be. Yet, if ye leave, he will come after ye."

Cat said nothing in response. It was not as if she could

explain the portal was an escape that would leave no trace and no trail to follow. Her thoughts raced to what she had left behind, her own century, her own life.

Samuel was twenty years older than Cat, and she had been fascinated with him from the very first class he taught her at UCLA. She had been determined to complete the hours needed for her degree. He had a brilliant mind, and she was attracted to him from the very beginning. Cat had met him the first week she had arrived in LA, incredibly naïve. His brutal honesty had saved her innocence. Samuel used intellectualism as a weapon, making sure she understood their relationship was temporary. The experience had devastated her, and she went back to the ranch in Texas. It was one of the many times in her life she needed her mother. Her father knew she was in pain, but never asked why.

Howard Terril was a fair man, and she knew he loved her deeply, but there was a part of him that was extremely distant emotionally. His was a world of exhausting work and rough men, a third generation cowman from Texas, and he had worked diligently all his life to care for his family. Cat was determined to give the same effort on the ranch as those who worked for her father, and it was her talent with horses that was instrumental in securing her fist job as a stuntwoman. She studied choreography, then found it easy to combine the two careers. After the disastrous episode with Samuel, Cat had a fear of depending on a man too much. She was intelligent and self-sufficient, but when she fell in love there was a longing to immerse herself in the relationship, having done so with Samuel. Once he made it clear he felt smothered, Cat made every effort to bury that part of her as if it didn't exist, and she rarely dated. Taking extensive classes in sword fighting and fencing, she worked single-mindedly on her career. Finding an antique cutlasss at a flea market, she began to collect them, and took classes in medieval history to learn more about the weapons.

Her first job as a stuntwoman was on a television series, and it was there she met David. He offered her a job since his company contracted work from film to film, and she got to travel on location. She would miss her job, and although the movie work took her away from home, she seldom saw Howard when she was at the ranch. He was much too busy, and she was strangely bereft at the realization that she rarely had a conversation of any length with her father. The closeness, the connection, the feeling that she belonged, did not exist, neither with Howard, nor Samuel.

Roderic returned late in the evening, and Edna visited Cat to tell her he would soon come to her.

"Please forgive me, child. There is no way to sneak you away. There be too many of his soldiers about. I wanted to save your life. The Mackay is a viper! Montwain will care for ye as his wife. He has mercy in his soul. He let Angus go, though he could have done as he pleased. He called me 'old woman' as if I were honored, not scorned. He willnae mistreat ye. Does your heart belong to another? Is that why ye be so troubled?"

There was guilt and compassion in the old woman's expression.

"No. There is no one else," she replied, and let the memory of Samuel go. "Don't fret, Edna. I will find my own way out of this tangle."

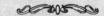

Roderic had just finished his bath and was donning his boots when there was a knock at the door. He stomped his foot down into his boot and opened the door to see Mary with a tray of food.

"Ah, Mary, enter," he said. She walked swiftly into the room and set the tray down on a small table by the window. She moved back and watched him warily as he sat down to eat.

Roderic took a drink of ale as she stood silent, wringing her hands. "Fear me not, lady. May ye have peace."

"Aye, Sir Roderic," she said, raising her gaze to his hesitantly.

"Your child continues to fair well?"

"Aye, she is no longer hungry, and I thank ye for your forbearance with Kenneth."

"How long has it been since the death of his mother?"

"Kenneth is four and ten summers. Edna decreed that he would stay at the keep when Judith died. Edna runs the keep and saw to Mackay's comforts, so he dinnae deem the child worthy of courting her displeasure. How I wish she could have stopped his interest in wee Judith 'afore it became a danger to her."

"May your sorrow for her pain abate in time," Roderic said.

"Ah, Sir Roderic, ye know not what it is for a woman to be defiled in such a way." There was a pensive shimmer in the shadow of her eyes.

"Think you I am intent on rape this night?"

She raised a brow. " 'Tis little to stop ye."

"I willnae harm her, Mary. Brianna has been given to me by the King, yet I shall not force her to come to my bed. Rape is an act of war. I am bent on seduction. If I am not to win the lady this night, there are many nights in the future to make it so."

She heaved a heavy sigh.

"Thereupon, sir, may ye fair well in your quest."

She turned and left the chamber, and Roderic paced for several minutes, his face tight and grim. He turned as Cameron, one of the King's loyal men, entered.

The man was one of the first to pledge loyalty to Duncan's plan for the Mackay lands, in spite of the command being given to Roderic. Cameron was a distant relative of the King, and a fierce warrior with superior skill. Roderic trained his men well, and Gavin had boasted that Cameron had joined them because he longed to fight beside the strongest armed force in the Highlands. Roderic respected the man's loyalty to Duncan, and Cameron had backed him in battle often. They were more than comrades, for Roderic trusted him, and valued his counsel.

"What has ye so vexed? A mon just wed should ponder the comely lass he is to bed this night. Were she mine, I would make haste to be with her."

"Ye find her tempting?" Roderic's expression clouded even more. Cameron had merely favored his bride with a compliment. Was he already experiencing jealousy?

Cameron shrugged. "With respect, I do, Sir Roderic. Yet, I forget ye dinnae want to wed."

Roderic shook his head. "Aye, I did not. Still, in time, I had hoped to marry. Every man holds dear the thought of his own sons. I had hoped to have a bride that would deem me her lover, not her owner. I had judged this marriage a yoke I must bear. I had not believed that I would be looking forward to bedding the lady with such joy that I seek to revel in it."

Cameron's eyes danced when he laughed. "So, ye be flesh and blood now, not merely a leader who must please the King? Ye need a wench. A mon gets too muddled about with duty when he doesnae gift himself with a woman's touch. Ye seek to be more Scot than the Scots ye lead, and a commander full of charity to the Mackay clan. Ye are as cautious as an altar boy hoping to please a priest, when there be no need of it. Were she Gavin's, the lass would be screaming her pleasure at this moment."

"Mary thinks I will make her scream, not in pleasure, but when I rape her. They all distrust and fear me. I know it will take time to win this clan's loyalty, yet I am sickened by the assumption. I sought to remove her from her father's dominion, not to torture her with my own."

"Aye, and they will see it in time. Ye think as an Englishmon. We Scots be stubborn. We must be shown proof, with coin in our hand, 'afore we shear the sheep."

Roderic smiled, considering the apt declaration. He leaned forward with quiet assurance. "Thereupon, I will give the clan and my bride their proof. Rather than ravage her as they hope to see, I shall treat her as a cherished gift and break down the wall of their lies."

Cameron shrugged. "Ye fancy the wench. Go to her."

Roderic's brown eyes contained a sensuous flame. He turned and left the chamber, resolving to do just that.

Gavin walked briskly through the keep. He had seen the new bride steal out of the tower room and down the corridor, and he had an arrogant grin on his face when he found Roderic making his way to the tower.

"She willnae be waitin' for ye. Your lovely bride has

made an attempt to flee."

Roderic frowned. "And you did nothing to stop her?"

Gavin's eyes twinkled, making an attempt to stifle his amused chuckle.

"That be the husband's chore. She went hence forth." He pointed casually over his shoulder toward the stairs.

Roderic marched to find her, doing his best to ignore Gavin. He saw her on the balcony moving with silent haste, and ran to catch up with her.

"Brianna!"

She turned at the top of the stairs. He had startled her, and she looked frantic. There was very little light from the candle she carried, and he didn't want her to take a fall.

"Roderic, I have to go."

He folded his arms casually and leaned into the wall, smiling.

"You are not very prepared to go out of the castle, sweeting . . . you're barefoot."

Cat noticed his hair was damp. It was evident he had just bathed. Roderic took the candle and set it on the stone step beside them. Cat glanced down at her bare toes peeking out from under her cloak.

"I couldn't find my . . . shoes . . . those slipper things," she whispered.

She was embarrassed and flustered. His stare was bold and assessed her frankly, his gaze falling to the creamy expanse of her neck. He could see the quickened pulse there and stepped closer.

She was frightened, and he meant to calm her. He could see the silky white undergarment near her feet under the cloak. Was that all she was wearing? The thought immediately aroused him.

"Come, Brianna. Come with me." His voice had a rasp of excitement.

"You don't understand. I'm not who you think I am," she said.

Roderic reached out to her, his strong hands clasping her waist gently. "You are my wife. Brianna, sweeting, come to our chamber now." He bent his head to place a feather light kiss on her temple.

She was overwhelmed by his warmth, his clean masculine scent. She wrestled with the desire to completely surrender to this strong, handsome man.

"You don't understand. I'm not prepared to make love. We can't do this."

She spoke with quiet desperation, stammering and struck with the ludicrous nature of her remark about preparation. It was a knee-jerk reaction. She had used the excuse to many a date in her own time, for everyone understood the need to practice safe sex. It was meaningless here and now.

Roderic touched her cheek and spoke in a fervent whisper as he slipped his arm under her cloak to encircle her waist.

"Beautiful Brianna, you needn't proclaim your innocence to me. This I know and bless God for the gift." He felt her tremble when he moved to kiss her. She turned her head away, and the kiss fell on her cheek, next to her lips, now parted.

"You are my wife. Don't push me from your arms, when I have thought of little this day save the softness of your mouth under mine."

He kissed her then, his lips urging hers to open for him. His moist, firm mouth demanded a response. She tried to resist him, and he felt her struggle with her own longings, and found it intensely exciting when she whimpered, a soft sexy sound, and opened her mouth to him. Groaning at the subtle invitation, he coaxed her, gently moving his hand to the back of her neck as his mouth pleasured hers.

She pulled back from him in a brief attempt to elude his embrace.

"I can't," she whispered.

He felt bereft at the loss of her mouth. Untying the cloak, it fell from her with one sweep of his hand, and he pulled her to him gently, kneeling to wrap his arms around her legs under her buttocks. When he lifted her, she grasped his shoulders.

Her breast brushed his mouth, and she gasped sharply as she was held, suspended above him. Laying his cheek to her bosom, he nuzzled the pillow of her breast, and looked deeply into her eyes.

"Gentle virgin, do not fear me. Trust me. Let me drink of your beauty and get lost in you. Open your mouth for me."

The fear was there, glittering in her emerald green eyes, although her cheeks were flushed with desire when she touched his mouth to stop his words.

"Roderic, we mustn't," she whispered.

Moving his tongue to her finger, she shivered when he drew it into his mouth and began to suck gently. He watched the nipples of her pretty breasts pucker with desire beneath the soft white gown, and she cried out with passion when she bent down to rest her forehead upon his.

"You . . . are a master of seduction," she whispered.

He kissed her again, and she responded by placing her hands on his face to hold him. He reached up to stroke her backside while he plunged his tongue inside her mouth. He pulled back enough to speak, breathing hard as if he had been running.

"Who better to seduce than my wife? Your body tells me it enjoys my touch, Brianna."

He moved his hand up to her breast and brushed the back of his knuckles gently across the nipple. He watched her body shiver with pleasure, and saw the evidence of her desire as her breast swelled to his touch. Cupping it, he kneaded gently.

"You see? Tell me now you don't want me."

He brought his hand down slowly between their bodies from her breast to the apex of her legs. He brushed his thumb over the soft nub of flesh that was the heart of her desire.

"Oh!" she cried out and grasped his shoulders firmly,

digging her nails into his skin.

"Here?" he groaned.   He watched her as she opened her eyes to him. She was breathtaking in her passion, green eyes shimmering and glazed, heavy-lidded with desire. Her mouth parted in a soft gasp when he stroked her again.

"Tell me you don't want me here. Pressed closer . . . deep inside you."

She whimpered again, helpless as he overruled her with his passion. She closed her eyes as if she were in pain, leaned her head back, and bit her lip before she answered.

"I can't."

The two words were a desperate whisper, a reluctant surrender. She was set on her feet, and she scarcely took a breath before he picked her up with one swift movement, one strong arm at her back, and another slipping under her knees. Holding on, she put her arms around his neck and tucked her face in the curve under his chin.

Roderic marched purposefully down the hall to their chamber.

Chapter Five

Rejoice with the wife of your youth; let her breasts satisfy thee at all times; and be thou ravished always with her love.

~Proverbs 5:18-19

Roderic was infinitely gentle as he lay Brianna down on the bed beside him. "You are freezing, little one." He stroked her skin from ankle to knee. "I will do my best to warm you." He pulled her close, gently massaging her feet and legs.

By all above, she was a vision as she lay before him. Her hair fell in a thick curtain of curls to her waist. The thin white undergarment did little to conceal the dark red curls where her legs met. He could see the blush that stained her cheeks even in the firelight. She tried to cover herself, but he caught her hands to hold them on the quilt beside her.

"Don't hide from me . . . Brianna, let me look at you. I won't take you with haste. I want your pleasure, your joy."

He held her hands gently, brushing his thumbs over the back of her knuckles.

She spoke in a trembling whisper. "I'm afraid of what I want."

"Why?" He frowned.

"Because I want you to kiss me again." She said the words as if admitting a grievous fault. He took her right hand and placed it on his chest. He brought her left hand up to kiss the palm.

"Do not fear your desire, Brianna, for I want to kiss you, little one, so much I ache with it."

Her small hand was caressing his chest, exploring and lightly tugging the hair there. It was driving him mad.

"Where do you want me to kiss you, sweeting? Tell me. Let me hear you say it." His words were whispered, tantalizing, sensual. He kissed her hand, then nipped her fingertip. He sucked gently just to watch her reaction, and she spoke his name in a gasp.

"Ah, yes . . . you like that. On the stairs you liked it so much your breast swelled to my touch. Let me kiss you there, Brianna. This beautiful garment is in the way. Take it down."

He slid his hand over the white gown. It was becoming an agony to allow his wife to set the pace. He wanted to be inside her, and at the same time wished to slowly touch and caress every inch of her.

He stood by the bed and undressed. Her eyes moved over him, and he felt a ripple of excitement when she dropped her gown to her waist and held out her arms to him. Her breasts were full, white, and pink tipped. He watched the rise and fall of them with her panting breath.

"Kiss me, Roderic," she breathed.

He covered her with his body while his mouth came down to hers, and he stamped down his desire, determined to take time with her. She was very small, and he wanted to give her as little pain as possible when he rid her of her virginity. He stroked her warm, satiny skin, brushing her nipples with his thumb. His tongue mimicked the movements of lovemaking while he kissed her. She held nothing back from him, and he nearly lost his control when she began to sensually suck on his tongue. Her kisses could bring a man to his knees, begging to be inside her. He pulled back to cup her face in his hands.

"Tell me, sweeting . . . where do you want my kisses?" he whispered intimately.

"Roderic, please . . ."

Her voice was thick and unsteady.

"Tell me," he insisted.

Her hand was shaking when she reached up to touch her breast. His smile was tender, approving of her acquiescence. He bent down to lavish her breast with soft kisses, and when he sucked her nipples her hips moved restlessly. He stroked them, and brought his mouth to her other breast, while pushing the gown away, and she put her hands in his hair to hold him.

She was shy of him in spite of her desire. His lovely wife

trembled when he gazed at her hips and long, pretty legs. He bent to kiss her silky belly, and her hands gripped his shoulders when his tongue laved her navel. His fingers went to the heart of her desire, the soft red curls that veiled his goal, and she made soft, whimpering sounds of passion while he stroked her, slipping his finger inside.

"How moist you are, my angel. So wet, hot, and tight. Yes . . . let me feel you move."

She obliged, undulating her hips with the motion of his hand. His warm mouth touched the pulsing hollow at the base of her throat, then her ear, while she opened her mouth on his chest, licking, tasting him. Stroking his belly, she closed her hand gently around his erection. Closing his eyes, he groaned as she caressed him, tracing the length, circling the tip. Her touch was sweet torture that lit a fire to his loins and threatened to consume him.

"No. Sweet."

He delicately pushed her hand away. "I shall spill my seed too soon if you persist. Forgive me, but I can wait no longer to be inside you."

He parted her thighs with his knee, then prepared her for his entry with his fingers. She embraced him, and he watched her face as she tossed her head on the bed.

"Roderic . . . please."

"I don't want to hurt you. Do you think you are ready for me now?"

She whimpered when he kissed her. "Yes, please, Roderic,

don't tease me anymore."

Positioning himself, he carefully moved her legs over his hips. Cat wound her arms around his back as he plunged inside her, and she cried out. The expression of pain in her pretty eyes wrenched his soul, and he lay very still, when all he wanted was to plunge into her sweet, hot sheath again and again.

Though her eyes welled with tears, she refused to let them fall, making a valiant effort to hide her pain from him. Roderic studied her reaction, his brown eyes troubled when she caressed his arms and shoulders.

"It's all right," she whispered hoarsely. "It doesn't hurt . . . that much."

He kissed her tenderly again and again and then gently nipped her earlobe. "What a wonderful liar you are, sweet," he whispered.

She reached out to take his face in her hands. She moved, and he groaned as she squirmed against him, the fiery sheath of her body sending a thrill through his.

"Please, little one. Be still now. I don't want to hurt you more. Be still."

His hand slipped down from her hip to caress her thigh, cupping her knee to bring it high on his hip.

Reaching down to grip her hips in his strong palms, he smiled. "Look at us. See how we are joined?" He kissed her deeply, then gently nipped her shoulder.

"Say my name. I want you to know who's loving you.

Tell me who you belong to." It was a gruff command.

"Roderic. I belong to you, my gentle knight."

Welcoming him with her entire body, she reached out to hold him, hands moving over his buttocks. Cat rubbed her feet on the back of his legs. "Come to me . . . yes, now. Come to me now," she said.

The plea sent him over the edge, moving to the age old rhythm of love. Roderic reached down to hold her firm backside as he thrust inside her again and again. A glowing image of fire, passion, and light exploded in his body. He said her name in a lusty groan. Although consumed by his orgasm, his hand moved between their bodies as he touched the soft red curls, stroking while he continued to move.

Cat was frantic for release. How did he know just how to touch her to drive her wild? She felt poised outside a magnificent realm of pleasure, so close; then suddenly, she felt it, pure and intense.

Roderic held her tight as he felt the wonderful spasms, her inner clenching that signaled the peak of her pleasure, watching her intently as she threw her head back and cried out. Her nails scored the heavy muscles in his upper arms. Beautiful, weak from her pleasure and breathing heavily, she slowly relaxed in his arms.

Cat reached up and touched his lips with her fingertips, her other hand stroking his chest, resting above his heart. Roderic was moved by the look in her eyes when she opened them, full of trust and caring. Catching her hand, he kissed the palm.

She fell asleep while he cuddled her to him. He moved from her body very slowly, but still he noticed her wince. It was then he saw the stain of blood on her thighs. Rising, he went to find a cloth and soaked it with water.

She slept like the dead, for she made no protest when he made her more comfortable by washing her. Keeping the blanket over his hands, he worked deftly in case she awakened. His wife was extremely modest. She turned over in her sleep, lying on her belly.

Roderic sucked in his breath in an angry hiss. On her back was a black bruise the size of his fist. He was instantly furious and wanted to shake her awake to demand who had done this to her, but he did not. She was exhausted, and he did not wish to disturb her. It was not necessary, for he knew the answer to his question. Mackay. Trying to fathom any man capable of slamming his fist in her back with such force, he lightly touched her silky skin near the discolored spot.

Roderic had been taught about honor and justice by a man that believed such was not an opportunity, but a responsibility of all men. Alexander took Roderic into his household long before he was the King of Scotland. The man made every effort to instill in him virtues that included seeing to the safety of women and children. Any man who would beat a woman was a despicable coward. Yet, Mackay was also a murderer, so that sin would hold no fire to his conscience.

He bent down, placing a kiss on the dark patch of her skin, and pulled up the blanket, folding her in his arms, his hand resting under her breast. Intoxicated by the scent of her hair as it lay in a swirl upon his chest, he picked up some of the silky strands and brought them to his nose and inhaled.

His thoughts were a chaotic tangle, and Roderic could not put a name to the anxiety he felt. His gentle little wife was responsible for the most overwhelming session of love-making he had ever experienced. No timid virgin, she did not weep and expect to be cosseted, but was a woman who reached out to touch and build his own desire with her every movement. He had just discovered that her virgin's pain must have been worse than he had known, considering the injury on her back, yet she said nothing, and even tried to ease his guilt at inflicting it. That concern inspired a deep and abiding tenderness for his bride. The lady was beginning to mean too much to him. He could not allow it.

Women served a purpose. A truly wise man kept his emotions far removed and safe from any woman, even his wife. Warriors did not permit a woman more power than she should wield. Roderic was a warrior, and he would not allow one small female to turn him into a lovesick squire.

The sound of rain awakened him. Sitting up to find himself alone in the bed, he looked about restlessly. His sword was in his hand and he was up making ready to defend her before his gaze fell on Brianna across the room. Taking a deep breath, he relaxed. It was raining, and she had pulled back the leather on the window. Wrapped in a blanket, she sat on the floor there, her head in her hand, silently listening to the rain. He put down his sword and went to her, kneeling down beside her.

"Brianna . . . what is it?"

She held up her hand in protest.

"I'm feeling slightly dismayed. I am not accustomed to being . . . married."

Sitting down, he pulled her into his arms so she sat on his lap instead of the cold stone. She pulled the blanket over his chest.

"You need not fear this marriage, Brianna. I want your happiness. I will take care of you."

"Will you do something for me, Roderic?"

He stroked her hair and cupped her face, brushing her cheek with his thumb. "If I can, at all cost, little one. What is it?"

She looked away from him into the rainy night. "Would you call me Catherine?"

"Catherine?"

His dark eyes were full of compassion, confused at her request. The sound of her pain, though it was a small worry, was intolerable, and he wished nothing more at that moment than to do all he could to remove it.

"It's a name my mother used for me on occasion," she whispered. "I was thinking of her and feeling lonely."

Suddenly, he understood; she missed her mother. He

had learned from King Alexander that Elizabeth Mackay was a kind, caring woman. It was certainly just that Brianna should miss her on the day she was married. That love and acceptance was replaced by cruelty from the moment her mother died. Roderic would indulge his wife.

"Very well, Catherine. You must come back to bed, sweeting. It's too cold by the window."

"Not yet. I like the sound of the rain."

He began to warm her by massaging her limbs and pulling her close. She reached out to him, nuzzling her cheek to his chest. There was a subtle desperation in the way she clutched him.

"You washed me, didn't you? You cleaned me up?" It was a shy whisper.

"Yes, little one," he said tenderly. He stroked up and down her back.

"You must have been very gentle. I didn't wake up."

Roderic shook his head and smiled down at her. "You slept so soundly, a broadax battle would not have awakened you. Come, let me get you back to bed. We must prepare for a journey, and you need to rest."

"A journey?"

"Yes. Our marriage has sealed an alliance. As soon as it can be arranged, we will go together to see the dear friend of your mother. He wishes to speak to you."

There was an amused glint in his eyes. He stood up in a fluid motion and carried her to the bed.

"A friend of my mother's?" she exclaimed, and turned to him as if confused, her gaze apprehensive.

He smiled and kissed her forehead.

"Forgive me for my jest. You have been heartsore because you miss your mother. Now is not the time for jesting. Do not give way to fear, for your mother's friend is your own, and your Sovereign. We will soon meet with the King."

"Please, Roderic! I don't wish to meet with the King! I am certain he will not remember me, and I have no wish to go! Please, promise me!"

He wanted to give her comfort, yet he did not understand her fear.

"Hush, hush now. We must go, but we will wait a few days if you need to make ready. Brianna, he means you no harm, and you needn't fear the King. He was very fond of your mother."

As he held her in his arms, he was aware that his gentle words had not swayed her foreboding.

Chapter Six

Withhold not good from them to whom it is due,
when it is in the power of thine hand to do it.
~Proverbs 3:27

Cat stood beside the bed and stared down at Roderic. Having an air of authority, his face was strong and handsome even as he lay relaxed, sleeping deeply.

I need to go home! What am I doing?

Cat muttered to herself while she searched for her clothes, pacing as if she were late for work. "Merlin, if you think this is funny, I'm going to punch your lights out! I can't stay here! I hate being without my cell phone! How do they communicate here? Smoke signals?"

She bent down on all fours, searching silently for her boots, continuing to mutter in a furious whisper. "My first thought when I woke up was 'I need to check my e-mail.' Then, I remembered where I am. I'm supposed to trust my heart, you say? Let's just examine my location, shall we, Merlin? I'm in bed with Mr. Gorgeous, but he's my husband!

Husband! The translation of that in this time period is he owns me like a horse!"

Cat sat up carefully, then stood. "Calm down, Cat, and think. Where the hell are those boots? Oh yes, the trunk!"

Cat tiptoed over to the trunk while keeping a cautious eye on the bed. Roderic slept on. Opening the trunk, she frantically pulled out clothing. Finally, she found the boots, buried deep under the clothes. Carefully, she shut the trunk lid, watching Roderic all the while. Dressing in a chainse and dark bliaut, she strapped on her sword and tiptoed out of the chamber. As she went down the stone steps, she found the black cloak she had worn and threw it on, pulling up the hood. One of Roderic's men, Alec, stopped her briefly. Implying that her husband knew she was going for a walk, she asked that Roderic not be disturbed.

Cat was relieved when the stable boy was still asleep, and thus made no move to stop her. Choosing a small sorrel with a dark mane, she walked out of the stable.

Having awakened with the thought that maybe the portal was not at the castle at all, she decided to ride to the stream where she landed. With desperate hope she could not abandon, Cat hoped to find it there, wanted to find a way out before it was too late for she was becoming far too immersed in her life here as Brianna.

Cat walked the animal past the clan's small stone cottages and went east through the trees. Once she was out of sight, she swung up on the horse and quickened her pace.

Riding bareback, she controlled the animal with her knees, the mare giving her little trouble.

Soon Cat sensed that she was being followed and, unsheathing her sword. She turned the horse. The rider made no attempt to hide his approach, and heaving a sigh of relief, Cat recognized the shock of red hair and the slight form on the brown horse. "Kenneth! You shouldn't have followed me! Go home! Now!"

He smiled as if it were a game, shaking his head.

Pointing toward the keep behind him, she did her best to look stern. "Go! How can I make you understand? If I have to go away, you can't come with me!"

The happy expression fell from his face as if she had slapped him. Cat urged her mount forward until her knee brushed his, and placed a comforting hand on his shoulder.

"Very well, I don't suppose it will matter. You can find your way back if I find the portal. If not, we can go back together."

As they rode deeper into the woods, Cat watched for familiar signs, having taken careful note of her surroundings on the ride with Angus. Kenneth seemed to be in a joyful mood as he listened and watched the forest around them.

"Edna said you fear most people. I'm glad you're not afraid of me. We're misfits, you and I. They think we're crazy, and unlike my world, that doesn't mean a comfortable hospital where you visit a shrink every day. Here you could be shut away permanently, or even burned as a witch.

I've got to be careful, because superstition can literally be the death of me, especially if I talk about the mist and the door. I doubt even Roderic could protect me. His decree would serve me naught."

She paused. "I'm beginning to use the medieval speech!" Cat shook her head as if surprised. "It's probably best I do if I want to avoid trouble. They all believe I merely wandered from my clan."

Falling silent, the horses plodded on for another hour. Cat turned the sorrel so that she rode side by side with Kenneth instead of ahead of him.

"It just occurred to me, Kenneth. If you could manage an occasional phrase such as 'and how did that make you feel'? you would make an excellent psychologist. I can vent my feelings freely with you. I have to release them somehow, or I truly would go mad. I can't even grasp what I've done!" She shook her head.

"I have no excuse for it. None. Last night I was playing the part of Brianna. Somewhere in the back of my mind was this ridiculous rationalization. Cat Terril could not make love to a total stranger, even though she found herself married to him. But Brianna? Ah! Brianna could make love to her husband, for it was perfectly acceptable." Kenneth smiled softly at her, and Cat smiled back.

"How could I have let this happen? It was totally irresponsible of me. I don't care if I do think he is the most handsome specimen of manhood I've ever seen."

Her voice became whisper soft. "When he came to me on the stairs and took me to the tower room, he looked devastatingly handsome in the firelight, like something women fantasize about, not a real human being. That chest of his could sell millions of dollars worth of designer clothing in my time."

She shook her head as if disgusted.

"It doesn't matter. I knew better. I've been fending off cowboys in pick-up trucks since I was seventeen, and never once was tempted to let them take liberties with my body." Cat paused for a full minute.

"Liberties. That's a ridiculous understatement. The word doesn't even begin to describe it, because the man took total possession. There is nothing unconsummated about this marriage. Now, if I do somehow go back through the time portal, I could very well have a child to bring up alone. All the others in the past left me cold, Kenneth. I could always pull back and put a stop to it. Yet, when Roderic touched me . . . I . . . lost all thought or reason. I've never felt such an intense sexual need, such desire. He seduced me, but I allowed it, and I'm not going to pretend for one moment that I didn't want him as much as he wanted me. These feelings are scary, because I want to stay for a while, Kenneth. I want to be with him, if only for a short time."

Suddenly Kenneth raised his head as if alert to a sound only he could hear, and the horses became skittish. Cat reached down to stroke the mare's neck.

"What is it?" she whispered. She sensed the fear in her mount just as Kenneth slipped off his horse to walk around behind them.

The men came out of the trees. She and Kenneth were confronted by three mounted warriors wearing plaids of red, yellow, and blue. Their swords were drawn and ready, and Cat drew her weapon and forced her horse in front of Kenneth. The men stared at her in surprise and lowered their arms. Cat stared back, chin raised, and the large man in the middle spoke up.

"Be easy, lass. We won't hurt the boy. I am Robert Maitland. We have come for the priest, Father MacNair. He is the only one near, and we have need of him to perform last rites."

"He is at the Mackay keep. I am Brianna, Lady Montwain. The priest just performed my marriage."

Cat was quick to notice the man's expression was one of extreme emotional distress, despite his control. Frowning, she leaned forward. "Someone has died?"

The man sighed, and sheathed his sword. "I am Laird of the Maitland clan. My wife will die, soon, if she does not give birth to her babe. Helen has asked for a priest, and I'll have the man there with her if I have to go to war for it. It may be the last wish I can grant her."

"How far away is she?"

"An hour's ride to my land, to the north, then east," he said.

"Has she a midwife to help her?"

"Aye. 'Twas the midwife that has given me little hope my wife will live, never mind the child."

Cat sheathed her sword and pulled her cloak about her. It distressed her to think of the midwife's methods. "I'll take you to him," she said.

They turned to ride back to the keep, and Cat reached out to try to calm Kenneth. The boy eyed the soldiers with fear, but did not try to run away.

Cat's heart twisted for the young woman struggling to give birth under such conditions. She knew a lot about mares foaling, but had never witnessed a baby born, except in films. So many women chose to give birth at home in her own time. Natural childbirth was a popular choice, and two of her friends had taken Lamaze classes. What if it was a simple complication? What if she could help? Cat came to the conclusion that her knowledge, though hardly that of a medical expert, could be of help to others.

Her search for the portal could very well be a futile effort. This time was her reality, and she was much more adept at dealing with the practical aspects of her life here than longing for her past. Cat was never one to sit and whine for something she could not change. Merlin appeared to her twice. Maybe she would have to wait for him to appear again.

Afraid of being vulnerable with Roderic, she was running away from him, but he was, after all, her husband. Roderic might be a man of honor and integrity, but he was in a position of power over Cat, and she was not ready to accept that. A man could treat his wife any way he chose in this time. Cat remembered reading that the expression 'rule of thumb' came from a law in early England that forbid a man to beat his wife with any stick wider than his thumb; a stick smaller than that was, of course, perfectly acceptable.

Cat Terril would never tolerate such behavior, from Roderic, or any man. Lady Brianna, however, would be forced to suffer her husband's wrath. Cat knew it would be impossible to root out traits in her personality that would be unlike Brianna. Knowing her faults well, she acknowledged them; she was stubborn and, at times, reckless. Those traits had served her well in her time. Taking no note of the danger to life and limb in her work, she plunged in with abandon and was rewarded for being fearless in a profession dominated by men. It was not an attribute that would be appreciated in Lady Brianna Montwain.

Cat felt a sudden respect for all the actors she had worked with in the past. The part of Brianna was, for Cat, a creative stretch. A medieval wife would be submissive to her husband. Brianna would take these men back to the keep, to the priest.

Yet, what if Cat could help the woman? She pulled her horse up to stop.

"If your wife's condition is that serious, we have no time to lose. Send these men with the boy. He will take them to the priest. I don't know if I can help, but I would like to try. You could take me to your wife."

The large man's expression was one of suspicion.

"You are the daughter of Calum Mackay, yet ye speak as though ye are English," he accused.

Cat did her best to lend a slight brogue to her accent.

"Nay. My husband is an Englishman. What does it matter if I can help? Please, let me try."

He stared into her eyes as if assessing her character while the other men admonished him not to trust her. He held up his hand to silence them. Cat was sure he looked at her for a full five minutes before he spoke.

"So be it. I have nothing to lose." He turned to the men. "Ye take the boy and do as she says. Fetch the priest. I will go back now . . . for if I am to lose Helen, and she leaves this world, I want to be by her side before it is too late."

❦

Cat rode swiftly with Maitland to his holding. He made haste to bring her inside and did not stop to make introductions, but brought her immediately to his wife's chamber. The Laird spoke briefly to the midwife as the woman sat at the end of the bed, her hands under the blanket, between the lady's legs.

"She's come from the Mackay holding. She married Montwain, but she offered to help, and I've sent the others for the priest."

The older woman stood to glare at Cat. She had long,

gray hair and was tall, large-boned, and looked capable of throwing Cat out of the chamber bodily.

"A Mackay that means to help?" The woman spoke in outraged disbelief.

"Aye, and if it be my decree, ye shall bend to it!" The Laird could be formidable, for when his eyes turned stormy and he pinned the midwife with his glare, she relented.

"Be you a healer, lady?" she asked. Cat knew if she was thought incompetent she would not be allowed inside the chamber, so she answered the midwife affirmatively.

"Aye, for many a birthing I've seen." Cat did not go on to explain that all the births were foals. Robert Maitland sat down behind his wife to prop her shoulders upon his chest. The young woman had long, chestnut-colored hair, dark eyes, and was obviously in a great deal of pain. Urgently, she grasped her husband's hand as he stroked her gently, kissing her hair.

"Robert, the priest . . . he is coming?"

"Aye, lass, Fergus and the others will fetch him. I've brought this one, she means to help ye."

The midwife turned to Cat, gesturing over to the side of the room, and Cat followed her a few steps from the bed. The older woman spoke in low tones, her compelling words meant only for Cat's ears.

"I fear that the helping ye will do, lady, will be with a burying. The babe is being slowly strangled in the womb. Helen has labored for many hours now, and I fear to lose them both. What say you to give the father false hope?"

"I did not. I only meant to help if I could. What do you mean the baby's being strangled?"

"The cord of life be wrapped about the child's neck."

"You could tell? You could reach it?"

"Aye, yet I couldnae move it. It pains her so, she screams and pushes me away."

"Did you try when the pains were not at their worst? She does not appear to have the urge to push yet."

"Nay, 'tis true, but it is coming soon, and when she does, that child will die."

Cat glanced down at the woman's hands. She was very tall and her hands were large. "Let me scrub my hands and get clean. Perhaps I can try to reach it. My hands are smaller."

"If it will help Helen, I will do anything. Yet, it be not wise to give the father a hope when there be none."

"We don't know that for certain," Cat said.

As the afternoon wore on, Cat was to bless every moment that she had spent with her father assisting with the foaling mares. Between one of the pains, the midwife brought Cat's hand to the spot where she could feel the baby's head. Pushing her fingers up inside, she felt the cord around the baby's neck, but could not maneuver to free the child, for too tightly was it wedged in the birth canal.

"Can we turn her over to a different position? Perhaps then we can reach it," Cat said.

"We can seek to try, for the child cannae be born this

way and live," said the midwife.

The young mother was at once seized with the urge to push and became frantic, crying out in pain.

"Laird, help us! Turn her over! Support her," the old woman ordered.

Both Cat and the midwife carefully helped the lady turn to her right side, and her husband reached out to encircle her in his arms. He put his large arm under her chest as she gripped the bedding.

They turned Helen, and Cat inserted her hand as gently as possible into the birth canal. She winced when the young woman screamed in pain, but she had no choice but to force her fingers between the baby's neck and the cord. Shifting position had granted her a bit of room to maneuver, and she slowly worked it from the grip around the child's neck. Finally, she pulled the cord down through the birth canal. The Laird did his best to comfort his wife, supporting her, holding her, and speaking to her tenderly through it all.

"It will be soon, love, it will be soon."

The midwife crowed in delight when she saw that Cat had indeed pulled the cord from of the woman's body. Cat was concerned about the bleeding and said so to the midwife.

"Nay, 'tis not much blood," she replied.

They had little time to speak after that, for the birth progressed very rapidly. Robert helped his lady once again turn over, and she pushed in earnest. The midwife snapped orders to Cat, and she obeyed.

Each of the young woman's efforts to push the baby from her body was agonizing. The midwife put a hand on her belly and pressed with every contraction. The second time she pushed, the baby's head emerged, and Cat watched with amazement as the midwife pushed the liquid away from the baby's nose and moved the little babe's shoulder.

The pains came close together, and the young mother was weak, yet could not help screaming when they ripped through her body. Robert sat behind his wife and slipped his hands under her knees, his arms supporting her as would a birthing chair. Helen was at the edge of the bed, and the midwife kept her hand down below the baby's head.

"Lean down here. Get on your knees; if the shoulders push through on the next pain, the child could fall to the floor!"

Cat dropped to her knees as the next contraction gripped Helen. She pushed with all her might, and the baby slipped from her body. The tiny, slippery baby boy ended up in Cat's lap, still attached to his mother by the umbilical cord, and Cat's eyes welled with tears as she was overcome with emotion. Handing Cat a soft cloth, the midwife instructed her to push the membrane and the liquid from the baby's mouth.

Cat cleaned the baby while the midwife took a knife and cut the cord. Tying two knots in each end, she pressed on the young mother's stomach again. Robert let out a shout of joy and pulled Helen back into his arms where she collapsed, weeping.

"It's over, my love, it's over." The man kissed her again

and again, overcome with joy. He had feared losing his wife and child, but the dire outcome had not prevailed.

Cat hummed to the baby, wrapping him tightly, stroking him. She gazed on the couple and was struck by the love between them, for the Laird wiped away a tear and continued to hold his wife to his chest. At one point he closed his eyes and interlocked his fingers inside hers to make a fist. Cat suspected that he was saying a prayer when he rested his cheek next to his wife's. At that moment she was very grateful she had come to the Maitland holding; she knew she was in the presence of love.

Roderic had been in a temper from the moment he had awakened to find his wife gone, then learned Kenneth was missing as well. His wife was turning out to be an unusual amount of trouble.

Half his army riding with him, Roderic came upon the clansmen with Kenneth, but was far from consoled. They needed a priest for Robert Maitland's wife, who lay dying he was informed. Cat had offered to help in the meantime.

Gavin, astride his mount, spoke quietly to Roderic.

"Your wife is either an angel of mercy, or she has more courage than sense. She's walked head on into another clan's territory, and may have started a war."

Roderic sent for the priest without answering Gavin.

They rode hard and fast in pursuit, the two Maitland warriors in the lead. Almost two hours behind Brianna and the Laird, it was late in the afternoon when they arrived.

They were surrounded at once. Maitland had prepared for them, and his warriors stood ready to fight as Roderic rode in alone with Gavin. He had left the others behind, hoping to bring Brianna home without bloodshed.

The man met him on the steps of his home, a structure of gray stone.

"You have my wife, Maitland," Roderic said, his voice ringing with command.

"Aye, I do, Montwain, but it was by her own free will and mercy she came! I'll not need the priest. My wife is alive. She is alive and well, as is my son! Would you like to meet my son, Montwain?"

Roderic was shocked at the question. The man did not appear hostile in his manner, although the men of his clan stood fully armed for battle.

"We Scots hate the English, no matter how verra dear ye be to our King. We dinnae want ye on our land! I see the question in your eyes. To answer it, I wish no war. Lady Montwain has made this a happy day for me. I'll not be buryin' my Helen, nor the boy. Your wife is a fine midwife. It be hard to trust anyone a part of Mackay, yet she was not afraid to do her best. She is with Helen now. Come."

Roderic left Gavin to wait outside and followed the Laird into the great hall. Cat came walking down the steps holding the bairn. The weak little mews from the babe soon became a strong wail.

Cat looked up at Roderic and smiled sweetly as she handed the boy to his father.

His wife was not at all concerned with his anger. She sighed as if she had just finished a good meal.

"Helen and I said our farewells," Cat said to Maitland. "She is sleeping soundly now, and Rachel is with her. Helen is very weak, but she should be well and sound in a few days. Rachel is a fine healer, but she needed another pair of hands."

" 'Tis true. It took both of them to bring this lad into the world," Maitland said as he stared down at his son.

"Roderic. Isn't he a handsome bairn?" she said.

"Yes, indeed. He is a fine son, Maitland. I'll take my wife home now."

"There will be peace between us, Montwain. Your wife's act of kindness will not be forgotten. Think ye to need my aid, ye ask, and it will be granted. Your wife has courage."

The bairn stopped its crying when his father touched him tenderly.

"One that can draw a sword of challenge to me would have need of it," he said. The Laird was smiling at Brianna, a teasing glint in his eye.

Roderic was incensed by this bit of information, and stepped forward to grip his wife's elbow none too gently.

"Go, now, Brianna. Get on your horse. We leave

immediately."

Roderic thought it absurd that she should look so affront-ed. He was the one who had a right to his anger. Her pretty face flushed with humiliation while she said her farewells to Maitland, and abruptly stomped out of the great hall.

"She is a proud, strong woman. Comely, too. Many of my warriors would have kept her, and damn the war it start-ed with an Englishmon. But debt for my own overshadowed my desire to appease my men. If ye give her a lickin' for the worry ye suffered, be sure to soothe her pride after. May-hap she lacks caution, but dinnae forget the kind heart that moved her to such folly," Maitland said.

Roderic would never have believed that after one day of wedded bliss, he would be taking advice about how to beat his wife and actually relish the prospect.

He walked outside to the horses, where Brianna, ignor-ing Gavin's offer of assistance, hurled herself onto the back of her mount with the speed and grace of an arrow. She sat astride the animal trembling with indignation, eyes flashing green fire.

Roderic got on his mount and came before her. Reach-ing out with his dagger, he cut the sword from her belt and tossed it to Gavin.

"Was it absolutely necessary to humiliate me in that manner?"

She made her demand in a cold, hard voice. Roderic leaned toward her and gripped her wrist.

"Brianna . . . do . . . not . . . speak. I am very close to beating you right now, and I am sure if it is to be done, you would want it done when we are alone. You could have started a war here today. Many men could have died because of your actions. You are my wife, and you will obey me. Be silent!"

"Well, excuse me, your worship!"

She said the word "excuse" as if it had three syllables. He was in no mood for her jests.

"Enough! You endangered your own life by running away! You also endangered that of the boy . . ."

"Kenneth followed me! I tried to make him go home before we came upon the Maitlands," she said urgently.

"It matters not! I did not permit you to leave the castle! Even if your motive was one of mercy, it can not be excused. You left with a strange man to cross another clan's borders! That alone can start a war! Knowing it, you took no heed of the consequences and drew your sword in a challenge to a Laird, who could have hacked you to pieces! For that and more I will punish you, and you will accept it as your due!" His tone was cold and furious.

She stared him down and one brow quirked haughtily. Sarcasm dripped from her like venom.

"Sir Montwain, I have only one response to your arrogant assumption." She paused before she spoke again angrily. "Accept it as my due?"

Cat pushed his hand away. "As they say in England . . . *like bloody hell!*"

Chapter Seven

For no chastening for the present seemeth to be joyous, but grievous: nevertheless afterward it yieldeth peaceable fruit.

~Hebrews 12:11

Gavin urged his mount closer to Roderic's. "Your temper has cooled?"

Roderic glanced briefly behind him. His wife had gone to ride with the rest of his warriors, placing ten riders between them.

"Nay, I still wrestle with the desire to beat her before you all!"

Gavin chuckled. "Ah, once I kenned how a lass could twist a mon's purpose and duty. Yea, though, a wife? 'Tis true of a bride hundredfold. Still, mayhap there is good to come of what happened today."

"You seek to defend her?"

"Nay. But, if Maitland is now an ally 'tis a boon that should be heeded as you do your duty." Gavin grinned without remorse.

"My wrath amuses you?"

Gavin laughed. "Aye, to see ye at last befuddled by a woman, I be vastly amused."

Roderic rode back to his wife. Grabbing the reins of her horse, he kicked his own to a canter , and returned to the front of the group. Turning to Gavin, he raised his voice.

"I wish for some time alone with my wife. We will stay parallel with you."

"Aye," Gavin said.

When they were a comfortable distance from his army, he turned to Cat. "Is being my wife so abhorrent that you would rather be raped or dead?" he demanded.

The look of shock and disbelief on her face could not have been feigned.

"No! Why would you ask that?"

"To run away as you did would certainly lead to your capture by a rival clan. Robert Maitland could have kept you hostage if the circumstances had not won his loyalty, and he could have held you for ransom. You must know this!"

Momentarily confused, she glanced away. "I don't. I had no idea."

There was a puzzled frown on his face. Could she truly be unaware of the danger?

"How can this be, Brianna? Every young woman in the Highlands is taught of such danger from the cradle. You must understand the hatred for your father is so great many would kill you to avenge those they have mourned."

"I have been allowed more freedom. I can't tell you why I ran away; you wouldn't believe me. But I wasn't aware of the danger, and I certainly wouldn't have gone had I known it would bring you trouble."

"The Mackay gave you so few rules that he cared not if you put yourself in danger?" His tone was laced with disbelief.

She didn't answer, but merely looked away and shrugged. "You saved my life. I suppose I should learn to listen to you."

He studied her expression, and she appeared truly repentant, even vexed with herself.

"Aye, and so you shall. You will obey me, Brianna. For if you do not, you endanger not only yourself, but my army as well. Gavin has told me to consider well the alliance you have created with Maitland. But, I will have your vow to never leave the keep without my permission."

Her manner was somewhat calmer as she took a deep breath and sighed. "All right already. Fine. I will be the little woman of the manor."

"Jest with me not, lady. We must return to the others, but we will discuss this again when we arrive at the keep."

They rode back to his men, Roderic facing a dilemma of his own making. Having told his wife earnestly that he would never hurt her, he had made a promise he would be unable to keep. Though he was disgusted by the very thought he had no choice, for he read well the contempt his warriors directed at her. She had not only forced them to postpone the journey to meet with the King, she had put them all in danger.

The Scots who made up his army were good and loyal men, and they believed in harsh justice. He had fought beside them, but their loyalty was hard won and a burdensome struggle to maintain. In their eyes he was still born an Englishman, and they had buried many kin killed by the English.

Roderic thought back to the circumstances that placed him, a boy of ten years, in Alexander's care, and remembering the old warrior who found him when his family was killed by the Saxons. He could smell the smoke of his home burning, hear the sounds of his mother and sisters screaming as they died. The old one had saved him, hiding Roderic away, stealing a horse. Then they had traveled for three days without stopping for food or drink. Roderic took little notice, for his heart closed up inside his body. Having no tears, he had faced the worst he could suffer, losing all who had meant love, warmth, and safety, and he had not even the will to struggle.

He became hungry on the fourth day and ate the food offered by the old man. Losing track of how long they traveled, Roderic did as he was told and walked where he was led. At last, the old one came upon a band of Scottish warriors, Alexander among them, and he urged Roderic to go to them.

Alexander looked after him, and in time he grew stronger. He had been trained and loved by the man, but never once did Alexander allow his hand to become slack and permissive. If he disobeyed, Roderic was beaten for his own good and well-being.

Catherine had endangered them all by her actions, and he would be expected to correct the matter. His men's loyalty was unquestioned, but never far from Roderic's mind was the fact that he was not born to Scotland. The command of this army was a responsibility he held sacred, and he did not risk the lives of his men for foolishness, but for right and truth as Alexander demanded of them all.

His wife had a compassionate woman's heart, but she did wrong putting the safety of one woman and her child above that of so many others. A perplexing mixture of child and woman, she had no fear, as the Maitland Laird had said. It seemed true as she had spit at Roderic like an angry cat when she should have been begging his forgiveness. She had then plead ignorance of her danger. It was impossible. He could believe such of the simple minded boy, Kenneth, but not of her.

A healthy fear was necessary, it was a hard life in the Highlands. If she did not have a fear to exercise caution, she must be taught one, and soon, or it could mean her life.

Convinced she was attempting to escape him and their marriage, he had been prepared for her denouncement. Roderic's pride was dealt a blow at the thought, making him angry enough to carry out her punishment. Her denial and confusion baffled him. His wife forced his logical mind into a tangle, and his problems with her were as a flock of birds he wished to catch scattered on a hillside. He didn't know which one to capture first. Still, capture them he would, for his wife would obey him at all cost.

They stopped to water the horses, and Gavin approached him.

"I must speak to you. Alec has brought something to my attention. It may explain much. One left behind by Mackay has said that your wife is not what she appears. They say she is mad."

Roderic frowned and then scoffed. "What nonsense. Who said this?"

"An older man who was left with the women. He implied to Alec you best not relax your guard, and beware of Mackay, who has tricked you by giving you a madwoman as wife."

"He said this of Brianna?"

"Aye. It could be the reason why she put herself in such danger. If her mind is weak as the boy's . . ."

"You don't believe such tales. The woman is headstrong . . . but intelligent."

"It would appear so. Long did I consider the wisdom of bringing this to your attention. Yet, dinnae allow her beauty to blind you to what could be the truth."

Roderic shook his head. "She will not blind me to my duty, and will be disciplined if need be. I must make certain she cannot put herself in danger again, and I will know her reasons for leaving. I promised I would never hurt her, yet her actions today could have started a war."

" 'Tis verra true. What if the Maitland babe had died?

What if she had been unable to help? We would have had a bloody battle, indeed. Still, she must have a way as a healer to have helped the lady with the birthing, and she did win the Laird's loyalty."

"She knew we were to go to the King, but did not wish it. I sought to calm her fears, and then she ran. If that was the reason, why would she dread meeting the King? Most ladies would love to go to court."

"True," Gavin said. He looked reluctant to speak his thoughts. "Did all go well on your first night together? Some women can be very timid," he said, glancing away.

Roderic was immersed with the memories of that night, and had no intention of sharing them with Gavin, or anyone else. He held them too precious.

"All was well, and she was far from timid." His tone was coolly disapproving. "She is never timid, and one could wish it! Catherine drew her sword on the Laird," Roderic said.

Gavin's eyes widened in shock.

"Aye," Roderic said. "For that alone she deserves a hiding as any child would get for doing such a foolish thing. He could have killed her." There was a tremble in Roderic's deep voice.

Gavin understood that the anger in his friend was not unlike that of a parent pulling his child out of the way of the hearth. The pain of a beating on the backside would be much less than the horrible pain of being burned or scarred by fire.

"Aye. I don't envy your task ahead. Your new bride will need to be watched closely. Guarded. If she is treated as a prisoner, it will hardly warm her affections, nor will the punishment you must see she receives. Ye also must ask yourself if her loyalties truly lie with you."

Roderic looked at Gavin sharply but said nothing in return. Had his passion pushed out all other thought or reason? Had it clouded his judgment? Did he have her loyalty? He did not have an answer.

"Tell me where to find this man. I must speak to him. I will go there first. Take my wife with the men and return to the keep."

It was late when Roderic left the stone cottage, more frustrated than when he arrived. He had gotten few answers from the man, who was vague with his replies, refusing to say more than to beware of the Mackay and his tricks. Roderic remembered his own uneasy feeling that Mackay was much too smug on the day he was driven from the holding.

The woman Mary ran to him as he was about to mount his horse.

"Sir Roderic, ye best get to the keep, there be trouble. Make haste," she said.

He left, concerned at the urgency of her request.

Roderic could not believe his eyes when he entered the

great hall. His wife had crossed swords with Gavin. The man was standing relaxed with a grin on his face until his half-hearted defense suddenly vanished.

Cat attacked with a grace and speed that stunned him. She held her skirts in one hand; the other held her sword, which she wielded with a skill that dazed him, for all at once Gavin had to defend himself in earnest. On the floor was a leather strap, and near the table stood Kenneth. The boy stared as if seeing nothing, unaware of his surroundings. Edna stood with her arms around the boy to keep him still.

"Brianna, stop!"

She ignored him, and he realized the only reason Gavin had failed to disarm her immediately was her light step and quickness. Unable to keep his weapon to hers long enough, he could not use the power of his heavier sword.

Suddenly, as if it were a game she tired of, Brianna lowered her sword. Her green eyes spit fury at Gavin when she spoke. "Try to beat Kenneth again, and I'll do more than scratch your face! I'll run ye through, laddie!"

Roderic's gaze flew to Gavin's face and at once saw the scratches that left a trail of blood on his cheek.

"You beat the boy?" Roderic said.

"The old woman bid me do so!" Gavin burst.

Cat whirled to face Edna. "What? Why would you do such a thing?"

"I always beat him when he runs away." Edna spoke softly to the younger woman, then turned to Roderic.

"He has run off since he was a wee lad, going to the woods, and I feared he would get lost. This time he took a horse, something he has never done. I beat him in the past, but it was my hope that Gavin could beat him hard enough he would never leave again. I fear for him. Kenneth has no sense of bearing. It was just a mercy he followed Brianna, and she found him. Dinnae blame her for this. She be protective of Kenneth."

Roderic immediately considered the rumors and accusations. Could Brianna be like the boy in her disregard of caution?

Edna turned to Cat. The girl's eyes were angry still.

"I don't care! You had no right to treat him so! Look what it's done to him!"

Roderic, too, frowned at the boy's blank expression.

"It's just his way. Kenneth goes oft to the world inside his head," said Edna.

Cat walked to the boy and put her arms around him, stroking his hair softly.

Roderic spoke in a low tone. "Kenneth?"

"He won't answer or look at anyone, and I know he hears us," Cat said. She turned to speak to Gavin.

"It appears this wasn't your doing. I'm sorry about your face."

She gave Kenneth a gentle pat on the shoulder and bent down to pick up the leather strap. "I went a bit mad when I saw you hitting him with this thing. If you want to hit someone, hit me. At least I can fight back!"

Gavin let out a loud, boisterous laugh. "All too well, lass."

Roderic stepped forward and took the sword from her. He spoke to Gavin while he held her gaze. "Would you tell me how she managed to take this from you?"

"I had one arm on the boy, and the other on the strap. She let out an angry scream coming at me from behind, and pulled it from my waist before she took her nails to my face."

"I should have told ye. 'Tis for his own good in the coming," said Edna. She addressed Cat.

"I don't agree," she replied, her voice cold.

"Don't you?" Roderic said. " 'If you want to hit someone, hit me.' You say this because you know what you did was wrong! Yet, I, too, was at fault for trusting you."

Roderic gave the sword to Gavin and took Brianna's hand, then bent down and hauled her over his shoulder. Gavin continued to laugh as he handed him the strap.

"You will need this."

Roderic had taken her by surprise, and she squirmed because of her indelicate position, but she did not fight him. He walked up the steps to their chamber and set her down on her feet. Turning, he shut the door, then faced her.

"I am asking you to give me a reason for your leaving. Were you trying to reach Mackay?" His eyes narrowed in suspicion.

"No! It's not what you think! I wouldn't betray you, Roderic. You can believe I was foolish in deciding to trust

Maitland, but I am not sorry I helped Helen and her baby."

"Brianna . . ." He heaved a heavy sigh. "I am English by blood, but I lead five hundred of the King's warrior's. They began as misfits from many clans, and were outcasts so they accepted the King's effort to join them.

"These men wear the kilt. I do not. I dress as an Englishman, for Alexander taught me not to fall into the trap of pretending to be what I am not. I risked their lives for you today; they have a right to their anger and live by a harsh code of justice. If any one of these men would have put others in danger, I would have had them flogged. You are my wife, but the daughter of an enemy. I cannot ignore what you have done without jeopardizing their loyalty. I told you I would never hurt you, but I did not foresee your putting me in this position. You have given me no choice."

"Let me understand you. If I let you beat me with that strap, the men of your army will feel I paid my debt and hold no ill will toward me?" She was incredulous.

"Yes. It is not just that you endangered their lives, but your own. What possessed you to raise your sword to the Laird?" he demanded.

"They came out of the trees! I was protecting Kenneth!"

"They threatened the boy?"

"Well, no . . . not exactly."

"Will you swear to me never again will you use a weapon in such a manner?"

She sighed and shook her head, refusing to give him the

answer he longed to hear. Roderic's eyes narrowed when he spoke.

"You give me no choice. You must be punished." He picked her up by the waist and strode to the bed. His little wife was remarkably strong as she fought him. Bending her over one knee, he pinned her flailing legs down with one of his own.

"It will help in this ruse if you manage to scream at the proper time." He spoke in a sly tone as if conspiring. Holding her at the waist, he raised the strap again and again to hit the side of the bed. Brianna squirmed to look up at him when she realized what he was doing.

"Ruse?" she demanded in a startled whisper.

He was not hitting her at all! At once she understood. Her green eyes were full of mirth and laughter when he continued to slap the belt with a loud pop. She cried out, but it was hard to keep from laughing when he winked at her. Turning her over as if he were really spanking her, she did her best to let out an outraged scream with each of his strokes, and he kept it up a good while. She drummed her fingers on the bed and put her face down to muffle her occasional giggles. After thirty strokes, Roderic threw down the strap.

She turned over to face him, her head propped, resting on her elbow. Extremely provocative, she looked up at him, her green eyes warm and sensual.

"Why, Sir Roderic . . . as a brutal husband, you fail miserably."

He pulled her close and cupped her cheek. "Do you think I *want* to hurt you?"

She licked her lips and stared at his mouth. "No, you are too gentle. Kiss me, Roderic."

"Don't mistake me, Brianna. My wish to keep a promise to you so early in our marriage does not mean that you will dictate to me in any way. Endanger yourself or my men again..."

He brought his hand down to land a stinging slap to her backside. She gasped and rubbed her bottom.

"And you will feel enough pain to make it memorable!"

"I'm sorry I displeased you. Forgive me," she pleaded. She put her arms around his neck, stroking his hair when his mouth came down to hers. Their passion exploded with the first touch. Her hands caressed him while he pleasured her mouth.

Roderic all but tore her clothes from her. Her hair made a glorious veil over the pink tips of her breast when she took it from the braid and shook her head. He pulled the silky chanise from her, and held her waist in the span of his hands. Shifting, he brought her up to straddle him. His gaze quickly found hers, hoping he wasn't handling her too roughly.

Eyes glittering with excitement, she was as aroused as he. Placing her hands on his shoulders, she took a deep breath, thrusting her soft breasts to him. He sucked her nipple into his mouth and stroked the soft skin of her legs and hips.

"Roderic, it feels so ... wonderful." Cat whimpered as he

gave both her breasts the attention they craved. He reached down and slipped a finger inside her, his thumb stroking the soft, red curls. Speaking in between open-mouthed kisses, he went on.

"Tell me, how does one discipline an erring wife? A very beautiful ... headstrong wife?"

He kissed the soft joining of her neck and shoulder. Her body responded to his touch with abandon. She held nothing back.

Resting her forehead to his, she panted. "I know you don't understand me. I don't understand myself at times ... the way you make me feel."

She cupped his face and placed her cheek to his. He kissed her jaw and forced her to meet his gaze.

"Like a fire inside. Do you burn for me, little one? Do I make you hot?" His voice was warm and tender.

"Yes. You know you do ... when you touch me ... I ..." She made a soft sound of pleasure as his thumb caressed the small nub at the head of her sex. He was impatient to undress quickly, so he removed his tunic. Cat licked and nipped his neck and shoulder. Groaning, he wrapped his arms around her, caressing her hair and skin. She looked like a temptress, a wood nymph who would be more at home out in the forest. Vowing one day he would make love to her on a bed of green grass, he held a vision of her there, white creamy skin and red hair lying on her shoulders as she reached for him and opened her pretty legs in welcome.

Cat kissed him with an abandon that enticed him. He reached out to grasp her hips when she sucked daintily on his tongue. She held him tightly, brushing her nipples across his chest, but he struggled with his desire, wanting her desperate, even to the point of begging.

He reached down and adjusted his clothing, freeing his aroused body. She made a move as if to cuddle his sex with her own, but he held her hips still when she tried to join them.

"Roderic, you're so hot and hard . . . please?"

"You belong to me . . . say it." He made the demand in a voice raspy and harsh with passion.

Cat, too, was vulnerable. Mouth wet from his kisses, her breasts puckered, her green eyes cloudy and pleading, she answered him. "I do belong to you . . . only you . . . please?"

Her plea ended on a sob when he lifted her. Resting her hands on his shoulders, she gripped him hard when he impaled her. Cat gasped and winced, for her body was still not accustomed to his. Roderic hated hurting her, so he coaxed her with tender words.

"There now . . . there. You can take me. You were such a small . . . tight little virgin . . . now. Now."

Words were no longer possible. He lifted her again and again, and when he saw that he increased her pleasure by pulling her forward, he did so. She found her joy, and he watched her, delighted in her inner spasms when she cried out helplessly. Joining her thrust for thrust, he was then consumed by his own orgasm.

Cat collapsed on him, her breathing labored as if she had run a long distance. Cupping her face, he stroked his hand down to the rapid pulse of her heartbeat in her throat. Shifting, pulling the bedclothes up to cover them, he held her, caressing the beating pulse of her heart, and despaired. It was his own heart that concerned him. It was most assuredly in danger.

Chapter Eight

Put not your trust in princes, nor in the son of man, in whom there is no help.

~Psalms 146:3

Roderic called together some of his men for a counsel. They sat at the large table in the great hall. Alec spoke somberly.

"I wish to beseech your pardon for being lax in my duty."

Roderic silently observed the distress of the younger man. Alec's handsome face reflected a remorse that was indisputable.

"Of what do you speak?" Roderic said.

"Had I detained your wife and made verra certain she had your leave to go away from the castle, we could have stopped her before she made the grave mistake of crossing Maitland's border," Alec said.

"My wife is a headstrong woman. I have taken steps to correct that flaw," Roderic said.

Gavin smirked before he broke into a wide grin. "We

heard the noise of it! Yet, I trust ye gave her the comfort a mon should after the beating."

There was a lascivious sparkle in Gavin's eye. Roderic was not amused when the others broke into a ribald laughter. He stood at the head of the table, shaking with anger.

"Enough!"

There was an immediate silence.

"My wife was wrong to go to Maitland's land. She will not make that mistake again. It is to be understood that despite suspicion because of her father, there is no proof of her disloyalty. Lady Montwain will have the support of every man in my command as part of his duty to me and the King. Be there any cause for complaint, so let it be spoken now against her."

Each man in turn at the table expressed his support by brief words or gesture. At last it was only Alec and Gavin that had not spoken. Alec coughed and cleared his throat.

"I serve you, Roderic, and my King. I would do all in my power to protect Lady Montwain if need be."

"I have but one complaint of your wife," Gavin said.

"If you speak of her defending the boy . . ."

"Nay! 'Twas wrong of me to strap the lad, for his mind is too simple to know better. But, let her raise a sword to me again, 'twill be my own hand that beats her!"

Roderic's expression changed to a scowl.

"Aye, even if we cross swords," Gavin said with a deadly calm.

"Your complaint?" Roderic demanded.

"She be too comely, and fair," Gavin said. He had a wicked sparkle of amusement in his eye. "She should be mine."

Roderic sighed with relief when he spoke. "I gather from your jest I have no reason to doubt your loyalty to Lady Montwain?"

Gavin's eyes darkened with a brief cloud of resentment and hurt. "Nay, my friend. I should cuff ye about for your doubts. Ye have my loyalty, my fealty, a promise born of love and trust. Although, I fear, and I pray ye also have God's help with this alliance. Ye will have need of it."

Roderic nodded to his friend, then turned to Alec.

"Make ready to go to the King. I am sending a message to him, and I need a courier."

Alec frowned. "I shall send someone."

"Nay," Roderic said. "I wish you to go."

Roderic's brown eyes pinned the younger man with a compelling plea. Alec was obviously perplexed, but he quickly acceded to his wishes.

"I shall go within the hour," Alec said.

Setting the grinding pace of a soldier on march, Alec traveled for two days with little respite. Closing the distance between himself and the King, on the third day he slowed his gallop and vowed to rest until dawn rather than a brief nap.

It was twilight, and he had no desire to move on when he came upon the couple. He raised his hand palm up to imply he meant no harm when he approached them. Sitting near a small fire was a young woman who looked vaguely familiar. She was not alone. A large warrior in a pale green and black plaid stood before him, shielding the young woman vigilantly.

Alec spoke respectfully to the lady.

"Ye address my wife, sir." The warrior's words were spoken as a warning.

"Ah," Alec said. "Ye be a mon favored by the gods to have a wife so fair."

His eyes moved over the lass, appreciating her beauty. She had dark red hair the color of fox fur, and glanced down demurely while she allowed her husband to speak for her. Though the warrior had a suspicious nature, he graciously invited Alec to share their camp.

Alec smiled warmly. "I am grateful. 'Tis a long way I go and a comfort not to sup alone."

"Your journey is just beginning, sir?" the lady asked.

"Aye, milady. I must travel a bit to greet the King," Alec said.

She sighed as if relieved, and smiled. "You, too, then . ."

Her husband reached out to her, and with a quiet motion of his hand stopped her speech. Alec observed the silent communication of husband and wife. She seemed perplexed, even hurt. Then a subtle fear replaced the emotion in her expression. It was a warning, there was no reproach in his glance when the warrior looked at his lady. An intense gentleness was conveyed as he directed his silent command.

She returned his look with one of love and trust. This woman cared for her husband deeply, and wanted very much to please him.

"I have seen no plaid with your colors in this part of the highlands," the warrior said.

"Aye, for my clan is in the low country. And yours?" Alec asked.

The man did not answer him.

"Ye think me an enemy?"

"If that were so, ye would have had a taste of my blade as we speak."

They did not trust him, but Alec gave it little thought. He would not tarry long in their presence.

The warrior did not sleep. He sat near his wife where she slept, his hand upon his sword.

Leaning up against a tree, Alec sat across from him wrapped in his plaid, and did the same. It was not a restful night, and although at times he feigned sleep, Alec thought it best to be on his guard.

The couple feared an enemy. Alec was aware that the mention of his destination was a mistake, and he could have very well threatened his own safety. He was no Englishman; word would have traveled fast in the Highlands of Roderic's victory.

He hoped he would not be forced to kill the man, for

what then would become of the woman? Alec would be forced to take her with him as a prisoner. Long before first light, he took his leave.

Throughout the day as he traveled he became suspicious that he was being followed. The tracks he found told him it was one lone rider, and he traveled on his way, watching his back but the day wore on, he became impatient. Doubling back, he hoped to engage the man and fight, but the enemy was clever, constantly keeping him at a disadvantage by staying near, but undetected.

Waiting for him to attack did not set well, but Alec changed his direction, determined to allow no delay in his mission.

Returning to his former trail, he found a sign of two riders. One was much heavier than the other. The two people he had met last eve?

He slept little that night, guarding his small camp with care. Taking a slower course through the thick of the forest, he made an advantage of the woods about him. By afternoon he was heartily sick of the man.

"Let us fight now, and have done with the games, coward!" His angry bellow echoed through the trees. Alec did not sleep, but kept ready for battle, and was surprised as the night passed uneventful.

At first light he was immediately alert. Traveling on for several hours, he came out of a thicket of trees to see in a camp in the distance. His horse became agitated when he drew his sword, and he crooned to the animal when he came upon the camp. Recognizing the soft lavender gown worn by the woman he had met on the trail, he approached the couple. They had been attacked. Glancing about through the deep forest that surrounded them, he saw no evidence of an intruder.

His mind screamed a warning to flee when he saw that the young warrior was dead, but he had an immediate concern for the woman. Knowing he must give her assistance, Alec rode closer. Nearby she lay face down, arm outstretched to her husband. The two were covered with blood, but she moved one leg restlessly. She was alive.

Alec dismounted and first examined the body of the man. The back of his skull was visible; it had been split open by a sword. Confirming the man's death, he heard a deep moan from the woman.

Striding to the young woman, he sheathed his sword, knelt down, and gently took her in his arms to examine her injuries. He swallowed the bile in his throat when he saw her distress. Her complexion was gray and she gasped for breath. Above her breast, on her shoulder, was a large, gaping wound. She had been pierced through, and her small white hand fluttered near his chin as she uttered a choking gasp.

He felt her warning before he saw it. Her body shook with a tremor that he mistook for death's grasp, and she shook her head violently, green eyes filled with horror as she stared past him.

Trying to draw his sword, he turned, much too late. Alec felt the harsh, thin piercing of a dagger through his ribs. No sword this, but just as deadly.

"No . . ." he protested, staring into a familiar face.

"You!" He ground the word from his throat, feeling a great dismay at his own carelessness. His enemy pulled the dagger up, skillfully slicing his heart and ending his life with one thrust.

He looked up to whisper one word.

"Why?"

The darkness enveloped him when the weapon was pulled from his body. Slumping forward, he fell with his cheek resting on the woman's breast.

There was very little pain when his grip relaxed from the handle of his sword. He had failed Roderic, and he could not warn him. His last thought was of the woman, and he rested his head on her soft body, still warm.

It came to him then. He knew why her face was so familiar. The resemblance was eerie, especially about the eyes.

She looked like Angus Mackay.

Chapter Nine

The heart of her husband doth safely trust in her so that he shall have no need of spoil.

~Proverbs 31:11

Roderic was summoned very early in the morning by one of his men. Having left Catherine sleeping, reluctant to leave her side, his manner was disgruntled.

"Pray forgive my intrusion. The young boy is gone. Wandered off, he did," Nigel said.

"Can you not have Gavin see to it?" Roderic asked.

"Nay, for he has gone to the training field after breaking his fast, and he hoped to travel to visit the father of Lady Gwyneth."

Roderic smiled with little humor. "The lass spurned him once. Why would he further his quest when so many others flutter about him?"

Nigel was tall and blond with a ruddy complexion. He displayed a wide grin when he replied.

" 'Twas not the lass who spurned him. Gavin turns their

heads with no effort. He puts them in a swoon with a wink. 'Tis her father that will not hear of his proposal, for Gavin holds no title, no lands."

"Aye," Roderic said. " 'Tis a familiar plight. Mayhap Cameron will see to finding the boy?"

"He, too, is gone, hunting; he left early, before Gavin. I told the woman, Mary, I would see to it. But she demands to speak with you. Her cottage is the small one, just south of the hill west of the keep," Nigel said.

"I'm on my way," Roderic said. After two paces he turned at the top of the steps.

"Nigel."

"Aye."

"My wife still sleeps. Guard her until I return, for her own safety."

"Aye, Sir Roderic, as ye wish."

He found the woman Mary with her daughter, a lass of perhaps twelve summers. She was very thin and pale. Mary held her bairn, also a lass. The babe was fretful, and Mary paced the small cottage trying to hush the whimpering of the little one.

"I beg your indulgence, Sir Roderic. Please go to fetch Kenneth."

"My lady, any of my men would go with you to help you fetch him."

"Aye, but Kenneth is verra swift eluding others in these woods. He fears your men. You, he does not. I fear if I sent others, it would frighten him. 'Tis a special hiding place, and I know where he has gone."

The bairn she was holding continued to cry. Roderic's brows gathered in a frown.

"The child is ill?"

Mary shook her head. "Nay, I merely need to feed her, and Kenneth brings me the wood for the fire."

"I will see that one of my men brings it," Roderic said.

"I cannae leave her. My daughter, Janet, will take ye to find Kenneth. He plays near this cottage. An old one of our clan died there years ago, and the mon built it away from others, preferring his own company. 'Tis a pretty spot in the woods. Kenneth goes there to be with his own world, his own thoughts. Edna doesnae know he has left again. 'Twill save him a beating if you get him back soon."

Roderic sighed as he answered. "I will do my best, but first I will send someone with the wood. Come, lass."

"Lady Montwain."

Cat sat up in bed, recognizing the voice at once.

"Merlin!"

She scrambled up to throw on her cloak. "You should know not to call me by that name!"

The old man smiled, blue eyes twinkling. "Should I not? Very well. Catherine, if you prefer it. My lady is . . . content?"

"You can ask that of me, when I have traveled back in time and have no idea how I have done it? Are you real, or part of my imagination?"

"Does this feel as if I am a spirit, an apparition?"

He reached out to her and grasped her hands. She sighed wearily.

"Then how? How did we do such a phenomenal . . . unbelievable . . . ?"

"Catherine." He interrupted her, aware of the fear laced with her curiosity.

"Do not fear the portal. It comes not from an evil source."

"Then it is possible to travel through the space time continuum?" Her eyes sparkled with the possibility.

He snorted as if disgusted, and dropped her hands. He shook a very long, thin finger in her face.

"You have been peering into that ridiculous box people stare at endlessly in your time! Allowing it to think for you! It matters not how!"

"You're not going to tell me, are you?"

"You have been given a great gift," Merlin declared.

Cat opened her mouth to argue, but thought better of it; for he had spoken the truth.

" 'Tis true, Merlin. I wouldnae care for ye to think me ungrateful."

He smiled. "The speech of this time is not all to which you have grown accustomed. My lady has taken a husband?"

An unwelcome blush crept into her cheeks. She had

slipped into the medieval speech without being aware of it, but she discarded her embarrassment.

"I have. And shall we discuss it, old man? You seem a bit too smug about my marriage to Roderic. Why is that?"

"Smug? Aye. Meddlesome? Aye. Repentant? Nay." He smiled as if delighted, having bested someone at a game of chance. Cat's eyes sparkled, suddenly astounded; she understood.

"You want us together!" She spoke the words as an accusation. He did not answer, but made an attempt to change the subject.

"I must go now, Catherine."

"Why? Why did you want me to marry Roderic?" She threw her head back and placed her hands on her hips.

"May you be a virtuous and faithful wife to him. Treat him with tenderness, for I have only loved one more than that boy. I know you will, for I have searched long for this solution. Do not allow your fear to stifle your courage. I must go." He turned away.

"No! Not yet. You must show me where the portal exists here and now. Stop speaking in riddles! My being here is a solution to what?"

"You must find your own answers. You are needed here," said Merlin.

"What if I want to go back?"

"If that be true, you would have answered my question."

"What question?"

Merlin walked to the door. He turned and spoke one sentence.

"Milady is content?"

He disappeared silently, walking through the door with all the finesse of a true apparition.

Roderic followed the young lass through the woods. She moved swiftly, her small form darting through the trees, brown hair flowing. The forest was dense, and Roderic had to duck beneath some of the branches while he kept her in sight, the child was so fleet of foot and agile he had to bend frequently to follow her. They trotted through the forest in this manner until Roderic began to fear she did not know her goal. Suddenly she stopped and turned to him, and reached out to take his hand. The look on the child's face was one of joy, her eyes dancing with anticipation. Roderic smiled and took her tiny, delicate hand in his own.

"Come, we have arrived," Janet said. She pulled him forward past the trees to a clearing, and Roderic gasped, for the sight before him was appealing.

The cottage lay nestled among many small trees and wildflowers, and understood the look of enchantment upon the young girl's face when he looked about him. When mothers spoke to their wee ones about fairies as they spun a tale, one could easily suppose they would spread their wings in such a place. The mist hung heavy near the cottage, and it conjured up the fancy of childhood dreams and laughter.

Janet called out, "Come, Kenneth."

Roderic stood, still taking in the surroundings, while the girl sought his attention by pointing up to the roof. Kenneth crawled up over the top of the thatched roof, and smiled at them, shaking his head as if it were a game.

"Yes! Ye must come," Janet said. "Mother said we must fetch ye. She wants ye home." The boy continued to smile at her and made no move to come down.

"Climb down now, Kenneth," Roderic said. There was a silken thread of warning in his voice.

The boy, his expression defeated, scrambled over the roof. He shimmied down to the corner of the cottage, hooking his feet over the stone as a spider would climb down a wall, and soon dropped to the ground.

Janet rushed forward, and taking Kenneth's hand, followed the trail back to the keep.

"Halt, lass," Roderic said. Entering the small dwelling, he pushed the door open with his shoulder. He looked around at the condition of the place, and though the door had a broken hinge and was in need of repair, the roof was sound and the hearth was fitting to keep out the cold. He vowed some in the clan could make use of the shelter.

Returning to Mary's cottage with the children, he then made his way back to the keep. He set another warrior on the task of guarding Brianna, and summoned Nigel.

"We must speak of the needs of the clan. Give me your report on how they fare."

" 'Tis bleak, Sir Roderic. They were unable to rebuild or shore up their defenses from the last attack made on Mackay."

"What must be done at once?"

"Shelter. We have given them all food and assistance to those ill. Many of their homes are no more than half standing, near burned out on the last attack."

Roderic sighed. "We shall see to it at once. Set the warriors about the repairs now, and have those who can see to building new quarters. It seems we cannot go to King Alexander at this time. My hope was that I could give Brianna the joy of being at court and allow Alexander to see her once again, but I fear it must wait. Far more do I wish to lay before him proof that our goals were met here. My bride will have many occasions to go to court to be with the King and Princess Joan; we must give the clan proper shelter before the winter.

"The cottage where I found the boy can be restored. I wish to go there with my bride for some time alone. We shall return in three days. I give you the command until I return."

"Aye, Sir Roderic."

Cat had little time to ponder her dilemma and her encounter

with Merlin. Roderic returned to the keep and commanded her to make ready for a short trip, and to pack for three days.

They were less than an hour from the keep when they reached their destination. The stone cottage was tiny, nestled in a lane of trees, and mist lay softly around the clearing, creating an ethereal beauty.

Their first day alone was immensely enjoyable to Cat. Roderic was a very compassionate man. He treated her tenderly with kindly humor, and her feelings for him became more intense with each passing moment. Their time together was marred by only one disagreement.

She was steadfastly unrepentant of the incident concerning the Maitland child. His anger was brief, however, and dissipated quickly in the light of their passion for one another.

At the end of the second day, long into the evening, Roderic turned to her.

"Brianna, some of your own clan have called you mad. Are you bewitched?"

Her face clouded with uneasiness, and she floundered before the brilliance of his gaze. "Who has told you this?" She spoke with a tremble in her voice.

"One who has no use for an Englishman in his midst, and prefers me to the cruelty of the Mackay. Why would he lie?"

"Roderic, do you see me as simple-minded? Or bewitched by the devil?"

"I know only that you have bewitched me ... filled me

with lust." He reached out to hold her cheek, his eyes soft when he went on.

"I am in awe of your beauty, intrigued by your spirit. You are a mystery, though, no evil abides in your heart. You are too caring for those helpless and in need. I hope I possess your loyalty. King Alexander wants your protection by this alliance, and he will have it, I will do all in my power to see it done."

"Even if it means you have married a woman who you believe to be mad?" Cat was dubious.

"Aye. Make no mistake, Brianna. You will obey me. If there be any effort from you to be loyal to your father, I will not hesitate to stop you. If you be in like mind of the boy," he paused before he finished his thought, "I will take care of you both."

She was rankled by his cool, aloof manner.

"You could be speaking of a pet you were given but didn't want! I am not like Kenneth! You are too quick to judge him. He is mute, but I don't believe he is lacking in intelligence. Having learned to fear most people, he shuts them out, but that does not make him stupid. As for my father, why would I be loyal to him? The man has never expressed empathy in his entire pathetic existence!"

"I want to believe you, the people here cannot withstand being taken prisoner and driven from their homes. Three Lairds have reason to kill Mackay on sight. Do you think Kenneth and the others will not be included in their wrath?"

Her angry expression was replaced with one of apprehension. After a long moment, she spoke softly. "Nay, they would not spare them. I know I cannot begin to make you understand, but I am not mad. I will do all I can to protect my people, even those who tell you these stories of my being bewitched. Their needs are so great. You have given them food, and I am grateful, yet their homes are in such a state . . ."

"Aye, wife, you speak the truth. They need warm homes for the winter. I left orders for my men. They work as we speak. The elderly and infirm will have their cottages built first. I left my many duties to be with my wife."

Her green eyes were bright when she turned her face to kiss his palm before she answered. "I do treasure this time alone with you. I appreciate the sacrifice. They will come to give you their loyalty in time, Roderic. How long did it take for your army to follow you without rancor? They must have resented an Englishman as their leader."

"Aye, they were misfits, too. My army embodies those from many different clans. Some were cast out, bastards with no holdings, no ties. Some lost their loved ones to war and had nothing to go back to, as I. Perhaps they accepted me in spite of their prejudice because I led them, gave them pride and integrity by beseeching the King on their behalf. He thought to give them a home here, too, a purpose. If the people have the discernment to trust in this alliance, they will have the benefit and protection of the finest warriors in Scotland."

"How proud you are of them."

"Aye, they are fine men, worthy of praise," he said.

The following day was relished, for it was the last day of their respite. They hunted together and returned with birds to cook for the evening meal. Later, Roderic made a fire in the hearth and put a bed of furs before it. When he informed her that they would return in the morning, she could not hide her disappointment; for she had treasured their time alone. He took her in his arms, urging her to lie down.

"Come, do not pout. We can stay here no longer, but do not allow that to ruin the joy of this night."

"Pray sir, I do not pout!" She spoke with a mockingly outraged expression while her eyes danced with laughter.

He grinned. "Aye, you do, lady."

She took his hand and knelt down beside him. Cat did not care for the uncanny ability he had to see her character so vividly. Smiling at the man who was her husband, she felt a strong desire to be in his arms, to experience the comfort to her spirit which the act would bring. Opening her arms to him, she was almost ashamed of the gesture.

Roderic observed the change in her, be it fleeting. Embracing her by wrapping her snugly in his arms, he stretched out by the fire.

"Why are you troubled?"

Shaking her head, she tucked her face under his chin. He made love to her very slowly, each touch and caress savored. Cat lay in the afterglow of their passion, aware that in the desperate seconds before his climax, Roderic called out her name.

He had called her Brianna. There was no unease in her spirit at his use of it, no nameless anxiety to give her grief. Slipping her arms around him, she caressed his hair as he rested his head on her chest.

She lay awake for a while after it was obvious he slept heavily. Taking a deep breath, she sighed, and then spoke softly into the night.

"Aye, Merlin. I am content."

Chapter Ten

The wisdom that is from above is first pure, then
peaceable, gentle, and full of mercy and good fruits.

~James 3:17

Cat spent the next two weeks listening to Edna as she
tried to teach her about the managing of the keep.
Accustomed to her own time, she never realized
how diligently a woman must work to be peacemaker in the
castle. She was called upon to settle disputes of the women
of the clan who were disgruntled with the constant appearance of the men who served Roderic in his army.

Cat did her best to speak for the women in these disputes. The soldiers found that Roderic himself championed
the women, and agreed with his wife. Being a virtuous man,
he set down the decree that no woman was to be coerced to
bed by any soldier should she be unwilling. The clan had suffered enough, and their mission was one of restoration, not
of pillaging.

Cat was relieved to see that almost all the soldiers

accepted this command. Her husband had their respect, and they were eager to show him their fealty and obedience.

Gavin returned from his trip and never failed to remain loyal to Roderic in these concerns. Cat soon became used to the people requesting her judgement on even small matters, so she was not surprised one afternoon when Edna sought her out.

"Ye must come, lady. Two women have come through the soldiers to our gates. They have traveled a bit, and wish an audience with Sir Roderic. Half-starved they be, from the look of them."

Cat's brow creased in a frown. "Where is Roderic?"

"He be training with his men."

"Send someone to fetch him, and bring them food and drink. We will make sure they are fed before they tell us what they want of Roderic."

Edna hurried away to obey her. Cat had been salting meat to preserve it, she took the time to wash before she went to meet her guests. When she entered the dining hall she was appalled at the sight that greeted her.

A young woman barely in her teens sat at the table. Hugely pregnant, her limbs were thin to the point of emaciation. Humming to herself, she sat stroking her long hair. The girl had been pretty once, for her eyes were a lovely blue, with long black lashes. But now her skin was pale, her hair dull, and her breathing shallow as if it took all her strength to sit in the chair at the table. Although she ignored the other woman when she tried to coax her to take a bite of bread, she did drink the cup of milk when it was held to her lips.

"Aye, good lass. Drink every drop."

The older woman girl looked up, and Cat was startled by her penetrating gaze. Her eyes were silver and her hair was black, long and straight, falling to her waist. The gown she wore was black velvet, and though she was dusty and the worse for traveling, the woman was striking.

"Lady Montwain?"

"Aye. I would like to extend my greetings, and I have sent for my husband. You wish to speak to him?"

"Aye, lady. I do thank ye for the food. We have come a long way and hope to seek shelter here. I am a healer, and can be a help to Montwain, should he wish it. I can set bones, stitch wounds, and heal a lesion if it isnae too far gone."

Her hands were thin, Cat noticed when she stroked the girl's brow with long delicate fingers. The girl leaned into the woman's touch, but said nothing.

Cat frowned.

"I see ye seek answers, but if I may beg your indulgence, I prefer to wait until Montwain arrives. 'Tis a sad tale, and healer that I am, lady, I cannae cure a broken spirit."

The last was spoken with anger and resignation, as if she were loath to admit the truth. They sat silently while the woman ate and tried to feed the girl.

Finally, Roderic arrived, sweating profusely as he had come from the practice field, still carrying his sword. He smiled briefly at Cat before he spoke.

"You seek audience with me, lady?"

The woman stood. "Aye, Sir Montwain. I have heard of your victory here, and they say ye be a mon of mercy. I am Glyniss Gordon from the Gordon clan to the south, and this be Meggie. Her mother is a Macpherson, but we both came from the Gordon clan. We were cast out, ye see, and have nowhere to go."

Meggie dropped her gaze from Roderic and turned, as if apprehensive, to wrap her arms around the woman's middle, and emitted a frightened whimper. Glyniss stroked her shoulder in wordless comfort as she went on.

"I was banished for helping and healing Meggie, unwed and forced to starve when her parents abandoned her to the man that ruined her. I've helped many women the Church would have condemned. The clan took no heed of them, if I chose to help, but not so Meggie. She loves the father of her child, but he was the pampered only son of the Gordon Laird. He wouldnae accept the child was his, and when I spoke to the Laird on her behalf, he sent me away. I knew they would let her starve if I left her there, so we set out, Meggie and me. Some of the Gordon people have spoken of your mercy to the Mackay women and children. Think ye daft, they do, but I allowed ye might take us in.

I have a bit of coin ye can have for your coffers, and I will work as a healer. All I ask is shelter for this poor child and myself. If ye say we are not welcome, and ye decree that we should be gone, so be it. We will make our way to Melrose Abbey and the holy sisters."

She turned to Cat. "Ye think her simple, lady, but it isnae true. Ahh, such a bright, beautiful lass ye had never seen, so full of joy. It was stolen when that pampered boy spurned her. He took her joy and spirit, and she be like a tree that no longer has the sap running through it to make it strong and alive. I can get her to put so little food past her lips I was afraid she wouldnae survive this journey. Still, her babe lives, is healthy and kicking. If Meggie gives up on life, it willnae be for lack of all my strength and healing ways. She speaks not to anyone, so dinnae mind her. I am not one that believes all those a bit mad should be locked up or burned."

Roderic lifted his sword and put it in the scabbard at his waist. "Nor I, lady. Sanctuary is granted, and you may keep your coins. Though you may not have a cottage of your own for a bit. We are still building for the people here." His brown eyes were troubled and filled with compassion as he stared at Meggie.

"Ah, a cottage? Sir, I wish for no such luxury, just a few pallets for Meggie and me. We could sleep in the stable, though I fear 'tis too cold."

"I agree. We don't want you in the stable. You both need a room of your own with a fire," Cat said.

Glyniss gazed at her, and the hard, brittle look of fear was gone, replaced by warmth and gratitude.

"Bless ye, lady. I'll not forget your kindness." She turned

to Roderic. "Nor you, sir. Englishmon or no, ye have more integrity than many a Scot."

Cat went to work seeing them settled. The girl's eyes almost never left Glyniss. When Edna brought up some pudding, Cat was encouraged to see that Meggie took a wooden spoon and ate half the cup before stretching out on the bed. Pulling Glyniss down to lie beside her, she went to sleep at once as Glyniss hummed softly and stroked her hair.

"I can get up once she is sleeping. She becomes frightened if left alone. Meggie is quite weary from our ride this day. I thank you again for the warm bed, for she will sleep better now."

"You are welcome. She's so young," Cat said.

"Aye, only five and ten summers. I fear for the size of this babe, though she eats so little. My prayer has been that she can manage to push it from her small body when the time comes."

"You are a midwife?"

"Aye. I helped bring all those born to the Gordon clan these last seven years."

"I helped one of the ladies from the Maitland clan when her son was born with the cord still around his neck. The midwife and I barely managed to save both the mother and the child."

"And the Maitland men dinnae keep ye?" There was a sparkle of amusement in her bright silver eyes when Glyniss spoke.

Cat sighed. "No, though my husband was near forced to go to war. The lady was wed to the Laird, and he was grateful for my help, so we left peacefully."

"A blessing, that," Glyniss said.

Kenneth ran into the room, coming to an abrupt halt by Cat. He stared silently at Meggie and leaned down near her on the bed.

Glyniss put out her hand as if to push him away.

"Be not alarmed," Cat said. "This is Kenneth. He is mute, but he will not hurt her; he is very gentle."

Kenneth leaned down and sniffed the girl's hair. Touching her cheek lightly so she did not awaken, he stared at her belly, and placed his hand on it. Cat wanted to laugh at his dumbfounded expression when he smiled and looked up at her, a query in his eyes.

Glyniss smiled and covered his hand with her own. "The babe stirs," she murmured.

Kenneth leaned down to press his cheek to the girl's belly, and laughed out loud when the baby kicked his face. Cat made signs as if to quiet him.

"Leave him be, 'tis no worry. Meggie sleeps deeply now she is warm, and 'tis good to hear laughter of a young one."

"How long were you with the Gordon clan?"

"Seventeen years. My mother took a second husband after my father died. He was a Gordon, and treated her well. Ten summers I was then, and now I am twenty and seven. I never married, for I chose not to. Too many men wouldnae sanction my gift of healin'. They want a lass at their beck and call, warming their beds when they want her there. Most have no sufferance for a woman who is apt to leave them at a moment's notice to nurse others.

"I was a year older than Meggie when I knew I had the gift. I held my baby sister in my arms when she was ailing. My mother said she had given her up for dead. Mother could feel the healing power coming from my hands, and that was when she told me I had been given a great gift. God had chosen me to heal others, she said, and was verra stern as she instructed that I was to revere the power He put in me, to use it for good.

"The older Gordon Laird favored me. I healed his shoulder wound, and he allowed that no one could make his legs feel better than me when the gout pained him. He respected me as a healer, no matter I was a young lass.

"The old man has been dead now five summers. His son, the present Laird, can be harsh to his people, and he be proud and vain about that young boy, who willnae defy his father. Douglas sought to marry another more comely lass, and he kenned that to accept Meggie and her child would mean the loss of the other."

Glyniss fell silent while she stroked the girl's hair. Cat took note of the extraordinary delicacy of the woman's touch.

"Rest well, Glyniss," she said, and rose to leave the chamber.

Cat did her best to help Glyniss in the days that followed. The woman was devoted to Meggie, and although the girl rarely responded to anyone else, she was not as fearful as when she arrived.

It was only a matter of days until Glyniss was called upon to heal one of the soldiers, who had been injured on the training field by a less experienced lad he was teaching. The wound was in his thigh, and he was resigned to the fact that she would have to burn it with a hot iron.

Cat was inwardly cringing. "Must you do this? May we not simply clean the wounds so he'll not have to suffer the burns?"

"Nay, lady. We cannae get all the dirt out," Glyniss said.

"Do we have any strong drink about? Stronger than ale?"

"We can beseech the soldiers. Some always have a bit of strong brew to ward off the cold. In Scotland there are barrels of that to be had, or to be bought for the right price."

"Have it brought to us, Edna. Send Nigel to fetch it," Cat said.

When he returned with the flask, Cat went to work cleaning the wound. The man moaned low in his throat as they worked, and he gripped his other thigh and grimaced in pain.

"I fear he would prefer the iron," Glyniss said.

"Yes, I know it hurts, and I am sorry for your pain, but you will see, there will be no need for the iron," Cat said.

"No matter, my lady. Get it done as ye see fit," he said.

Glyniss' gaze turned penetrating when she looked at Cat. "And how do ye know this, lady? Have ye seen this done with wounds before?"

Cat dropped her eyes. "I didnae think to instruct you of healing, Glyniss, but aye, I have seen it done."

"Ah, dinnae beg my pardon, lady. I trust you to do right by this mon as ye did by Meggie and me. We may try this and watch the wound closely on the morrow, and I can use the iron if need be."

Three days later the skin continued to heal around the wound, and the soldier complained of little pain.

"No red lines or signs of trouble," Glyniss said. "Must ye clean it as steadfastly as ye did?"

"Aye, but once you have, you have only the pain of the wound, not the burn," Cat said.

From then on Glyniss occasionally trusted Cat to sit with Meggie. A bond was formed between the women, as Glyniss could see that Cat had the heart of a healer. Cat would sit with the girl at times, Kenneth at her feet. Meggie slept most of the day, much to Glyniss' worry and concern.

One afternoon, weary of the sickroom and the confinement of the castle, Cat took Kenneth for a riding lesson, with Cameron tagging along.

"This lad is like a cocklebur under your saddle, lady. Mayhap you would like to take the air without his presence?"

"Nay, Cameron. I enjoy Kenneth. I don't mind him

coming with me at all."

Cat laughed out loud at the arrogant, impudent look Kenneth gave Cameron over his victory.

Cameron rolled his round brown eyes and laughed along with her.

Cat amused Kenneth by playing a riding game. He would lie on the ground as if he were sleeping, and she would ride at a full gallop, bend down, and pick him up to hoist him behind her on the saddle. It was one of her classic stunts, and she performed it in part to prove to herself she could still perform. She also galloped the horse and stood in the saddle, the reins in her teeth, grinning at the astonished look on Cameron's face.

She pulled her bow and, reins still in her teeth, shot an arrow at a nearby tree. She dropped down in the saddle before coming to a halt at Kenneth's feet.

Cameron hailed her as he approached. "My lady, never have I seen such a feat performed by any woman on a horse, but I must take a risk and chastise you. I have undertaken your safety in a solemn vow to your husband. Ye must know that my base blood would be worthy to be shed at his hands should ye come to any harm."

"I beg your pardon, Cameron, I am really in no danger. I have ridden this way hundreds of times before, and Roderic does tend to hover."

"Aye, as any mon would hover, cosset, and protect ye, hoard ye to himself like a miser does his gold. Think ye he willnae toss me from a window in the castle should I allow ye to come to the slightest harm?"

Cat sighed and inclined her head. "I concede, sir."

She spent the rest of the afternoon working with Kenneth, helping him learn to stand in the saddle. Admonishing him to be patient, she walked the horse slowly while he grew accustomed to the animal's movements. Holding the reins, she did her best to help him balance.

When the sun dropped low into the sky, Cat decided it was time they got back to the castle. Cameron had grown weary of waiting and started back ahead of them, although still in sight. Helping Kenneth mount behind her, she walked the horse slowly back, enjoying the lovely shadows of the end of the day.

When she entered the keep, Edna came to her immediately. "Glyniss is gone; she went to look for herbs that will tempt the poor lass to eat. But, she should be back by now, lady."

"I'll go. I'll find her," Cat said.

Kenneth followed her as silently as her shadow. They walked in the forest down the trail Edna had pointed out and made quick time, as they would soon be in darkness. Cat's step faltered when she heard a startled scream. She turned quickly to Kenneth.

"Go for help!"

She pointed behind him toward the keep, and ran through the trees following the sound of the woman's frantic voice.   Running down the trail, she saw Angus Mackay and Glyniss struggling on the ground. He lay on top of her, holding her down, and tried to rest between her legs. He fumbled with his clothing, and Cat knew at once he was bent on rape.

Chapter Eleven

Behold, I set before you this day a blessing and a curse; a blessing if ye obey the commandments and a curse if you will not obey.

~Deuteronomy 11:26

As he raised his kilt and tried to maneuver his erection into her body, Glyniss screamed in rage, beating at his back with her fists. He held her arms as she tried to fight him.

Cat ran up to them and kicked Mackay hard in the ribs. Grunting in pain, he rolled away and Glyniss scrambled up.

Mackay came up to his full height and faced Cat. The hatred in his eyes was like a blow. "Ye unworthy bitch. Ye have shamed me and interfered with me for the last time. Better I have ye as I wanted from the start." He drew back his fist and tried to pound it into her temple.

Although Cat dodged the blow enough that it did not knock her senseless, her cheek felt as if it had exploded. She lost her balance and fell hard to the ground. Mackay covered her body from behind and the weight of him impeded her efforts to move him off. He pulled her hair back, and she whimpered in pain. Glyniss tried to help her, reaching out to pull him off. Angus turned and, backhanded her brutally.

Cat screamed as Glyniss hoisted herself to a standing position.

"Go, Glyniss, run!"

Angus turned back to Cat, flipping her over to face him and putting a hard hand on her throat.

"No," she wailed, reading the intent in his eyes. Angus had not forgotten the humiliation she and Roderic had dealt him. He cared not if he died, but rape her he would. Knowing it was hopeless, Cat screamed Roderic's name. Angus controlled her movements with his weight and pressed down on her throat while his hands groped at her breast.

"Ah, lass. Call for him, scream his name. It will be me that rides ye. Do ye sigh in pleasure when he takes ye? When you rut with that Norman, does he give ye your woman's joy?"

He put even more pressure on her windpipe, and though Cat continued to fight him, it was getting harder to breathe. From a distance she heard Glyniss cry out.

Deprived of oxygen, Cat became dizzy and faint then Cameron appeared out of nowhere and let out an unholy growl of rage as he lifted his sword. The blow was so strong Cat felt it ripple through her own body when the sword breached the back of Angus' head.

The stroke was true, for although it was now dark and she could see little, she felt the tension leave his body. Cat was certain Angus had just died upon her; his head slumped forward, and she felt a warm splash of blood.

Cameron pulled the body from her like so much refuse and pushed it aside, then put out his hand to help her stand.

Cat ignored it, turning away on her hands and knees. Feeling a desperate nausea clawing at her middle, she was retching on the ground when Gavin came running through the forest holding a torch to light his way.

Roderic was behind him, sword drawn. He stopped suddenly and lowered his weapon when he realized that Cameron had already removed the threat. Cat raised up, taking deep breaths, and Roderic turned in a rage to Cameron.

"Curse you, where were you? You stand too long at the privy? Beseech me why I should grant you your life!"

"Roderic, no. Please, don't be angry, just hold me," Cat said.

He felt her trembling and bent down to pick her up in his arms.

Gavin stepped between Cameron and Roderic. "See to your wife." He turned to Glyniss.

"Ye be well, lady?"

Glyniss nodded her assent.

Cat refused to cry, but she held tightly to Roderic while he carried her back to the castle.

Roderic took her to their chamber, and called for hot water, then directed the healer to see to her. Cat sat silently in the hot tub of water and tried to come to terms with what had happened, while Glyniss sat near her on a stool, gingerly trying to see to the injury on her cheek.

"Ah, lass, what ye must have suffered in this keep. Edna said that one was your brother. What manner of a mon would try to rut with his own sister?"

Cat looked up, concerned at how it must have appeared. "Roderic knows he was bent on raping me, too?"

"Nay, for Cameron was told by me only that he was hurting ye. He swung his mighty weapon with haste, though we could see little. Gavin came with his torch, and we all could see better, yet Cameron had disposed of the lout. Sir Roderic will be even more angry if he kens why ye were losing the food in your belly."

"How could I have done this?" Cat spoke as if to herself. "It's not safe here."

Glyniss snorted. "Where be it safe for any lass when a man wants a taste of what lies between her legs? Men are lusty, and a lass is at risk to a mon if they choose it. He thought me cast out, belongin' to no one, just as I am, or even a whore who follows the army of Montwain. If a woman has no husband, he could expect no retribution for his deeds. If he is a renegade thief, forcin' a lass to a quick tumble in the grass is as common as the sunset."

"Aye, and he had reason to want me dead. You see Glyniss, I am not Brianna Mackay."

She whispered her tale when she told Glyniss of her abduction by Angus.

"Ye must tell Sir Roderic the truth. Lies only breed more of the same!"

"I can't. What will happen to the clan if I do? Roderic is helping them, and the King wants the clan to have the protection of the soldiers. Roderic believes they are the finest in Scotland, and they can defend these people and give them a chance to build anew."

Cat sighed, shaking her head. "Angus is dead, and all this will hurt Edna. She loved him. She raised him."

"Ah, then she raised herself a viper. Ye fought for us, lass! There was no other way to go. Think ye he would have let ye be once he was done with ye? Nay! He would have killed ye, too. Fie! The way he hated your husband he would relish the deed. We cannae wish it undone unless ye wish he had his way with ye, mayhap even stealin' your life."

"I had no choice but to do as they asked when I came here, Glyniss."

Cat was surprised to see no judgment in the other woman's eyes.

"Aye, I ken. Many is the time a mon has forced marriage on a lass. Most do it for land and gold the lass may own. I am certain he thought it a righteous cause indeed to save his neck from a stretching.

"I care not from whence ye came. Ye risked your own hide for me, and I will not forget it. 'Tis all the more glad I am that mon is dead. Ye helped Montwain sting his pride in front of his clan? Ah, lass, men can wreak not a small vengeance for such a slight."

Cat stood, bone weary, and although she felt better now that she was clean, she was exhausted. Glyniss continued to work at daubing some medicine on her cheek, and Cat pushed her hands away. "Stop fussing, Glyniss. You were hurt, too."

"Aye, but not on my face. Men never notice others as they do the lady they take to their own beds. Ye are his wife, and I dinnae want these bruises to stir Sir Roderic's anger to an even hotter fire, for Cameron will be punished this night."

"Punished?"

"Aye, I heard talk from the soldiers. He's to be flogged."

"Flogged? You mean whipped?!"

"Aye, lady, though how many lashes none can say save your husband. They speak of it now in the great hall."

Cat stood up from the tub in a rush. She searched in haste for her gown and dressed, leaving her hair hanging wet down her back. Her heart wrenched with guilt when she considered Cameron's efforts to protect her. One word from her in the kitchens, and he would have stopped speaking with Nigel and followed her. Cat realized that her own independent nature was truly more than a hindrance to her adjustment in this time. It was a danger to Cameron, who would be punished severely. Putting on her shoes, she turned to Glyniss. "Come with me.'

She all but ran down the stone steps to the great hall, and several soldiers were clustered about the long table. Gavin stood facing them all; Roderic sat at his right, Cameron at his left.

Roderic made a brief sign with his hand for Gavin to begin.

"I call a tribunal," Gavin said. Facing Cameron, he went on. "You stand accused this day of abandoning your duty to Lady Montwain. How then do you testify to this charge?"

Cat tried to walk forward and speak, but Glyniss reached out to grasp her firmly by the arm and haul her back. Cameron stood to face Gavin and Roderic.

"I plead guilty, sir. I was lax in my duty. Lady Montwain had entered the keep. I knew not that she had left once again in search of the healer. I kenned she was putting her horse away in the stable. Hence, I was derelict, and I stand guilty as charged. Sir Roderic, I submit to your will."

Cat suddenly gripped Glyniss' hand on her arm and whispered low under her breath, "No."

The noble knight had a pained expression on his face; however, he stood resolved. Gavin spoke once again. "Do we all stand in agreement that this hearing was fair and just?"

Roderic's men one by one nodded an assent. Cat rushed forward.

"I would like to beseech this council to be heard. Although I am but a woman, I plead your indulgence that you grant me favor to speak."

All then turned to Roderic, silently waiting for his decree.

"Permission granted."

Cat took a deep breath and plunged ahead. "I beg that

you grant mercy to Sir Cameron, for I, too, was at fault. I should have run for help when I saw that Glyniss was being attacked, but I tried to intercede, and the attacker turned on me. I should have run back to the keep to plead for assistance. I did not inform Cameron that I was leaving."

Gavin folded his arms before him, eyes narrowed when he spoke. "Think ye, lady, it be your duty to inform the mon to make his responsibility a light one?"

Cat heaved a heavy sigh. "Nay, sir, maybe not, but I cannot be silent if he's to be flogged." She turned to Roderic. "Is this true?"

"Aye, the punishment will be twenty lashes."

Cat grew pale at the thought. Turning to look at Glyniss, her expression was one of disbelief and astonishment, and she whirled back to Roderic.

"You mustn't do this!" she cried out. "You can't!"

"Brianna . . ." Roderic interrupted.

"Aye, lady, we can," Gavin said.

Suddenly, Cameron spoke up. "Hear me, my lady. Say no more, for my duty is a sacred trust. You could have been killed, and I embrace whatever punishment my comrades decree."

Addressing Roderic, her eyes pleading with him desperately, she spoke. "Please. May you lessen the punishment?"

"Why would I do that when I could have lost you?"

"Because I ask it of you . . . nay, I beg it. You are my lord, my husband, Roderic, and I beg you, please."

"Enough!"

She had pushed him too far. No one spoke, and the silence stretched for a long moment as Roderic considered her pleas. Finally, Roderic spoke.

He turned to Gavin and bit off four angry words. "Five and ten lashes!"

The soldiers took Cameron to the middle of the courtyard and tied him up. Cat forced herself to stand and watch, though every stroke of the whip was a lash to her conscience. Cameron bore it all stoically, never once crying out. Roderic stood beside her, and at one point he spoke in a low murmur. "You needn't watch this."

"Would it be any less cruel if I did not watch it?"

"Show me your displeasure in our chamber, lady, but here I will have your loyalty."

Cat looked away, took a deep breath, and nodded. Later, she was silent and solemn when she entered the sick room, and began tearing strips for bandages for Cameron's back. Glyniss silently crushed up the herbs with mortar and pestle, and mixed the unguent that she would use on the wounds, then asked Cameron to lie down so she could have better access to the cuts.

"Have you anything you could give him for the pain?" Cat asked.

Roderic entered the chamber as Cat had just spoken the question. "Brianna, I will speak to you in our chamber now. Leave him to the healer."

"Be at ease, Lady Brianna, for I will mix up a potion that will have him sleeping shortly," Glyniss said.

Cat nodded, putting the bandages near the table by Glyniss' medicine, and followed Roderic silently down the hallway to their chamber. When the door closed behind him, Roderic immediately pulled her into his arms. He trapped her chin gently in his hand to examine her cheek.

"Does this pain you still?"

She made futile little moves as if to push him away, but he held her fast.

"I'm in very little pain, Roderic. Not like Cameron. 'Twas my folly that brought down every stroke of that lash."

He nodded, uncompromising. "Aye, 'tis true."

She snorted. "I see you're not going to ease my guilt."

He shook his head very slowly. "Never, lass. With your title comes duty, and the two go hand in hand. Your manner as lady here may foster these people or give them tribulation. 'Tis time you yield to that knowledge. Gavin will take Cameron's place in keeping you safe until his back is healed."

"Why must I have one of your soldiers take time out from his duties to follow me about? I am not accustomed to having a man guard me."

"You are accustomed to having your own way, Brianna, but heed me in this you will. I'll warn you, Gavin will stop you from leaving the keep at all, even to hunt if you continue to risk yourself. Nor is he to allow you to please the boy with standing in the saddle." Cat was not surprised Cameron had told him.

"I cause no harm when I ride standing in the saddle!"

"You harm me, with worry for your life and limb. Find another way to entertain Kenneth."

She pushed away from him and sat on the edge of the bed. He sat beside her and took her gently in his arms, massaging her shoulders and stroking her back. Perversely, at this moment, Cat resented his touch.

"What are you doing?"

"Mayhap I seek to give you ease, to show you tenderness after being so roughly handled and abused."

Cat felt tears come into her eyes. She didn't like her vulnerability, or his gift to comprehend her needs. Angus had inflicted upon her a loss of power and control even of her own body. In her own time Cat had accepted the belief that if a woman were capable and strong enough, she could, in fact, defend herself. Angus had proven that to be a lie. Though she was competent with her sword, she was not allowed to carry the weapon, and was defenseless in this time by the very nature of the culture. Her husband was her protector, and though in her own time she would have taken offense at such a presumption, it was necessary here.

Despite Cat's longing to blend in at the castle, it was a struggle. She had to fight against her inborn need to be independent and move freely, to do what she wanted when she chose to do so. Roderic would never understand those needs, yet he refused to punish her and allowed her own remorse to be a full recompense. He was trusting her to make the changes necessary in her own behavior. For now, it was enough.

Chapter Twelve

*He that walketh uprightly walketh surely: but he
that perverteth his ways shall be known.*

~Proverbs 10:9

The old, thin Scot struggled as he walked up the short hill to the stone cottage. His crippled leg gave him pain in spite of the crude wooden cane he leaned upon, and his disposition was surly as he banged on the door.

Mary answered, her baby girl on her hip. Blue eyes were sharp when she addressed him. "Enter, Tobias. I have gathered them here as ye bid me."

It was a bit before she could close the door. Tobias walked very slowly, but Mary knew better than to offer assistance. The old Scot had the pride of Lucifer, and he chose to go his own way, though slowly, rather than accept help. Some of the wee ones of the clan, having been taught their manners, had tried to help him in the past. They were given a harsh reproof and a whack on the backside with his stick for their trouble.

Tobias was a kind old one at heart, but he was suspicious by nature. He had done his best to help the women when Mackay's men were gone reaving. Once, although wracked with pain when he mounted a horse, he had taken two of the strongest lads and raided a neighboring clan for food and blankets. They had managed to eat for a month after his return. 'Twas he that made the grave judgment to kill the horses for food, yet soon the hunger had weakened them all. The women had been coming to him with their worries, and he had done his best in Mackay's absence to keep them all alive. Such efforts had spurred a loyalty and willing obedience when he voiced a request.

Dorcus, Elsie, and Emma were there with their children. Tobias glanced briefly at Elsie's eldest daughter. The child was four and ten summers, and although she was heartbreakingly thin, her blue eyes and black hair were striking. Tobias feared the soldiers in the army of Montwain would take note of her beauty.

"Have the bastards let ye be, lass?" he asked abruptly.

"Aye, Tobias. They jest with me a bit, but they dinnae seek to hurt me."

"I keep her close to me," Elsie said, folding her arms over her chest. Elsie was a tall woman, with a wide face and a shock of gray in her dark hair.

"See that ye do," Tobias said.

"I vow his men may even stop it, for there be one less rapin' Mackay about us now. Tried to have his way with the healer, he did. Did ye hear?"

"Aye, Angus was a fool to come back here, but, the wench gadding about alone brought on her own folly. She put herself in harm's way. Trust an Englishmon to put an outsider above the loyal Scot he was given to rule, and nae punish the one deserving."

"She saved the healer," Mary said.

"Aye, one more burden for us all," Tobias said.

Mary gasped. "She isnae a burden! We have need of a healer so close to us!"

"Aye, we do. But, she will bring more trouble with the Gordon clan. Lady Montwain has no fealty for Mackay. Why did she stay, if not to lord it over us all?"

Dorcus snorted. "She is no lady, that one; she is from humble folk. Mayhap even the daughter of a stable peasant. And she thinks to look down on us?"

"Nay, Dorcus. She does not. The lady has been good to Edna and Kenneth," Mary said.

"I see that is true," Tobias said. "Howbeit, she is not of our clan and we cannae trust her. We know not if her virtue be that of a nun, or of a whore. 'Tis bitter enough to bear the King's gifts to the Englishmon. Where is her loyalty? She helped the Maitlands, and they hate us. Why did she leave and force Montwain to fetch her? Who was she tryin' to meet that she would court starting a war for the risk?"

"The lass dinnae have to help us," Mary said.

"Bah! Her own hide she wished to keep hale and comely.

Calum threatened her. Think ye she wished to wed Mont-wain? Thereupon, after the deed, she slithered away to Maitland. Nay, Mary. Ye favor her for she spoils the boy, but she will betray us as she does the Englishmon."

"If that were what she was about, why did she not stay with the Maitlands when she reached their lands?"

Tobias rapped his cane against the table, making the children jump. "I know not! But she willnae say from whence she came! She hails from no clan in the Highlands? How can that be? She appeared before Angus and Graham in a stream with no horse about? Who left her? Who sent her?"

"Mayhap the lass was cast out. Edna helped her and gathers this to be so. To be wed, even to an Englishmon, is a comfort to one used to cold and hunger. We have borne it ourselves, so shall we judge her for wanting a full belly and a home with a strong warrior by her side? She fancies him, and even a small temptation from so fair a lass would lend the mon to come at her like a stallion. Montwain be as lusty as any mon. He willnae let her go, so best we welcome her if we dinnae want the wrath of Montwain upon us."

"Mary speaks the truth," said Emma. "Montwain is here and approved by the King. I am happy to be feeding my wee ones, and I want no part of bedeviling him. I be too weak and tired for any fight."

"Aye," said Dorcus. "I agree."

"Elsie?" Tobias waited for her answer, frowning.

Elsie shrugged. "She hasnae earned our support or our

hatred in my judgment. We should give Lady Montwain and Glyniss time to see if they mean us any harm."

Tobias studied them all thoughtfully for a moment and sighed heavily. "So be it. Yet, we wait only until we be strong enough to defy them. I hope she will be the means to break him."

Glyniss worked diligently tending to Cameron's back, soothing the wounds with a salve she made from plants. Meggie wandered into the room and, jealous of her attention to him, made an attempt to pull her away. Glyniss shook off her hand.

"Ah, go to the kitchens alone, lass! Ye are no bairn. Sit up and eat from your trenchers! I cannae spoon feed ye. Go and sit in the dining hall, and wait for me."

Meggie looked mulish as she glared at Cameron. He winked at her, and smiled when she left the room, stomping.

"That was a pretty pout," he said.

Glyniss bit back a grin. "She is eating better, yet clings to me. Why get up and walk if someone will carry ye? I allow it is time for a bit of firmness. Meggie cannae act a babe if she is to bear one."

He closed his eyes and sighed. "What is that brew ye made me drink? I feel as if I've long been in my cups of ale."

"It is a wee potion. Did ye hear the lady? She dinnae

want ye in pain."

He shrugged as she worked, deftly stroking the medicine on his back. "Ah, Glyniss, the touch of your soft hands is balm to me."

"Weel, ye bore this with a lot of courage. Many a mon wouldnae stay in the service of Sir Roderic after such a judgment."

"He did right, Glyniss. He strives hard to be fair to us all. Roderic dinnae even bring forth the charge. Gavin stepped up to it while he was still taking his own council, working it out in his mind. Though I willnae lie, I wish Lady Montwain would have taken care, for she would have saved my back and her own pain. His anger was a righteous one, for she was hurt."

He chuckled. "She slipped away from me, but she willnae play that game with Gavin. Never was there a lass he could not bend to his will, be she five summers or twenty."

It was a week before Cat ventured away from the castle. Arranging for Gavin to escort her to do a bit of hunting, she let Kenneth ride with her on her horse as they were to be gone a short time.

Cat pulled at the reins and stopped her mount beside Gavin to rest the animals. The hunt had been successful, and she grasped the satchel of birds behind her to feel that it was still safely secured and Kenneth had not dislodged it.

"I know there are other duties you would prefer," Cat said. Gavin turned to her in the saddle.

" 'Tis a fine duty, and I will not shirk it. Ye would balk to know my thoughts of ye, lass. Ye are a blessing to Roderic in spite of being a stubborn handful." Smiling, he took a deep breath, exhaling slowly.

"Ye make him happy. Ye have penetrated that heavy shield of mistrust he holds for all. Do ye yet bear me ill, lady, for the strapping I gave Kenneth?"

"Nay, but I was angry at the time. He's such a sweet boy."

"I was in a temper myself. I wished you were mine, so I could thrash you as Roderic did."

Cat was tempted to mention the so-called thrashing was a ruse, but thought better of it.

"Ye are too soft, lass, for all your bluster. Ye would spare Cameron, and the boy. 'Tis a hard life we have here in the Highlands, and Kenneth wasnae cuffed about any more than Roderic as a lad."

Cat looked troubled. "Because he was English?"

Gavin shrugged. "In part. In part for being so verra favored by the King. He took him in, and many coveted his place. The holy scrolls say envy is rottenness to the bones, and I agree, for I have seen its perfidy. Roderic was tormented as a boy, as was I, for I am a bastard. We joined together and sought to watch one another's back. Two staff rods coupled be more difficult to break." Gavin winked at Cat.

"I'm happy you watched his back, Gavin. I thank you."

"You're most welcome, Lady Montwain."

"Methinks you are gifted with an abundance of charm, Gavin."

"Aye. I, too, am a humble mon, as the Lord wants us." His eyes were dancing with mirth. She laughed aloud. Cat could only guess how a woman would manage to resist him if he actively pursued her.

Kenneth fell asleep on her shoulder with his arms around her waist.

"It's time we returned to the castle, 'afore this one falls off the back of your horse in a slumber," Gavin said.

Cat shifted Kenneth to wake him, then urged her mount forward, following Gavin.

Graham entered the tent of Laird Mackay with little hope he would favor the message brought to him.

"Where is he?" Calum bellowed.

Graham smiled, trying to take the sting out of the message. "He hasnae returned. The boy went off for a bit of wenching. Too long has Angus been without a lady to give him ease."

Calum growled deep in his throat. "There be whores a plenty in this camp. I need him here if I am to plot that mon's defeat. Sooner I would hold a serpent to me bosom than a child with no loyalty."

"Angus is not disloyal to ye. Call to mind a priest once said that as arrows are in the hand of a mighty mon, so are sons."

"Aye. Yet mine falls bent and crooked from my quiver! What of the emissary from MacKirdy?"

"He returned last eve, but he wants no part of going against Montwain."

"Be he so rich he would turn down the gold offered?"

"Mind ye, he dinnae see the color of the gold ye promised, and your word be not one to take to Church in the Highlands. He wants no tuck with Alexander over this, Calum. MacKirdy kens the Scots in Montwain's army are sound and hearty warriors, some of the strongest men about, and if Alexander sees fit to give them your land, MacKirdy kens they willnae be crossing his own borders."

"So he be content to let the English mongrel have a hold here? Have all the warriors of Scotland become women? To bow down forever to their English oppressors?"

"Nay, they merely heed their own King. Alexander wants peace with the English."

"Aye, for he married Henry's sister. He beds an English bitch and gives that wolf pup my land, but his lair isnae safe. An ally I have; close to Montwain, one that wants him dead and the King sorry he gave such trust to an Englishmon. This mon sent me to find an army. We must find a clan to fight and move hence against Montwain. These clans could fill their coffers with enough gold for three winters, and have the pride of a victory against England. Did ye send a messenger north to Forbes?"

"Aye, but he hasnae returned. 'Tis a far way northeast to that clan."

"Aye, then, so be it. We ride to the Sinclair holding on the morn. Sinclair be a true Scot, for the English killed his father. He kens there will never be peace in Scotland until we rid the English vermin from our soil."

"Aye," Graham said.

Graham turned to leave the tent, and Calum barked, "Graham!"

"Aye."

Calum took a long drink of ale, then lowered his tankard. "Bring me that little cooking wench, the one with the long dark hair. She shall warm my bed tonight."

When he arrived back at the castle with Lady Montwain, Gavin was informed by Nigel that he was needed outside the gates to settle a dispute. They had a visitor and he was causing trouble.

"He wears Gordon colors," Nigel said.

Cat dismounted from her horse and a soldier came to take the animal to the stable. She felt a tremor of alarm when she realized the messenger could be the Gordon Laird. Cat hoped fervently that he was not going to demand Glyniss and Meggie return south. The child Meggie carried was indeed his grandchild, and blood ties were very important to the Scots. Many a bastard was given the entire responsibility of a clan at the death of his father. Cat said a quick prayer that the Gordon clan would not make war on Roderic.

"Go inside, Lady Montwain," Gavin said. Seeing that he was troubled, she forgave him his harsh tone.

Gavin turned to Nigel. "Take me to the messenger now!"

He returned to the keep within the hour, accompanied by a young man, tall, handsome, and wide-shouldered. The boy had bright, red-blond hair and deep brown eyes. When Cat gazed upon him she could find no other word for it; the young man was beautiful. His features were perfect; nose straight, jaw strong, and his brown eyes had long black lashes. He wore a plaid of dark blue, yellow, and green.

Glyniss and Meggie sat near Cat by the fire, Meggie handing Glyniss threads to work on her tapestry. When Meggie caught sight of the young man, Cat, for the first time, heard the young girl's voice.

"Douglas!"

Cat's heart wrenched at the desperation and hope in the one word. Meggie threw down the thread and ran to him. He stepped around Gavin and swiftly met the lass to hold her in his arms.

"Meggie, my Meggie." He kissed her again and again then lifted her off her feet, holding her tightly.

"My love, my own. I feared ye were lost to me forever."

The young man spoke in between kisses, joyful kisses. He held Meggie effortlessly and swung her around and around in pure joy. Glyniss stood, setting aside her tapestry, and walked forward, her movements stiff with anger.

"Be at ease with the lass! And her big with your babe!" Glyniss was angry, but the young man seemed unconcerned. He even smiled at the older woman as he set Meggie down to her feet, arms still holding her fast.

Bending to kiss her forehead lightly, he spoke. "Sheathe your claws, Glyniss. I could never hurt Meggie. I love her."

"Ah, ye be a wee bit tardy with that declaration, lad! Pretty words be easy to some, like a troubadour, but it takes a mon of integrity to stand up to the havoc he has wrought and make it right!"

"Aye, ye speak the truth, and I am here to do so. 'Twas my father's plan that I marry Jane, for she be prosperous, and would bring many a coin to the clan." Holding Meggie close, he gently stroked her huge belly.

"I had hoped our child would alter his plans and move him to let us marry, but relent he would not. I have beseeched him all these weeks for leave granted to come to Meggie. He held steadfast, thereupon I have come for her, and I'll take care of her. We will go to England and be married."

Roderic entered the chamber, but said nothing, silently observing the scene.

Gavin lifted a brow and smiled. "It seems the young lover seeks his lady."

Glyniss interrupted. "You will take that child not one step from this keep!"

Meggie bristled at the older woman's decree. "I will. I will go with him to England if that is the only way we can be wed!"

"That be brave talk, young lass! When ye stand weak as a sapling!"

The young man suddenly frowned with concern, as if he only at this moment noticed Meggie's body, so thin. "What has happen to ye, love?"

"Your own betrayal happened to her. She had all but given up on living," Glyniss said.

"Did ye not hope that I would come to you?" A devastated hurt was manifest in the young man's eyes.

"Truly, I did give up hope when your father sent Glyniss and me away." Her voice broke with emotion.

"Please believe me, Meggie, he told me not of his plot. Why do ye think he sent ye away when I was in Edinburgh? I would never let ye leave the clan had I been there. When I returned, ye had been gone many days."

Roderic suddenly spoke. "Young man?"

"Aye, sir?"

"Are you the son of the Gordon Laird?"

"Aye, sir, 'tis true."

"Are you the father of Meggie's child?"

"Aye, and I wish to marry her."

"And will your clan sanction this union?"

The young man sighed heavily before he answered. "Nay, sir. They will stand with my father. Yet, I will pay ye for her keep, she and Glyniss, if ye may grant us consent to stay until her babe is born. Once they both become strong enough to make the journey, we will go hence to England to be wed."

"And if I give it, would your clan accede to this?"

The young man paused and shook his head. "Nay, sir. I fear not."

In spite of the ladies present, Gavin shook his head and cursed. "Ahh! Another war!"

Chapter Thirteen

He that deviseth to do evil shall be called a mischievous person.

~Proverbs 24:8

Three days of hard riding brought Mackay to the Sinclair holding. The Laird would not bid them leave to enter his lands, so he arranged to meet where the Mackays had camped near the border. He came with ten warriors to council.

As they filed into the tent, the Laird, a large man with a dark red beard, spoke to Calum.

"Best ye have a fine purpose for this council, Mackay, for I near sent all my warriors to rid ye like a scourge."

"The scourge be the Englishmon! I will make a gift of gold to ye, if ye fight him with me!"

The big man folded his arms and looked down at Mackay.

"I care not that Alexander seeks to favor him. The King has his purpose, mayhap, even a righteous one if, in the end, it means peace for Scotland."

"Peace, ye say! With your father's blood on their hands!"

"On their hands and on their souls! I will seek no vengeance. Too many of Scotland's lads have died on the altar of war, and afore ye reproach Alexander, think ye of the clemency ye hold in your hand. It be wrapped in the King's mercy when many a Scot would see ye dead!"

"And be ye one of those Scots?" Calum spat the question.

"Nay, not I. But I'll not risk one drop of my clan's blood for your cause."

"And that my land! My own!"

"Best ye had taken heed to hold it and ceased robbing others of their stores at the point of your sword. Ye should have shored up your defenses and sought the respect of your King. Nay, ye seek no fine principle for this war save your own greed. The avarice in your heart will be the death of ye, Mackay. It has, thereupon, lost ye your lands. As for me, I shall trust my King, for he has my fealty."

The younger Laird turned to leave with his guard. As he beheld the hatred in the older Scot's eyes, he addressed Mackay again.

"Make no mistake, Mackay. We shall watch our backs when we return to the keep. Best ye make haste. Ye have a long ride ahead of ye, for I grant ye two days to be off Sinclair lands."

The big man marched outside to the warhorse held for him by one of his guard. He took up the reins and quickly mounted, again pinning Mackay with his glare.

"Two days, Mackay!"

As they sat in the dining hall, Cat made a special effort to silently observe Douglas Gordon. She was especially conscious of the way he interacted with Meggie. Kenneth, in a playful mood, pestered the newcomer, trying at one point to sit between Douglas and Meggie. Through it all Douglas was patient, and Cat had reason to hope that there was a great deal of kindness and compassion in the young man.

Kenneth's strange ways brought out both the best and the worst in people. Cat felt you could determine a great deal about a person's heart by how they reacted to Kenneth.

Douglas was patient with him throughout the meal. He made no effort to take back his tankard of drink when Kenneth took it from him in jest. Douglas also handed him his dagger when Kenneth made it known by signing with his hands that he wanted to hold it, and displayed a forbearance that many times was nowhere evident in men more mature than he.

As for Meggie, it was as if her happiness had been restored full measure, and she smiled at her lover throughout the meal, reaching across Kenneth to continue to hold Douglas' hand. Once, Cat even heard her laugh.

Later in their chamber, alone, Cat spoke of it to Roderic as they sat together on the bed. "I am so happy for Meggie.

She's no longer miserable and unhappy."

"Aye, Glyniss is wise to prevent them from leaving. Meggie is too close to her time. What if it came upon her during the journey? Glyniss needs to be with her when the babe comes."

"Yes; Glyniss fears for her. I'm glad you gave him permission to stay, but do you share Gavin's concern about a war?"

"Aye, but the Gordon's south of us may not be the most imminent threat. I have had no message from the King or Alec, and Calum Mackay is destined to learn in time that Angus is dead. Gordon will not make haste to attack us, for his own son is here and would be in the thick of the fighting. He, too, was one of three Lairds to the south that beseeched the King to sanction Mackay's death. Your father knows he will have no ally in Gordon, so there is little hope of them joining together to ride against us."

Cat nodded.

"Do you forgive me, Catherine? Have I redeemed myself with you?"

"For what would you need redemption, my lord?"

"You found our law harsh with Cameron. Have you more peace with my decree?"

"Roderic, I have come to know that your duty may be severe, but your army of warriors respect you. You could not hope to command them with disorder and turmoil. Cameron himself accepted the punishment as his due."

"But it is my command of you that rankles most, does

it not?"

Cat smiled softly. "Aye, husband. I was taught as a child ..."

She stopped, not really wanting to speak her thoughts, glancing away, but he would not be ignored.

Roderic reached out and took her hand. "You were taught?"

Taking a deep breath, she went on. "I was taught as a child to do what a boy would do. It has fostered in me an independence that men abhor. I fear you agree."

"Nay, Catherine, I do not. Never could I abhor you in any manner. I want no meek and humble woman simpering about me, but there are rules for everyone. Do you think I have total freedom? My many responsibilities weigh upon me, and the King awaits my unification of these warriors and these clansmen. If I favor one above the other, I risk mutiny. You, as my lady, must also adhere to my commands. I want you happy; I also want you safe."

She caressed his cheek. "I feel safe with you, Roderic. But, I fear at times I don't make you happy."

He looked deeply into her eyes. "Nay, lady. You are both a champion and a comfort to these people, and as for me, when I go about my tasks in the light of day, I must wrench my thoughts from your hair, your eyes, and the delight I feel when I plunge deep inside you."

Cat kissed him, and was once again engulfed in the protection of his embrace.

Mackay made his way to the Forbes' holding. The Laird of the Forbes' clan was called Laird "Jester" by many in the Highlands. Both respected and scorned, he was respected because he provided well for his clan; he was scorned for the way he went about it. His warriors were sneaky thieves bent on stealing grain for each winter. The Laird was compassionate and having no goal of leaving another clan in want, he bartered the grain by leaving something of value in its place. The Laird saw life as one huge jest following another, and he bartered with goods that never failed to provide amusement for the other clansmen.

In place of the grain stolen from the MacFarlands, he left a large bundle of cloth for the winter. It had been woven by a cross-eyed craftsman with no sense of color, and the combination of threads he chose was truly hideous. The MacFarlands, being unable to waste the cloth, were the joke of their fellow Scots the entire winter, their clothing proclaiming that they were duped by Laird Jester Forbes.

The MacPherson Laird had his grain stolen and in its place was a fine stallion, and the Laird boasted of the strong animal. The horse turned out to be blind in one eye, however, and when he tried to ride him at a festival, he tore down four tents, including one belonging to a lady the Laird had wished to court. The havoc that ensued left the lady covered in soup and ale, and her beloved pup injured by the stallion's hooves.

Calum thought the Laird in part a buffoon, but he had been left with little choice. The gold he offered would feed the Forbes' clan through the winter, and he would have no need to barter. Mackay hoped the Laird would be swayed by the gold; he was running out of time.

Calum and Graham left their camp and went alone onto the Laird's lands. Forbes' warriors immediately surrounded them and escorted them to speak to the Laird.

The man was tall with black hair to his shoulders, a square jaw, and many creases in his cheeks when he smiled. He was large and wide-shouldered like many of the warriors of Scotland, and had piercing blue eyes. Forbes' manner was cautious as he greeted Mackay, though indeed he did have a sparkle of amusement in his eyes when he watched Calum and Graham sit down before him. The man listened intently to Calum's proposition and did not speak, but appeared to be in contemplation of the man's words.

"Where is your camp?"

Calum told him the location.

"I vow I'd like to rest my head on this. I'll give ye my answer on the morrow."

Mackay went back to his camp with a more jubilant heart than he had in many a moon. Not having gotten a definite nay from the Laird, he had reason to hope.

The following morning, they awoke in their camp to

find that they were surrounded by Forbes' warriors.

"What is that stench?" Graham asked when the Mackay soldiers walked out of their tents they found, to their dismay, a very large, shaggy cow standing munching on some grain in the middle of their camp. The cow had the runs, the result of which was all over the ground.

"What are ye about, Forbes?" Calum asked. He angrily kicked at the cow and began swearing. The younger Laird turned to his own warriors.

"I vow this one has insulted my gift. Would you not say so, lads?"

The soldiers who surrounded the Mackays all answered with a resounding, "Aye!"

Laird Forbes took his rope from behind his saddle and hurled it, casting it over Mackay's barrel chest to bind his arms to his sides. "Ye be in need of a mannerly lesson, Mackay. That is no way to treat your host, scorning his gift." He jerked the line tight and dragged Calum through much of the dung. The Mackays fought, but soon found the Forbes' warriors had the upper hand and were forced to back down. Calum screamed his rage when he saw the Laird order his men to take a third of his coffers of gold.

"Steal what is mine with no promise to fight the English-mon?" he bellowed.

"Aye, you covetous coward! It's not to go in my coffers. I'll send it with your compliments to your bedraggled clan! You show up on my land again, and I dinnae care if our King hangs your clemency around your neck and laurels of heather from your arse, I shall hang ye myself!"

The Laird threw the rope at Calum. It came to rest around his neck as he sat in the dung. "Keep it, Mackay. I do not think I care for the smell!"

Forbes' warriors laughed heartily, and the sound was ringing in Mackay's ears when they rode away. Laird Jester had once again prevailed.

Chapter Fourteen

If it be possible, as much as lieth with you, live peaceably with all men.

~Romans 12:18

In the days that followed, Cat felt a special joy when she observed the delight the young lovers had in one another. Douglas took particular care to see that Meggie ate properly. Often he brought her treats from the kitchens, for he knew her special tastes. Now that the stores of the buttery had been filled to capacity with the food brought by the soldiers, Edna prepared the dishes that Meggie notably enjoyed. Her appetite returned, and she took long walks with Douglas. Although he spent time with Meggie, he often went to the training field with the soldiers.

Douglas and Gavin struck up a friendship, and the younger man was in awe of the warrior, because his skills with sword and broadax were not something Douglas himself had yet mastered.

The young man worked hard for Roderic, indebted to

him as he was. At times, when he returned from the training field, he brought Meggie stones he had found in the bed of the stream. The young lass had a fondness for stones and collected them if they had a pretty color. The couple was openly affectionate with one another, and when Douglas tried to follow Meggie to her chamber one night, Glyniss sought out Cat.

"I must leave them alone. I shall seek out a bed with Edna. She has offered," Glyniss said.

"Douglas needn't put you out of your chamber," Cat said.

"Ah, lady, 'tis plain be it love or lust, they are bound to be together. To keep them apart now is like throwing water on the ashes of a keep that has burned to the ground. I was stern with Douglas. There is to be no lovemaking, it be too close to her time, yet I ken they merely want to hold one another. Douglas wants them to wed soon."

Two weeks passed and Meggie grew heavier with child. She lumbered about, weary from the strain upon her body as the babe grew ever more active.

The child appeared to delight Kenneth. He watched with rapt attention when the babe moved in the womb.

Meggie became adept at seeking assistance from any one of the gentlemen in her vicinity when she needed to rise out of a chair. One and all, they smiled and hoisted her up if Douglas was not near to help. He was unfailing in his efforts to ease her discomfort, and stroked her or rubbed her back when she was in pain.

Cat was struck with the notion that they would soon have an infant in the keep. Meggie was excited that she would, in a short time, hold her babe.

Glyniss worked with her in preparing the wee clothing, using her softest threads to weave a blanket to wrap the bairn, and Meggie plied her needle to make three small tunics.

One rainy afternoon Roderic sought out Cat in a rush, his hair soaking wet from the rain. He did not heed it. "We must speak, Brianna. Father MacNair has arrived. Please have Edna bring him refreshment. He brings an important message from the Gordon Laird."

Cat took a sharp deep breath, and her expression was one of such alarm that Roderic reached out to grasp her forearm firmly.

"Steady, lass. Don't borrow calamity until we know we must face it. Douglas, too, must hear this message, and I have sent Gavin to fetch him."

Cat made the preparations for the food and drink, and in a matter of minutes they all had gathered to sit in the dining hall. Cat was not encouraged by the grave expression on the priest's face. He did not tarry long, but spoke to them at once.

"Greetings, young Douglas."

"May ye have peace, Father," Douglas said.

"Are ye a prisoner here?" Father MacNair glanced briefly at Roderic when he posed his query.

"Nay, Father. 'Tis my will that brought me here. The

woman I love carries my bairn, and I will not abandon her to make a gainful marriage as my father wills."

The priest sighed heavily and shook his head. "Ahh, what a tangle. Your father sent me here to give Sir Montwain the message that he intends to make war unless ye are returned to him. Gordon has accused Montwain and all here of taking ye prisoner. Lad, do ye ken what ye have done? Not merely to Montwain who has taken ye in, but to this child ye fornicated with?"

"I want to make it right, Father. I want to marry Meggie. My father knew of this child, but still he withheld his lawful assent, and Meggie's parents cast her out when they learned of the babe. Glyniss, our healer, brought her here, and Sir Roderic gave them sanctuary. Meggie was ill. Near starved herself, but she is under my protection now, and Sir Roderic's. He gave us leave to stay here until the child is born, for she is long in her time and could birth the babe any day."

Father MacNair stood and slammed his fist upon the table. "The stubborn old goat! He readies his warriors as we speak, bent on bloodshed."

"Let him come," Gavin barked, spoiling for a fight. "He will soon see it is no army of weaklings he seeks to attack!"

"Gavin," Roderic said. He raised his hand as if to quiet him, and turned to the priest.

"Do you have a solution, Father?"

Father MacNair did not at once answer, but paced, deep in thought for a full minute. His dark eyes pinned Douglas when he spoke. "Do ye truly care for this lass?"

"Aye, Father, and I seek her joy."

"I want to speak to the lass myself," he decreed.

Roderic sent for Meggie, and Glyniss came with her. Meggie appeared fearful as she sat next to Douglas, and he took her hand in comfort.

"Do ye wish to wed young Gordon here, lass?"

"Aye, Father. 'Tis my heart's joy and hope," Meggie said.

The priest stood, in quiet contemplation of her answer. He turned to Roderic. "Mayhap I have a resolution. I could perform the marriage now, and their union would be sanctioned by the Church. If ye return to Gordon land already wed, your father would have no hope to change it. If his quest is annulment, he would have to go through me. Should he petition a Bishop through the Church, I can bring forth testimony and plead mercy through the Church hierarchy. After I have joined ye both, I will return to Gordon and speak to the mon, and make all efforts to cool his ire and stay the hands of war. Do ye both agree?" He addressed the young lovers.

"Aye, Father," Douglas said.

"Yes!" Meggie was resolved when she spoke the one word and turned to Douglas, her eyes sparkling in anticipation.

"Edna!" Roderic called. When the old woman entered the hall, Roderic spoke to her, his voice strong. "It seems we must prepare a wedding feast."

The next week was spent in a joyful preparation of the

wedding celebration. Edna procured the things she would need to make special dishes. Cat wanted to learn how to make the berry tarts and small cakes, and she watched her prepare them.

Meggie was handy with a needle and worked at sewing a very pretty lace cutaway surcoat to go over one of her gowns.

"I think there's a bit of velvet in one of the trunks," Cat said. "Maybe we can make you a new gown?"

"I thank ye, Lady Brianna. But, I fear there wouldnae be enough velvet in three trunks to cover me now."

Cat smiled. "It will be over soon, Meggie, and I am quite eager to see the baby. I'm sure it will be a pretty child, for you both are fair to look upon."

"Aye, Douglas is surely beautiful, and I hope our wee one favors him greatly."

"Once the babe comes, we will go to work and make you a pretty new gown. Still, I could make you a garland of flowers to wear in your hair, and there is some ribbon in the trunks with the velvets."

The two women set about the task of making a garland of flowers, lace, and ribbon. Cat thought Meggie had infinite patience with the tedious work of sewing. When she pricked her finger for the third time, Cat winced, cursing under her breath.

Meggie smiled when Cat put her tongue to the injured spot on her index finger.

"Ye try to stitch too fast, Lady Brianna. Ye mustn't try

to rush through the task. Sewing is best done slowly."

"Sewing is best done by someone who knows a needle from a thimble. Me, I was always an 'off the rack' girl."

Meggie frowned in confusion, and Cat waved away the comment. "No matter, you wouldn't understand."

"Why did your mother neglect to teach you a skill that every girl child must learn?"

Meggie was so sincerely perplexed that Cat felt she should make an attempt to explain.

"My mother died when I was young. I was cared for by my father, and he cared not if I mastered these tasks."

Meggie shook her head as if baffled. "Isnae just the weaving to be done. A lady must do a great deal of mending for those in her keep. My mother and father were so poor, I had to learn as a wee girl how to sew and cook."

Meggie winked at Cat. "I have seen your struggles in the kitchens."

"Aye, but Edna has done her best to help me, and I am trying very hard to learn."

Meggie shook her head and laughed, a pretty, lyrical sound. "It matters not, lady. Ye are a fine hunter, I hear, with a bow."

Cat was curious. "Someone has spoken of it?"

"Aye. Cameron. And Edna remarks that when ye go hunting, she is safe to plan for a pot of birds to cook, for ye are near always abundant with them when ye return. I would-nae fret, the keep has many hands to cook."

Cat sighed. "Aye, now if I could just master this needle as well as I have my bow."

Meggie reached out and took her piece of cloth and began to sew where Cat had stitched. "Try working slower. Fold the thread around this way and seek to work the stroke with a slower rhythm."

Cat did her best to follow Meggie's advice, and after a few minutes, though her stitches were not nearly as small and pretty as Meggie's, she did a fair job.

"I'm so happy for you, Meggie. I know how much you want to marry Douglas," Cat said.

"Aye, lady, I do. For my hope of that dream had all but died when Glyniss and I came here, and I truly didnae want to live without him. Father MacNair is a kind mon of God, and I know he will do his best, but I fear Douglas and I must leave for England. His father will never accept me."

"But, why, Meggie? Is it merely the dowry of this Jane that Douglas spoke of?"

"Nay, though that is true in part. Laird Gordon had all but counted the gold in his coffers.

"I was a poor lass, my father and mother have little, and Douglas is his father's only son. Oh, how a mon can hang many a hope on one child. 'Twas as if Douglas had to be perfection in everything he did, right all his father's wrongs. He tried so hard to be smarter, faster, and more agile than all the lads of the clan. Douglas did his best to please him, but our Laird would never sanction the likes of me for his only son.

"I have loved him for as long as I can remember. It is not merely the beauty of his face. 'Tis what is in his heart. Douglas is very patient and kind, just as your own husband has been to this clan. Sir Roderic is an outsider, however, and had I not been so heartsick, so uncaring of what went on about me, I would have been fearful to come here. I was e'en afraid of you, lady. For your father is . . ." Meggie stopped speaking, afraid to go on. Cat finished the thought for her.

"A cruel monster?"

Meggie, a look of compassion in her eyes, slowly nodded.

"Be at ease, Meggie. For I heartily agree with your assessment of my father's character."

"Glyniss, too, had doubts when we came here. Mayhap all of the clans dinnae want to believe that Sir Roderic, an Englishmon, could be kinder to these people than one to Scotland born. 'Tis true. They may fight the King's decree to send him here, but it has been a fine thing, has it not, my lady?"

"Aye, Meggie, fine indeed."

Chapter Fifteen

I have prepared my dinner: my oxen and my fatlings are killed, and all things are ready: come unto the marriage.

~Matthew 22:4

M eggie's wedding day was cold and windy, though the sun shone brightly. Cat was happy that Roderic had given his soldiers his consent to take part in the festivities.

Father MacNair performed the ceremony, and the joy was evident in the young lovers, and when they kissed it brought a happy cheer from both men and women. The feast then began, and after everyone had eaten their fill, some in the clan came forth with treasured instruments for the music that was planned.

They danced, and Cat thoroughly enjoyed the celebrating. Douglas and Meggie taught them all a circle dance that was a favorite of his clan, and he led Meggie to the floor with pride in spite of the fact she was heavy with child.

The clan joined in the festivities, laughing for the first

time in many a moon. The ale flowed, Cat enjoyed dancing with her husband, and Kenneth, although his method of dancing was to spin around with no aim to his movements, enjoyed himself as well. As she watched him, Cat relished his expression of pure joy.

While dancing with Roderic, she noted that Gavin had offered Glyniss his hand. They moved together with ease and grace, and the older woman's smile indicated Gavin had charmed her. An hour later, Cat, exhausted after finding a drink of water at the feast table, sought out Glyniss. Eyes sparkling, she jested with Glyniss about being with Gavin.

Glyniss scoffed in response. "Women are to that one as strong drink is to others. I am not a babe as Meggie, to be swayed by his flashing green eyes and pretty smile. He wants under my skirts, but I mean to do nothing to muddle my hope of having a home here. I've grown to like your band of misfits, lady. Here it matters not that I dinnae belong, for all Sir Roderic's followers are the same."

"He has done a fine job of joining them. They have given him their loyalty," Cat said.

"Aye, lady, to blend stubborn, clannish Scots for one purpose? And he be an Englishmon?" Glyniss snorted. "Fie! One day soon I look for him to take himself a hearty walk across the water of the sea!"

Cat laughed at the analogy. "Ah, Glyniss, how you delight me. I wish they all felt that way about Roderic. You would think they would all be here for the feast."

"Ah, now, dinnae think it is only scorn for his command that has some of them staying away. They be vexed that Douglas and wee Meggie may bring them calamity. 'Tis little time they have had since Mackay, and they want no war with Gordon."

"I hope you are right, Glyniss. He may not walk on water, but he wants the best for them all. Take care not to make such a jest again. If Father MacNair heard such talk, he would deem you blasphemous."

"Aye, he true may admonish me, but the priest is a servant of God, just as I. And the Father of heaven's light who gave me this gift of healin' knows I mean no harm with my jests, and that I love Him with all my heart. Father MacNair is not a tyrant. Some priests rule the people with a harsh fist and would have flayed Douglas and Meggie in light of their sin, but MacNair sees himself as a servant to others. 'Tis a fine and happy day, lady."

Roderic came to claim Cat for yet another dance, and she lost herself in the celebration of the day.

Father MacNair left for the Gordon holding and took several of Roderic's soldiers with him. Roderic spoke to Cat of his mission.

"I pray Father MacNair can indeed find a hearing ear with the Gordon Laird, for Douglas has already petitioned me for a guard to take him and Meggie to England. He seems certain the man will not listen to the Father's pleas."

"Father MacNair has a noble goal because he wants

peace. Maybe if the Laird is made to know he could lose Douglas, he will relent."

"Aye, wife. We can but hope."

"Roderic, did the wedding call to your mind our own wedding?"

"Aye, lass, and that you stood beside me with your sword strapped to your waist, completely terrified. You were afraid of me, yet you did not kiss me like an innocent."

"I was innocent!" Cat was affronted. He smiled, lifting one haughty brow.

"I did not say you were not, merely that you kissed me as no virgin . . . would kiss." She read the look in his eyes; it was hot, dark, and sensual.

"Are you saying I was wanton, sir?" Cat said.

"Both wanton and innocent, a captivating blend of virtues for any woman. Now I will await and hope you contemplate the term 'obey.' " He sighed, his eyes dancing. "Mayhap, one day you will study the meaning of the command."

Cat growled, threw herself at Roderic, and tickled his middle, something she had found he was vulnerable to. He chuckled and wrestled with her in jest until he captured the offending fingers bedeviling his belly. Holding them in his hands, he wrapped her arm behind her when he bent his mouth to hers.

Cat was giggling as he kissed her. His lips feather-touched her with tantalizing persuasion, and she sighed.

Four days later, Meggie began her laboring. Roderic was awakened in the middle of the night when Cat left his bed at Glyniss' urging. She went at once, and both women were sequestered in Meggie's chamber the entire day.

Long past midday, Roderic knocked at the chamber door to check on the lass. Douglas paced, agitated, at times hearing the lass scream. It was difficult on them all, for it was plain the girl was in agony. Gavin gave Douglas a tankard of ale that he left untouched in front of him. It was as if Meggie's pain were his own, and Roderic did not know how to comfort the lad.

Cat had never in her life prayed for anything as intently as she did for Meggie to give birth. The girl's labor was heart-wrenching, and she grasped Cat's hands until they were bruised and sore. Glyniss tied a long towel to the foot of the bed, and Meggie gripped it like a lifeline. The vicious pain tore at her young body until Cat wanted to weep, and still it went on through the night, early morning, and afternoon.

Edna brought up some food in the afternoon for Glyniss and Cat, but they ate little. The labor intensified, and Meggie became totally incapable of dealing with the wrenching pain. She screamed until she was hoarse, though Glyniss and

Cat did everything they could to make her comfortable.

Cat stroked her brow and wiped the sweat from her body with a cold cloth, but she had never felt so inadequate in her life. The other birthing she had witnessed was nothing like this.

"Can't we help her, give her something for the pain?"

Glyniss looked apprehensive, but then a look of resolve crossed her face. "Aye, and the devil with the Church if they don't like it!"

"The Church?" Cat asked.

"They say 'tis every woman's pain she must suffer for Eve's sins. Know ye not, that healers have been burned for helping women in their time?"

Meggie let out another agonized scream as the contraction gripped her body.

"Enough!" Glyniss said. Turning, she walked over to the table and grabbed her mortar and pestle. Glaring at Cat, she spoke urgently.

"Speak of this to no one. Ye have my life in your hands, lady, for if Father MacNair or the Church knows of what I do, I will die. Do ye understand?"

"Glyniss, you can't think that I would cause trouble for you! Just help her!"

Glyniss worked quickly, stirring a small amount of potion, and rushed to the bedside. Meggie was in so much pain, it was hard for them to get her to drink it.

"Hold, lass, hold on to hope. Take this, take it now!"

Glyniss ordered.

Cat helped, holding the girl's head so she could swallow the potion. Another pain came, and Meggie bit down on the blanket to suffer through it. A few short minutes later she had another, then soon after, Cat began to see a difference in Meggie.

The drug was evident in the glazed look in her eyes. She had held herself tense as a bow string, but now she began to relax, and stopped tossing her head on the pillow.

"Glyniss, thank you," she sobbed. Meggie's breathing slowed, and Cat blessed the concoction that had finally given the girl some relief. Glyniss wrapped her arms around Meggie's shoulders and kissed the girl's forehead.

"Aye, lass, my dear, weary lass. 'Tis better?"

Meggie nodded, too weak to answer, and Cat let out a heavy sigh. The drug did not remove all the pain of the contractions, but it helped Meggie cope and allowed her to rest in between them. She even dozed at one point.

"Is it better now?" Cat said.

Glyniss shook her head. "Nay. This babe is too long coming."

Three hours later, Meggie's baby girl was born. Cat had taken the baby from Glyniss' arms to wrap it in soft toweling and clean the blood from the child. Her joy at finally holding the beautiful baby girl was coupled with an intense relief that the ordeal was over for Meggie. Washing the baby, she marveled at the softness of the baby's skin when she touched her cheek. Wrapping the little girl tight, snug and warm in the blanket, she moved to the door of the chamber hoping to take the child downstairs to meet her father.

Suddenly Glyniss screamed. "No!"

Edna had entered the chamber. Cat turned and put the baby in her arms, and turned back to Meggie, appalled. The girl was bleeding severely.

"Help me!" Glyniss said. "Push those pillows under her hips!"

Cat moved quickly to follow the orders. Glyniss pressed a soft cloth between Meggie's legs in a desperate attempt to staunch the hemorrhaging.

"Oh, dear God," Cat said.

"Sit with her, hold her hand," Glyniss said. "Make her stay awake!"

Cat took Meggie's hand and gripped it, looking deeply into her eyes. "Be at ease, you'll be fine," she said.

Meggie's beautiful blue eyes turned doubtful. "Nay, lady. Tell . . . tell Douglas to forgive me."

The blood continued to gush from the girl's body, faster than Glyniss could blot it. It covered the bed and dripped on the stone floor.

"I won't tell Douglas anything. You will tell him soon, when you present him his beautiful daughter. Meggie . . . Meggie!"

Her skin turned even paler, her blue eyes remained fixed upon Cat's. She took a deep shuddering breath, and Cat knew she was gone.

"No, oh, God, no!" Cat frantically turned to Glyniss. There was an anger, however futile, from Glyniss, in her eyes, her body. She climbed up and over Meggie, to press her hand to the pulse in her throat. Angry tears fell down Glyniss' cheeks, and she shook her head.

Roderic was alarmed when he saw his wife run down the stairs to the kitchens. Covered in blood, she ignored Douglas when he tried to beseech her. The young man was startled, suddenly afraid, and ran up the stairs.

Cat picked up a bowl from the buttery and hurled it against the stone wall, then turned and ran out of the keep.

"Catherine, wait!" She did not heed him, and Roderic followed.

Cat hurled herself onto the saddle of the nearest horse, put her heels into the animal's flank, and galloped away from the keep.

Roderic rushed to find his own mount and followed. Her horse galloped hard, but Roderic paced his animal to match hers. On and on she rode, and although Roderic had the ability to overtake her and pull her from the animal's back, he did not. He simply followed, watching her, seeing to her safety.

Finally, Cat reined the horse in and slipped from his

back. She threw the reins over the horse's neck and ran to rest underneath a tree.

Roderic was cautious when he approached her. She sat silent, dry-eyed, and the expression of pain on her lovely face touched Roderic deeply. He was concerned with the fact that there were no tears in her eyes. The pain she held fast inside her, and he steeled himself for the task ahead of him.

"The child has died?"

Cat silently shook her head from side to side.

"Meggie?"

"She's dead." The tone in her voice was hoarse, desolate, without hope.

Roderic sucked in his breath harshly; his fears for the young mother had proved true. He studied his wife.

"Does it not make you angry?"

Her green eyes turned to impale him. "Angry? What good would anger do?"

Roderic was loath to see the anguish Cat was feeling. It had not gone hidden, the blossoming friendship that Cat had with Meggie. She had found joy in the lass, worried for her health, championed her marriage, helped birth her babe, and now, must bury her. Roderic knew his lady had a deep need to embrace the grief, but she refused.

She tried to pull away when he bent down to sit near her, and he took her hands in his in spite of the blood that covered them.

"Catherine!"

"I don't want you here, Roderic. I want to be alone! Go back to the keep!"

"Nay, love. Embrace it or no, you need me."

Although she fought with him, Roderic continued to hold her fast.

"Are you not angry? Little Meggie, so bright, so beautiful, with all her life as a mother ahead, taken from us! Does it not make you angry?"

"At what?" She screamed the words.

Glancing down as he held her fast, he winced inwardly at her bloody hands.

"At the injustice! You sit covered in her blood; she was but five and ten summers, and now her life is over! Shake a fist at the heavens, lass! Rage if you must, but don't hold it inside, or it will poison you! Tell me you are angry!"

Cat pulled her hands away and screamed. "Yes! Yes!"

Reaching out, she slapped his chest, though the blows did not hurt him. Then she began to fight in earnest. Using her fists to strike out, Cat hit Roderic, and he allowed it before he grabbed her arms and tried to subdue her as best he could. The anger and pain were released from her with a vengeance.

"She's dead, Roderic! She's dead!"

Her wrath turned to weeping, and she could no longer speak. He felt some of the grief flow from her while he continued to rock and hold her.

Cat cried for a long time, sobbing desperately. But the

tears finally ceased, and she sniffled, took a deep breath, and relaxed in Roderic's arms.

He disengaged from their embrace, walked to his horse, took a canteen of water from the animal and washed her hands clean of the blood. Bending down, he kissed her cheek, then sat for long minutes holding her.

Cat was silent when Roderic pulled her up and led her to the horses. She did not speak all the way back to the keep.

Chapter Sixteen

But I would not have you be ignorant, brethren,
concerning them which are asleep in death, that ye
sorrow not, even as others which have no hope.

~Thessalonians 4:13

R oderic took charge of the burial when they returned, and did his best to spare Cat the task of preparing the body. Glyniss took charge, and though she had done it many times before, she cried silent tears throughout the task. Dressing Meggie in the lace gown that she had worn when she wed Douglas, she even put flowers and ribbons in her hair.

Douglas was prostrate, numb with disbelief, unable to accept that Meggie was gone. He had sat with Meggie, pale and quiet, and when Edna brought the babe to him, thinking the child would give him comfort, and he could not bear to look upon her. Edna took charge of the wee babe, for though Glyniss pronounced the child hale and well, she was too busy with the laying out of the body.

The following morning, Glyniss came into the room to

direct the three soldiers that were to take the body. She found that Catherine had come in very early to be with Meggie. Roderic stood to the side of the bed, staring out the window. Cat sat quietly holding Meggie's hand, stroking her cheek, and spoke in a low voice when she said her farewell. She touched Meggie's hair, and Glyniss came to stand beside her.

" 'Tis time, lady," Glyniss said.

The tears streamed down Cat's face and dropped on the bedding. "Aye, I know. I find myself . . . hoping I can somehow warm her. She's so cold."

Roderic turned as if he could bear no more and gently took his wife's arm, helping her rise from the bed. "Come, love. 'Tis time for the soldiers to take her."

Glyniss watched her friend, the lady who claimed to be Brianna Mackay, lean upon her husband. Always one to walk in pride and strength, she seemed to wither. He held her fast in his strong arms and, for once, there was no effort in his lady to stand alone.

The days passed slowly after Meggie's death, and Glyniss and Roderic despaired at the change they saw in Cat. She was withdrawn, ate little, and cared naught about the running of the keep. She referred Edna to Roderic about even the small decisions for the kitchens, and rarely ventured out, even to ride or hunt with Kenneth.

Roderic became harsh with his warriors on the training field. He came back to the keep drained and spent, and it was clear to Glyniss that he was fretting inwardly about the dismal sadness he saw in his wife.

Meggie's death cast a pall over the entire castle. One and all were tired in spirit, but Glyniss had more regard for Cat. The lady tried her best to avoid tending the wee babe, so Glyniss and Edna took turns caring for her. Cat saw in the child the painful memory of her mother's death.

"How long will she be so broken in her spirit?" Roderic asked.

"I ken not, but never should I have let her near when Meggie was birthing her babe. She reaches out to help others, and I thought not beyond having someone to help me. But some cannae see the suffering of others, as a healer does. Sir Roderic, how I wish I had sent her from that room long before the babe was born. But bear it now she must. 'Tis a hard way for a woman fully grown, least one as young and small as Meggie. By the time I kenned we should send her from the room, 'twas too late. I was too hard on the task to save the lass, to stop the bleeding."

"You did your best, Glyniss. Indeed, even Douglas knows it to be true."

"Does he still sit by the grave?"

"Aye, and with his own thoughts," Roderic said.

"My real fret is that he willnae look at that child. 'Tis his own daughter. Brianna Catherine will come to a place of tolerance of the child, yea though, Douglas is another matter. 'Tis as if he blames the child for taking Meggie away."

"Aye, that is true, therefore, the babe shall stay here. Douglas has entreated me to keep her," Roderic said.

"Ahh! What do ye say?"

" 'Tis true," Roderic said.

"The stubborn, selfish boy! Does he think her to be a pup that he doesnae want?"

"Glyniss, we must not put that child with him if he doesn't want her. It would not be safe for the babe. May Douglas walk through his struggle with God in his own way, in his own time. We must not allow the child to suffer for it."

Glyniss scoffed. " 'Tis the truth ye speak, but I cannae help but feel a hot ire at that lad's self-indulgence. The wee lass is all he has of Meggie now, and he spurns her."

"Aye. He leaves on the morn," Roderic said.

Douglas stood near the grave striving to control his rage. His dearest girl, his Meggie, was gone. In her place was a wee lass, a tiny babe that one day would grow to a young woman, but he knew not if he could ever look upon her without feeling a deep-seated resentment. She was the death of her mother, and Douglas could not find the strength to reach beyond his own pain.

Lady Brianna approached him. She stood silent for a

moment, the wind moving the flame-colored strands of her hair in a gentle circle about them.

"Roderic said you are to leave us?"

"Aye, Lady Montwain."

"And you do not plan to take the baby? Why, Douglas? Meggie would not want you to leave her."

The young man grimaced and swallowed hard, shaking his head slowly.

"I cannae bear it, not without her. The child is the cause of her death."

"Douglas!"

Ignoring her, he turned and walked to his horse, mounted, and returned to the keep.

Calum Mackay's messenger had ridden hard to catch up with him. He was carrying a missive scroll from Laird Kincaid.

"Alastair Kincaid is dead," Calum said. "Kincaid petitions me to come to him, but he seeks answers as to why the lad was killed."

"And your daughter?" Graham asked.

"He says naught of her. We go now. We ride for Kincaid's lands."

"He has an army!"

"Aye, a very steadfast, powerful army," Calum said.

Two days later Kincaid's warriors and sentinels allowed them to pass, they knew Mackay had been petitioned by their Laird. Many of their colors flew at half-mast on their staffs, they wore black arm-bands, and there was a mourning wreath on the door of the Kincaid keep. They entered the house of mourning with respect, and one of the men bid them in to the great hall. Soon the Kincaid Laird entered the hall with his wife beside him. He turned briefly to the beautiful woman at his side, and spoke.

"Leave us now, love." She nodded her assent and picked up her skirts to leave the chamber.

Kincaid ordered ale, and they sat down at the large table.

"May ye have peace in the time of your sorrow," Calum said.

The big man raised his dark head, and his eyes narrowed as he pondered the statement. "Best ye have no part in it."

"Nay, Kincaid, I did not. I sent my girl to your brother so that I would not have to give her to the Englishmon. Damn the King and his order!"

" 'Tis not the tale uttered by Alastair, for he spoke to me of plans to steal your Brianna."

"Scurried her away to him, I did," Calum said. "I put another lass in her place to give to Montwain, for he wouldnae know one from the other. His army has taken me lands with an iron fist, and his warriors move about as they please. No doubt he was told of the deception and sought to find them. If your brother lies dead, it be at Montwain's hand, for he was to have married Brianna. The English dog wanted revenge."

"And how do you know this, Mackay?"

"He is dead, is he not, young Alastair? And the girl is nowhere to be found. Methinks she has been killed by the Englishmon."

"Why would he kill a woman, even one that humiliated him?"

"I know not! I say I have pondered on the puzzle. The lass would know who killed Alastair. He couldnae let her live to go to the King with his deed."

"You have no word of your daughter from the King?"

"Nay," Calum said.

"Alexander's messenger came with Alastair's body. He has given me the King's vow to see Alastair righteously avenged."

"Think ye he will revoke the gifts he gives to the Englishmon? Take away his blessing? Ahhh! Nay, Kincaid. Ye be a fool if ye ken that."

"Call me no fool, ye old thief! If what you say is true, and Alastair did die at his hand, I will have his head on a pike, if I must go against Alexander to do it!"

"Aye, 'tis what must be done, and I will join ye. We must lay siege to Montwain. Surround him, we could. Force Alexander's judgment."

"I'll not attack a man before I know the truth."

"Who else but the Englishmon would want your brother dead? He gave ruin to Alexander's plan and disgraced Montwain before all in the Highlands by takin' the woman he was to wed." Calum laughed heartily. "I gave him a madwoman we captured. She be a simpleton that Angus dragged out of the water, but she be fair enough for his kind! Sooner would I see Brianna dead than have my blood blend with his."

"Ye have no army, so ye come in supplication for mine?"

"Better ye leave the murderer of your kin to grow fat and prosper in the Highlands?"

Kincaid's second in command, a very large, blond man, addressed his Laird. "Dinnae allow your grief to rule ye."

Kincaid slammed his fist on the table. "My grief is my own," he said hoarsely. After a very long pause, Kincaid addressed Mackay.

"We are in mourning here. I will take time to think on this. Ye and your men have leave to stay until I resolve yea or nay."

"So be it," Calum said.

The following day they held the ceremony of burial for Alastair, and after the long day was over and the sun had set, Kincaid once again sent for Mackay. As they spoke, they overheard the weeping coming from the chamber belonging to the mother of the Laird. She mourned her son, and the sound of it had a visible affect on Laird Kincaid.

Calum spoke as if searching for an answer. "If we send a message to Alexander to meet us at my holding, we can tell him of our suspicions, and mayhap he will hear our outcry for justice. We needn't attack. We can but surround him and wait for the King's decree."

The Kincaid Laird raised his hand. "There will be no battle, 'less I sanction it?"

"Aye," Calum said.

Kincaid sat silent for a long while, deep in thought. Mackay waited patiently for him to give his answer. Finally, he spoke.

"I made a vow to my brother's memory that put a sword, I would, to the mon that took his life. Best the King know, true to this vow I shall be."

The Laird took a deep breath and heaved a weary sigh. "Ye got your army, Mackay."

Glyniss walked from the keep to the stable, the babe in her arms. She was resigned to a difficult task, but she was never one to prolong a challenge in hope of a reprieve.

It was long in the evening. Meggie's baby girl held some of her hair in her tiny fist as she went to find Lady Montwain in the stable. Her friend glanced up, saw that she had the babe, and dropped her gaze.

"Tell me, lady, what be your true name?"

"Why does it matter? If you address me as such it will breed suspicion in my husband and the others."

"Think ye to go on with the lie?" Glyniss stood patting

the baby, her expression one of pained tolerance.

"I must. I have no choice," she said, shaking her head while she continued to brush the horse.

"So, ye think to do a better job of this than the soldiers?"

Cat went on with the task and did not answer. "I don't mind the work."

"There be plenty to do, lady, in the keep. I could use a bit of help with this babe."

"Can Edna not help you?"

"Edna has many a chore to do," Glyniss said. Sitting down on a large tub of grain with a heavy wooden lid, she put the babe to her breast and patted her gently.

"Lady Montwain?"

"Aye?"

"Thee is in agony."

Cat tossed her long red hair over her shoulder and turned to Glyniss. Tears welled in her eyes, but they did not fall.

"Aye," she said. "I feel a rage inside, Glyniss, as if I will never . . . ever understand why Meggie had to die."

"Think ye are to have the answers, do ye? Have ye lost your faith?"

Having no answer, she stood silent. Glyniss stood up, and beckoned her.

"Stop grooming that animal and come here."

Cat put down the brush and came to her. "Sit down," Glyniss said.

Reluctantly, she obeyed and settled herself on the

wooden tub.

"Many a tragedy have I seen as a healer, far worse than what happened to Meggie. Wee children beaten to death by their own. Young wives like Meggie who took a knife to their insides to get rid of another babe they couldnae feed, only to die of the damage they wrought. Young girls raped and abused. I heard once of a clansmon who hung his own wife because his food was too hot."

Cat turned her face and raised her hand briefly as if she could not bear to hear more.

"Be it all no matter, lass, I do ask your pardon, for ye are not a healer, and ye have seen too much death."

Cat shook her head in protest when Glyniss bent down and handed her the baby. She gave in and gently wrapped the tiny, warm body to her chest. Glyniss put her hand on the other woman's shoulder and went on.

"Grieve, lass. But never forget the beauty in life, or the love. Many tiny bairns have I helped to come in to this world. 'Tis wondrous, a new life, a new beginning. Should the melancholy overtake ye, but reach out and see God's hand. See the hope He gives us all. It's here in every sunrise, and in that child's eyes."

Glyniss walked regally out of the stable, twisting back briefly to speak. "Mayhap, we may christen her Hope? I favor the name."

Cat looked down at the infant when Glyniss walked out, and burst into tears. The baby girl had her mother's blue eyes.

Chapter Seventeen

He that oppresseth the poor reproacheth his
Maker; but he that honoureth him hath mercy on
the poor.

~Proverbs 14:31

C at found a unique comfort in taking care of the baby.
The little one was officially christened Hope, as
Glyniss preferred, and a lady of the clan, a wet nurse,
moved into the keep, making it was easier to feed the babe.
Once fed, Cat took over her care. At times, Kenneth was
sulky about her lack of time for him but, by and large, he was
as fascinated with the babe as he had been when she was still
in the womb. The baby became a particular delight to the
young man.

A month passed, and while the babe grew chubby they
all were relieved no further threats of war came from the
Gordon clan. As Douglas had returned to his father, the
Gordon Laird was content.

Cat had never experienced such an unusual burst of
love as for the baby girl, and stayed close to the keep, rarely

venturing out to hunt. Hope was lying on the blanket in front of the hearth one evening when Glyniss approached her. Cat was a bit embarrassed caught cooing to Hope.

"I'm being silly, I know," she said to Glyniss.

"Nay, not at all. This one is a sweet-tempered babe. 'Twould be one with no heart at all to be unmoved by her, and she quick has become the princess of this keep."

Cat picked the baby up and moved her to rest on her shoulder, smiling. "Aye, that's true. I think I even saw Gavin smiling at her last eve."

"Ah, but, lady, that be the first time for ye to take note of that? He loves to make her giggle by tickling her under her wee chin. And your husband? That mon is besotted!"

Cat kissed the baby softly on the top of her head. "She has a winning way about her, even with strong warriors."

"A month gone and still not a bit of word from Douglas. I confess I thought he would relent and want the child."

"Let him try," Cat said. "He'll not have her."

"Nay, I hope not. I, too, ken it best for the wee one to be here with those who love her. But Highlanders look out for their own, and mayhap one day the Gordons could come for her. They may wish someday to pledge her in marriage, for she be part of their blood."

Cat was to remember the conversation with Glyniss there by the fire, when Hope was only days past being four months old, Roderic was given the message that the Gordon Laird and his son were at their gates. They petitioned his command to enter, and he allowed them to come forth, entering the keep with three other Gordon soldiers.

Cat experienced fear and anger while she sat holding the baby at the long table in the hall, where Glyniss had joined her. The white-haired Laird lumbered in and sat down next to Douglas. Roderic and Gavin also sat at the table.

"I've come for the child," Laird Gordon said.

"No," Cat said. Roderic raised his hand to quiet her, and she immediately regretted her slip of the tongue. The Gordon Laird growled deep in his throat.

"I'll not be told no by an English woman. Ye have no right to my kin."

"That's enough," Roderic said. "My wife is but choked with fear that you will take this babe from her. She loves her."

Glyniss spoke up. "As we all do! Where were ye for counsel when this whelp of yours turned his back on her?"

"Ye have a sharp tongue, healer! Never have ye kenned a woman's place is not in a mon's council!"

"In the past ye wanted my place to be near you when ye be puking from a sickness! 'Twas holy, that, but not my aid to Meggie when ye wished her cast aside!"

"Glyniss!" Roderic spoke her name with quiet authority and, respectfully, she stopped her outburst. The lady sat back, though it was apparent she was furious; her eyes narrowed into slits of silver fire.

Douglas rose. "I know I was wrong, Glyniss, but my heart was too heavy. I could not look at her then. But she's all I have of Meggie."

"Sit down, Douglas," the Laird barked. "Mayhap, they want a war . . ."

"You want a war, old goat, you'll have one," Gavin said.

"Aye," the Laird roared, slamming his fist down on the table. "Be there not a more righteous reason for a war than to recover one of your own?"

He turned to Roderic and drilled him with his gaze. "Think ye long on this, Montwain. Will Alexander sanction the theft of a child from one clan to another? Douglas be the father of the wee one. She be a Gordon. Think ye of your own commitment to justice and weigh those scales against a promise of bloodshed. For a battle we will have, sir, do ye not turn the babe over to us on the morn."

Roderic turned to Douglas. "Do you stand by your father's promise?"

Douglas momentarily looked ashamed. "Aye, I know I was wrong to leave her. I have no defense save my grief and, aye, mayhap, I even blamed her for taking Meggie away. But she's my child. I want her, and I will stand behind my father and go to war for her."

The Gordon Laird also stood and turned to Roderic. "Ye put Mackay in his place, but he was a mongrel dog and a thief with no honor. Call to mind there are many in Scotland who dinnae want ye here. I have allies in the Highlands. I can be a peaceful neighbor to the south if ye give us the child, or I can be a bane that will be the ruin of ye. Think on that, Montwain."

The Laird and his son turned leave. Douglas dropped his gaze and would not look in the direction of the women while he and his father filed out behind their soldiers.

Cat began to argue with Roderic for, fearfully, she could see in his eyes that he was leaning toward giving the baby up. Heedless of Gavin and Glyniss' presence, she vented her discontent.

"You can't! You can't actually be thinking of giving her back!"

"Love, do you think it is my will?"

Cat hugged the baby to her chest as she began to fret and cry. "Then stop them, fight them if we have to!"

"Nay," Glyniss said. "Ye think with your heart, not your head. I, too, be heartsore for giving up the babe, lady, but we cannae start a war for it. The child be a Gordon, ye cannae change that."

"Glyniss speaks the truth," Roderic said.

"But Douglas abandoned her! What if they don't treat her right? Roderic?"

His expression was pained when he looked into her eyes. "Then I will make war on them myself. We may send Glyniss with a contingent of soldiers as often as they can be spared to see that the child is content and well."

It was all Cat could do not to cry when she spoke. "You've made your decision."

She thrust the baby into Glyniss' arms, whirled, and

strode from the hall.

The following morning when the Laird and Douglas came to fetch the child, Cat was pale as she packed some things in a satchel for Hope. She put the tiny garments that Meggie had lovingly sewed, and the blanket that Glyniss had embroidered. The two men brought along a nurse for the baby.

Roderic and Gavin stood beside Cat in the great hall. Gavin was trembling with anger. Cat and Glyniss said their farewells. Cat kissed the baby and, though she struggled to hold her tears back, they slipped down her cheeks and into the little one's hair.

"Goodbye, Angel. I love you."

Placing the baby in the nurse's arms, she turned, and ran from the hall. Roderic stalked to the Gordon Laird, and the big man glared at him.

"I shall send Glyniss with a company of soldiers. See to that child! If that wee lass is not hearty, not fat and smiling, you will die by my sword, and I will have my own war to rescue her."

Whirling to the younger man, he spoke vehemently. "And, Douglas, never let your foot fall again near the gates of this keep. For welcome you are not!"

Cat missed the baby, and it dragged at her heart. Unlike the futility of Meggie's death, however, she took comfort in the knowledge that they could travel to the Gordon keep to see the child. Throwing herself into spending time once again with Kenneth, she took him riding and taught him to hunt more accurately with his bow.

But the boy, too, mourned the loss of baby Hope. At times he would run into the chamber and stand silently, staring at the empty cradle. Glyniss, ever vigilant, dealt with her pain busying herself taking care of the people of the clan.

Five weeks after the Gordons' departure, Roderic sent for Glyniss. Cat was shocked when he gave his reason.

" 'Tis a messenger from the Gordon clan. They seek your help and beseech my leave to allow you to go to the Gordon keep. 'Tis a terrible sickness. It has befallen the Laird and many others. The messenger would not come beyond our gates lest he carry the sickness himself. Do you wish to go back with them?"

Glyniss did not falter. "Aye. I'll be away at once."

"Glyniss, what of Hope? Should I go with you? Would you like my help?"

"Nay," Roderic said. "I'll not risk you. The messenger said many have died from this fever. You will stay here, wife."

"Oh, Glyniss, be careful," Cat said.

"Dinnae fash yourself, lass, for I be a healer, and I have a wee angel hovering about me. Never do I fall prey to fevers,

216

though I have tended many stricken with them."

Cat protested once again, but Roderic held fast to his decision not to allow her to go with Glyniss. The healer took her potions and rode back to the Gordon clan with the two soldiers sent by the Laird.

Cat was extremely ill at ease; weeks went by before Glyniss returned. Riding in with five of the Gordon guard waving their colors at half-mast, she looked tired, her expression disheartened. Cat felt afraid as Glyniss got down from her horse with help from one of the Gordon soldiers, seemingly too weary to take another step.

"Douglas is dead, and the Gordon Laird. I did my best, but the fever took twelve of the clan."

Cat rushed forward. "Hope, the baby, she's not . . ."

Glyniss held her hand up and gestured briefly to the soldier who sat his horse behind Cat.

"Nay, lady, for I have news to bring ye joy."

The soldier reached down to hand a small bundle to Cat.

Hope was sleeping soundly and safe. She touched the baby's face immediately to feel that there was no fever.

"Nay, lady, she is well, and she is yours. As Douglas lay dying, he told me he kenned how much you love this babe, and as the sickness has so badly rent their clan, the other women have all they can do to take care of their own. Now I seek me bed, for I have not slept a full night in weeks."

Cat turned to Roderic, and the look of joy in his eyes mirrored her own. He put his arms around them both.

"Look how she has grown! Oh, Roderic, I'm sorry they are dead, yet I am so happy she is home."

"Aye, love. Thankful we must be that she and Glyniss have come back to us."

Chapter Eighteen

And ye shall know the truth, and the truth shall make ye free.

~John 8:32

F ather MacNair returned from the Gordon clan to reside with them for a short time. He planned to visit some of those who needed his help and encouragement.

Cat was sitting by the fire, humming softly to the baby when she was given an urgent message to go to Mary's cottage. She found the wet nurse to stay with Hope and went to fetch Roderic.

Nearing the stone cottages, they became concerned as there was a small crowd clustered around Mary's dwelling. A wave of apprehension swept through Cat as she made her way down the hill. Something was terribly wrong.

Reaching the dwelling, they pounded the door. Kenneth sat on a stool outside the stoop, his dusty face streaked with the tracks of his tears. They continued to flow while he rocked back and forth, and a low mournful sound emanated from the boy. He did not acknowledge them. Tobias, the old one with the weak leg, stood near with women and children.

"What's happened?" Cat urgently asked.

One of the women spoke timidly. " 'Tis Mary's bairn. The priest is here."

"The priest? Oh, no," Cat said. She entered the cottage, Roderic but a step behind her.

Mary sat with her babe in her arms; the child was much too quiet. The priest stood on one side of Mary, his hand on her shoulder.

Edna was attempting to take the baby from its mother, the picture of tormented grief. She rocked the child as her tears spilled unto the blanket, unheeded.

"Father, forgive me. Ask God to spare her. She is my sweet lass, and she hasnae seen but two summers. I cannae bear it. If she dies, let me die, too!"

"Nay, lass. Dinnae think such thoughts. Pray for God's strength," Father MacNair said.

"Mary, Angel, ye must let go. Let me take the child. Ye have not slept in two nights. If ye fall ill, what of your other child, Janet? She needs ye. Kenneth, too."

Edna took the baby, and Mary collapsed in a heap of emotional exhaustion.

"No . . . no," she wailed softly, a high keening sound. Father MacNair held her shoulders as she rested her face on the small wooden table near the hearth.

"Did someone fetch Glyniss?" Roderic asked.

Edna nodded. "Aye, she is mixing up a cure for the fever."

The woman's voice dropped to a whisper. "She fears it is too late."

The bairn coughed, a harsh barking sound.

Cat reached out to touch the child's chest and was alarmed at the heat she felt from the tiny body in the bundle.

Momentarily lost in thought, she whispered to herself, muttering softly. "The cough sounds like . . . croup. It's the croup. What was it Mama said . . . steam?"

"Brianna?" Roderic said.

She turned so quickly to face him, her long hair swirled over her shoulder.

"Steam! Boil some water in a large pot. Get several buckets. Edna, we need a few furs, or blankets. The baby needs to breathe in the moist air."

Glyniss came to stand before them. She held a small cup in her hand.

"Can ye help the child?" Roderic asked.

"I will do my best, Sir Roderic. This be a weak tea of the mountain willow bark with some herbs. We cannae give the babe but a small sip. The fever is so great, if it dinnae break soon, I doubt the child will live to see the morn." She spoke the last in a whisper, but still the young mother heard.

"No," Mary said.

"We can try the hot water in the air and see if it will help the baby breathe. Please Glyniss, you have to do as I say. Trust me."

Edna cuddled the bairn while she addressed the others. "I told ye we should have bled her."

"Bleed her! No! You can't. It will weaken her even more. She needs all her strength!" Cat protested.

"Why do ye ken this steam will help?" Glyniss made an attempt to help the baby swallow small sips of the tea.

"I hope it will, but please, Glyniss, don't bleed her. It is folly to rob the body of blood that makes it strong. I only want to help the child, and I am not certain it will cure her. You may indeed be right. The babe may not live past the night . . . so where is the harm in trying? Please?"

"Brianna, ye may not think to be a healer, but ye speak true. I have used bleeding on grown men and women. Never have I seen it help the way some say it should. I willnae do it to such a tiny thing. Better she leave this world in her Mother's arms unmarked, if it be the will of God."

Cat knew in her heart to tread carefully. The final say must rest with Glyniss. Those who already thought her bewitched would need little encouragement to accuse her, and if they could add the word of a healer, the claim would have further validation.

Roderic shook his head. "Why do you think hot water will help?"

"I don't think. I am sure of it. Trust me, Roderic, she will breathe better," Cat said.

"It willnae do to give the mother false hope. 'Tis cruel," Glyniss said.

"You are right," Cat agreed. Kneeling down beside Mary, she struggled to gain the woman's attention from her weeping. "Mary."

Mary raised her face, and there was bleak despair in her expression.

"I have a plan that may help your bairn. It is my hope that the hot water will help her breathe with more ease. I am not saying I can save her, but I want to try. Do you understand?"

Mary nodded. Cat went to boil water, and Roderic fashioned a pole in the middle of the room while they draped quilts around the pot. Mary dried her tears and seemed to find new strength, insisting on holding the baby while the others replenished the large pot full of boiling water.

Hours later Glyniss took the child, and Mary fell from the stool, utterly exhausted. Roderic carried her to bed, and the women helped make her comfortable. Cat held the baby and sat down near the water. The uncomfortable heat soon made her sweat profusely, but she sat and crooned to the baby, keeping her hand lightly on the little one's chest.

Roderic sat near the table. "You make a fine sight, Lady Montwain." His brown eyes bathed her in admiration.

Cat smiled wryly. "I fear I am not fit to be near, in truth. I am beginning to smell." She wrinkled her nose, wiped sweat from the back of her neck, and looked down at the child. Although the fever was still present, the child seemed to sleep deeply and the cough was not as frequent.

After an hour or so, Glyniss came and took a turn at holding the baby until she, too, was drenched in sweat. Cat fell asleep with her head on the table. When she awakened and looked about, she saw that Roderic was gone.

"Aye . . . little one. Fight for life," Glyniss said. She looked up at Cat. "This child is stronger than we thought."

"Where is Roderic?"

"He left a bit ago to see to his men. The priest and I can handle the buckets alone. Ye were sleeping, so he decided not to disturb ye. I must say, lady, that mon, English or no, is full of compassion."

"Aye. He is that," Cat said.

"Tell me, be that why ye stay? Ye care for him?"

"Do you wish to be rid of me?"

"Nay, but, if ye wish to run home to your own, ye could slip away," Glyniss said.

"But . . . I have no place to go," Cat replied.

Glyniss said nothing as she rocked the child for a moment, pondering Cat's words. Finally, she spoke. "No fault in wantin' a better life as a fine lady. If ye wish to be known as one of the high born, best ye act a bit more selfish. Not many who could be restin' in a fine castle would fash themselves about a poor woman's babe. Ye see how chafing it be to live with lies?"

Cat sighed. "I know you are right, Glyniss. Still, I thank you for keeping silent."

"Ye must tell them all, and soon, or I will," Glyniss said.

Cat folded her arms about her and sighed. She was trying to think of a way to tell Roderic the truth, and decided
once again to trust Glyniss. "Catherine."

"What say you?" asked Glyniss.

"My name is Catherine."

Glyniss huffed under her breath with an amused snort.
"May ye have peace, Catherine. Dinnae be so fearful; Sir
Roderic willnae toss ye aside." She stroked the babe in her
arms, touching the child's chest. "We have done well, the
child is resting better. But, I can think of many a finer way to
spend a night. I am sweatin' like I be in the fires of hell."

"You don't really believe it helpful. Why did you not
oppose me?"

"Ye kept Mary busy boilin' water, pourin' it in a pot,
making the tent. All these things are better to ponder for a
young mother than watchin' her bairn die," Glyniss said.

Cat sighed and shook her head sadly.

"Why do ye care? These aren't your people."

Cat was too tired to think of a better answer than what
was in her heart. It was something Merlin had said. "I'm
needed here."

Father MacNair stepped up behind her. "Aye, lady. And
ye are no witch."

"They have spoken to you of this?"

"Aye. I must ask you. Do ye love God?"

Cat spoke emphatically. "Yes."

"Do you serve Him?"

"Yes," Cat said.

"Is that enough for ye, Father?" Glyniss asked, her tone demanding.

"Aye," Father MacNair said.

"So be it, then. Dinnae speak of foolishness born out of ignorance and fear. Do ye know how many healers are burned as heretics for tryin' a new way of helpin' others? Bah! If it would save this child I would try anything, yet there are those so quick to see devils around every post they try to make healin' the church's business. 'tis not! Amen, I said it! Mayhap that makes me a heretic, too!"

Father MacNair smiled. "Nay, Glyniss. Ye are but out-spoken and headstrong."

"I'm glad you believe me, Father," Cat said.

They fell silent, and soon Cat could no longer stay awake. The small cottage was alight with the first warm glow of sunlight when Mary awakened her, gently shaking her shoulder. Mary held her baby girl, and the child was awake.

"How is she?" Cat asked. Reaching out to the baby, Cat felt the soft skin; it was still warm to the touch.

"She is much better. After ye went to sleep, Glyniss put a poultice of onions on her chest. It was not long she coughed up the tea, but her chest is mending, and the steam did help her to breathe."

"Oh, Mary, I'm so glad."

"The fever is much better. I do so thank ye, Lady Mont-wain. Glyniss said she willnae forget your treatment for other bairns, and she has promised to stay with me until my Hannah is well."

Cat heard the muffled sound of angry voices outside the cottage.

"Sir Montwain is here. He is outside, and there be some trouble," Mary said.

Cat stood and turned to the door, throwing on her cloak.

Roderic stood outside, four of his soldiers beside him. Tobias and several women of the clan argued before him. One of the women began to shout.

"There! She's evil! She must be burned to cleanse us all!"

"There will be no more talk of it! I've come to take my wife to the keep so she may rest. She's had little sleep helping with the sick child. You all go back to your cottages!" Roderic said.

"English fool! Ye be blind to her wiles! Mary's babe should be dead! Did she use her spells to save it? We heard of it! Boilin' water like the fires of hell for a child to sit near. And she wanted the Gordon babe! They took the child from her and ended up dead for their trouble!"

"Enough!" Father MacNair said as he shouldered through the group of soldiers.

"Why do ye judge this woman so? She wasnae casting any devil's spells! She was a help, and so was the poultice Glyniss made. The child is better, though there still be fever. Mary needs ye one and all to be an aid, not a hindrance. The child is ill, and Glyniss will do all she can to help, but this lady is not wicked. Ask the healer."

Cat watched Tobias at the head of the crowd of women. He leaned heavily on a wooden crutch made from a tree, supporting a leg bent and crippled, and he sported a scruffy gray beard. Thin, his eyes a bright blue, he watched Roderic suspiciously, then suddenly met her gaze. Cat took a deep breath and raised her chin defiantly.

Glyniss stepped up and put her hands on her hips when she addressed the crowd.

"If ye all aren't a pretty flock of game hens! Ye hate the Englishmon, but ye cannae drive him away. The lass served ye weel enough, as Angus Mackay stole her to keep the alliance with the King! She saved your lives with a lie!"

Cat had feared the moment of truth. Glyniss turned, an expression of compassion shining in her eyes. "Forgive me, I mean ye no harm, but never could I abide lies and deceivin'. Never knew a secret to be kept! I dinnae fear your husband means these people harm, so the truth shall be spoken."

Roderic looked at his wife with a gaze filled with new questions and suspicion. Cat dropped her eyes briefly, took a deep breath, and silently pleaded his indulgence.

Glyniss went on speaking to the crowd. "Now ye be done with her, so ye judge her a witch?"

"The Gordon Laird and his son are dead after taking the child away when she wanted to keep the babe!"

"Aye, and so are ten others from that holding, of the same fever! They knew not this lady, and she had no grudge to bear them! Say ye she caused them to be stricken, too?"

"She claimed to be from a different time!" Tobias shouted the accusation.

"Mary told me she was knocked senseless when Angus pulled her out of the water! Slapped her about, too! Mackay threatened to kill her if she did not pretend to be the real Brianna," Glyniss said.

"The real Brianna!" Roderic spoke the words in anger.

"Aye. The lass ye were to marry fled, and Mackay had to think fast, like the wily serpent he is. Angus stole this lass to give them a way out. She is not evil, and she is not a witch. Reached out a hand of help to those here, she did, ungrateful backbiters they be." Glaring at the crowd again, her eyes flashed her contempt.

"We dinnae ken who ye married, Sir Roderic. Verily we know this truth." She turned to Cat and folded her arms to her chest. "She is not a Mackay."

Chapter Nineteen

Confess your faults to one another, and pray for one another, that ye may be healed.

~James 5:16

Who are you? What clan holds your allegiance?" Roderic demanded. There was a bitter edge of determination in his voice.

They had entered the keep and spoken with the nurse to see that all was well with Hope. The babe was sleeping soundly with her in another chamber, so they entered the privacy of their own, where Roderic felt safe to vent his anger.

His wife was not listening to him. Wearily, she poured water in a basin and washed herself from the waist up. He knew she was exhausted, but he would know the truth.

"Must we speak of this now? I am tired, and I need to be clean. Can you not spare me the time to do this?"

Whirling from her while she washed, he paced, battling his rage at both the Mackay and the beautiful woman he had married. He waited until she finished changing clothes and came to sit on the bed. Folding her hands in her lap demurely, she turned to face him, as if refusing more wine at the table.

"Answer me, wife." The angry retort hardened his features.

"Would it matter so much if I were not a Mackay by blood?"

"Brianna . . ." He took a deep breath while his eyes narrowed in suspicion.

"That is not your name. What do I call you now?"

She shrugged, a wry smile teasing her lips. "I'm called Catherine."

He came to stand before her, and she was keenly aware of his scrutiny. "So it is true, then. Angus Mackay forced you to marry me? He threatened you?"

Nodding, she looked away to gaze at the fire. "Yes. Calum Mackay said he would kill me if I didn't agree."

"They beat you! I remember the mark on your back! Why did you not appeal to me? I would have protected you."

"I know that now. I thought I could get away at first . . ."

"So you were running away from me when you went to Maitland. Are you from another clan?"

She stood up and walked away from him, around the bed. "You don't understand! Don't ask me questions I cannot answer. I can't go home. I have no place to go! Then, after we were together, I . . ." Cat stopped speaking.

"Yes? After we were together?"

Turning to face him, she looked ravishing in her soft white sheath, the fire casting a warm, dancing light in her red hair. Trembling, her green eyes were shining brightly with emotion.

"I didn't want to leave you. If I would never again see family or home it mattered not. From the moment I looked into your eyes, I felt . . . I belonged to you, Roderic."

Coming to her, he gripped her waist tightly. She felt his anger and passion in every muscle of his body, and held his face in her hands. Closing her eyes, she sighed, and rested her cheek to his. "Please, please, forgive me. I will never betray you."

Roderic was caught off-guard by his emotions. Profoundly touched by what she had endured for him and the clan, his mouth possessed her, his tongue swept past the softness of her lips to caress her passionately.

He pulled away abruptly. Wrapping her hair around his fist he spoke hoarsely. "May God forgive me . . . though I know what true duty and honor would demand of me . . . I cannot take you to your home to appease any noble principle. Better to suffer recompense at any harsh altar than have you ripped from me body and soul. You are my mate, my woman, and I will not lose you to another, be it kin or clan. The thought of another man with right of ownership of you fills me with a blood lust to kill, if need be, to keep you at my side!"

Looking at him with apprehension, she did not answer. Tears spilled from her green eyes as she rested her cheek to his chest.

232

"Tell me you will never leave me!"

"I can't, Roderic." She swiped her tears away with the back of her hand. He shook her into gasping silence.

"So be it. You will be guarded day and night!"

He expected her anger, recriminations, and at last, an explanation. He got none, and was baffled by her response. She slipped her arms around him and caressed his back, embracing him. Bending down, he swung her gently up into his arms and carried her to the bed.

Roderic made love to her tenderly, with an inner rage and possessiveness. Lying awake long after they found their pleasure, he held her tightly and wrapped his body around hers when she slept. He held her all through the night, as if he were in danger of an intruder and in fear of someone snatching her away.

Roderic refused to speak to his men about his wife's identity. If there was a spirit of discontentment, they hid it well, and he was increasingly uneasy at the thought of explanations to the King. Alec had not returned, and he began to consider bringing his wife to meet King Alexander in an attempt to sort out the truth.

Being duped by Mackay did not sit well, but the woman he married was also a victim of the man's treachery. Catherine continued to insist she could not return to her home, but implied by her actions she would leave him in time. The more he pressed her, the more she fell silent. Catherine had no family, no clan, or they may have cast her out. Had they abandoned her? What would possess them to forsake their own? At the time of the marriage Catherine was a virgin and very beautiful. What father would not want to make a lucrative marriage with so comely a daughter to pledge?

Catherine was not only lovely, she was intelligent, if one could overlook her constant forgetfulness. She had to be reminded of the simplest things regarding the keep. He watched with interest as Edna patiently taught her skills that every girl child in the Highlands knew by twelve summers. Edna helped her make candles, salt meat properly, oversee the meals, and direct the servants. Catherine was often confused, and asked the older woman's help discreetly, but Roderic was extremely observant of his wife and her activities.

Working with his soldiers on one of the cottages one day, he noticed Catherine stomping toward the stable. There was stiff anger in her movements, and he followed her, determined to see why she was vexed. She plunged her hand down into the cold water of the barrel near the forge when he approached her. Roderic lifted a brow as if to inquire her purpose.

Catherine huffed under her breath. "It's nothing. I burned my hand in the kitchens."

Exchanging a smile with her, he shook his head and he stepped forward. He reached down into the cold water to gently pull her hand up to examine the burn.

"Mayhap you would fare well to give over the task to Edna."

She jerked her hand back from his touch and put it once again in the water. "Oh, and why do you say so?" Her green eyes lighted.

He grinned. "Your skin is not all that has been burned since you set your hand to cook, wife."

"Yes, well, that's very amusing. But I never said I could cook! You show me something to put in a microwave, and I can cook it!" Spinning away angrily, she strode toward the horses. "I'm going for a ride!"

Kenneth raced past them, and Cameron followed them to ready the horses, as he was once again entrusted with guarding Lady Montwain.

Roderic turned and made his way to the keep. Entering the buttery, he sought out Edna. "What manner of bird or fowl is a crow wave?"

Puzzled, she looked up at him. "Are ye daft? I know not. There be only crow. Why?"

Roderic shook his head, baffled. "Catherine. 'Tis what she claims to cook well."

Edna snorted. "Nay, crows be not tasty. The lass must be jesting with ye. Or she be confused in her head anew."

"If that be true at times, Edna, give my wife the respect her position demands. If her actions merit your concern, come to me," he said.

Edna smiled. "Aye, Sir Roderic. I mean no harm. I favor

the lass."

He sighed, and grimaced in good humor. "As do I." He made his way back to the cottage and the tasks at hand.

Roderic wrestled with treating his wife as a prisoner, always the uncertainty of her identity haunted him. She was the pawn in the Mackay's schemes, and was also the center of an intricate puzzle.

Nothing about the woman made sense. Roderic had determined that she was like the boy, then he found out that she was not a Mackay. Roderic decided she was reared more as a son than a daughter. Catherine rode with a grace and ease that he himself coveted, as if she were one with the horse, and Cameron reported that they fared well in their hunting. She often spent time teaching Kenneth to fight. Roderic was amused at the thought until Cameron went on to render an account.

Catherine worked with the boy for long hours teaching him to use her small sword. She reasoned with Cameron that Roderic had forbidden her own use of the sword, but Kenneth could make a skilled use of it. It was small enough he could wield it successfully and have a chance at defending himself.

Roderic allowed her efforts to ease his own conscience. Thought fey and simpleminded, the lad had not been taught as other young men. Roderic meant to remedy the situation himself in time. Catherine took it upon herself, and he was grateful, because it kept her occupied. She was forever bored with womanly pursuits and had no knowledge of sewing! The latter amazed him, for every lady he knew had been taught this skill.

Regretting the loss of his ideals, he had imagined that his wife would sew tapestries and busy herself in her efforts to make his hearth and home comfortable. It was a hope of his marriage not fulfilled. Although Catherine was diligent to care for Hope, Glyniss and Edna gave her assistance, and she was never idle, visiting the people of the clan every day. She cleaned Mary's cottage, brought food, and worked with Glyniss to aid those who were ill. Catherine asked one of his men, who was an excellent bowman, to build a new crutch for Tobias. The man had a talent with wood, be it making weapons, shields, or chairs. He made the crutch and gave Catherine his promise that he would not tell the old one it was a gift from Lady Montwain.

"She feared Tobias wouldnae take it from her, for he may fear she is evil. Still, it was her kindness, Sir Roderic." The man spoke earnestly, as if in awe of his mistress.

"Aye," Roderic said.

It was a help for the old cripple, allowing him to move about more freely. Catherine helped them one and all, in spite of the resentment harbored by many. She was a stranger among them, but soon, as the weeks passed by, the fear that had been evident in those who had accused her abated.

Roderic was given grudging respect as he helped the people rebuild. The devastation and the sickness slowly dissipated, and the people of the clan began to speak favorably of the man that Scotland's King had sent to them.

Roderic sent another courier to Alexander, spoke not of the fact he had married the wrong woman. He did not wish to impart that news in a message. Edna tearfully confessed that the Mackay daughter went to wed the younger brother of the Kincaid Laird.

King Alexander wanted what was best for the lass, and would not be pleased that she rejected the marriage he decreed for her. Still, Roderic was certain the King would not forbid the marriage did the lass prove to be content and no longer under her father's tyranny. Roderic would meet with the Laird of her husband's clan to make amends. He bore no vengeance for the woman he had never met, too obsessed with the lady who took her place.

Catherine gave him no reassurance she would stay, which infuriated him. Edna implied she was a poor lass with no means of making a good marriage. Roderic would gladly give her title of his holding, his lands, his name. He would defy even Alexander, should he rule their union invalid. The devastating thought brought a realization that he was loath to admit. His emotions were not logical about the red-headed vixen he had married.

Catherine was agile and as quick as Kenneth, as strong for her stature as many men in his army. The lady was unlike any he had ever met. She had a gentle wit that could be sharp and biting, accepted her own faults and laughed at them, and held no arrogance at her station as Lady

Montwain. Edna's theory that she hailed from humble folk was not to be discarded. Her gentleness with others, her unassuming manner brought his respect. She spoke to his warriors with courtesy, deferred to their knowledge in a way that won their loyalty, and infused them with pride and courage. Roderic concluded that their promise made to defend her was now won by loyalty, not only to King Alexander and himself, but to Lady Montwain.

Roderic had little patience for his own lack of discipline. A woman must not dictate to a warrior and leader what he must do, and he could not risk his honor. He must give her up if the King willed it. At the very thought, however, he despaired.

Chapter Twenty

I laid me down and slept; I awaked; for the Lord sustained me.

~Psalms 3:5

"Run, Kenneth! Run! We just lost Cameron, but if I know that burly Scot, he will be crashing through the trees any second," Cat said.

She pulled her bow from over her shoulder and took careful aim at the bird in her sights. Kenneth came at a dead run to slide silently to a stop, kneeling at her feet. Forever amazed at his stealth, Cat whispered to him as she took aim. "You could slip out a dagger and cut the blazon off a man's chest and never wake him, laddie." Letting her arrow fly to its target, the bird fell and she smiled at Kenneth. He smiled back and stroked his cheek upward with his fingertips. They had their own signs of communication, he and Cat, and she frowned apologetically.

"I'm sorry, sweet, did I give you no affection today?"

Leaning over, she embraced him and he held her tightly,

nuzzling her cheek. She kissed his forehead. Kenneth needed an exceptional amount of tenderness, and Cat freely gave it, for the emotional loneliness of leaving her own time had left her wanting.

Kenneth and Hope filled her heart when she felt bereft. Roderic was a strong and noble husband, but she constantly resisted the position of subservience which was thrust upon her. Careful to keep a bit of her heart tucked away, only with Kenneth was she free to vent her frustration in the adjustment to this time.

"You know what I miss, Kenneth? My cell phone! I used to view it as an electronic leash that David had on me, and now I would give anything to talk on one. I miss fried chicken bought and paid for, served to me in a cardboard bucket. I was so spoiled by modern conveniences! I miss my father, and my own independence. Here, I have to beg just to touch my sword."

"And dost thou suffer from the loss of these things?"

Kenneth startled and moved out of her embrace to look up in the trees. The booming voice had come down from above. Cat gazed up at the trees, squinting her eyes when the sun dancing through the leaves briefly blinded her.

"Merlin? Where are you? I know you are there!" she called out.

Kenneth looked about, and then closed his eyes as a gentle breeze caressed his face and brow.

Cat stood and walked about, searching the treetops for

a sign of her friend. The sky was bright, the clouds soft and white. The air suddenly turned cooler.

Kenneth scrambled up and ran, and she turned to see him bound into Merlin's arms.

The older man was dressed in full knight's garb. No drab robe this, but regal, in deep blue and gold. His white hair glowed as it flowed past his shoulders. Wearing no hat, he held a sword at his side. "You must address me as Sir Raven, Catherine," he said with a frown.

She smiled. "Very well, if you favor it. Kenneth seems to know you are a friend." Cat walked over them.

"Aye, lass. This one is a funny little frog, a bit of an amusing sprite content with his own magic. Go . . . boy. Leave us for a time. I need a moment with your lady."

Kenneth reacted as if he understood every word uttered by the old time traveler. Traipsing away to stand over Cat's kill, he picked up the bird and began plucking off the feathers. Cat kept him in sight.

"You have come to take me back, have you not?" A bit of frightened anticipation touched the tone of her voice.

"You must make a judgment as to your path, Catherine. I will come for you in three days. Forever gone, or forever stay; you must ponder and declare your resolve." He turned strode away from her.

"Why only three days' time?" Frantically, she tried to keep up with his swift pace. "Surely it can be postponed for a bit?"

He stopped with a flourish, and the color of his blue eyes turned a deep sapphire in anger. "You would bargain with me, lady?" he said in an outraged roar.

"Nay. Forgive me, Sir Raven. I did not mean to make you angry. But, it will be so hard to . . ."

"Leave forever the man that holds your heart?" His blue eyes were penetrating as they stared into hers.

"Maybe that's true. Still, I wish to be no man's property! My time gave validation to women. They were not treated as silly pets. They were listened to, valued."

"You speak, and he does not listen?"

"Nay, he does listen to me. But if he chooses not to, I have no recourse, no choice! I am only what he allows me to be in this time!"

"Bah! Did he ignore your love for the Gordon babe? Did he beat you when you disobeyed him to cross another clan's border?"

Folding her arms about her defensively, she huffed. "You know he did not! He made a pretense of it for the others, but he has never hurt me. Roderic is . . . very tender with me." She spoke the last in a breathless whisper as if the thought were a sudden one.

"Aye, and this tenderness is a precious gift. Most women would thank God, fasting, for such a man." He pulled out a small scrap of paper from his belt. "May this lend a help in your decision, lady, and your arrow be straight and true, as always."

Putting the piece of paper in her hand, he continued as he walked away from her, "Be at the east landing of the castle at sunset in three days time. If ye judge to stay here, know ye never to plead to go back, for this will be your home!"

Watching him disappear through the trees, Cat felt suddenly cold. She looked down at the paper in her hand. It was a newspaper clipping from Houston, Texas. The date was only six months from the date she worked in Scotland. Merlin had gone into the future! The article documented the tragic loss of Howard Terril after a long battle with cancer.

Her father was dying.

Cameron was vexed at the fey young boy. Kenneth had taken hold of his arm and dragged him to Lady Montwain. The urgency with which he conveyed his need of help was merited when Cameron observed her condition.

Her skin was cold and clammy. Tears streamed unheeded from her eyes as she sat rocking back and forth on the ground under the trees. He wrapped her into his arms and took her to Roderic.

Roderic sat in the great hall at the long table sipping ale.

"Sir Roderic!" Cameron shouted.

Roderic rose and moved swiftly when he saw his wife's condition. He ran to take her from Cameron.

"What has happened? Is she injured?"

"Nay! I found no wound. She is pale, and cold, and wouldnae answer," Cameron said.

Roderic shouted, "Edna!"

The woman appeared at once.

"Fetch Glyniss. Your lady is ill," he said.

"Aye, Sir Roderic," Edna replied. She went to do his bidding.

Roderic held Catherine tenderly and carried her to their chamber, placing her in their bed. Her skin was like ice, and she tossed about on the bed, crying.

Crooning to her, he tried to take her in his arms and give her comfort. He begged her to tell him what troubled her so he could make it right.

Glyniss came to see to her and pronounced her illness not one of body, but of spirit. She was inconsolable. Another mystery flogged his brain as he viewed his wife. She lay on the bed and cried as if her heart had been rent in two. He made small attempts to give her comfort and affection, but she would not be consoled.

Roderic sat with her throughout the night, wrapping her in blankets hoping to warm her. Wanting no further outcry of her madness, he allowed no one else near, explaining only that she was ill. Her constant tears wrenched his heart, she whimpered, cried, and continued to speak two words again and again as if they beset her with a quandary.

"Three days."

Chapter Twenty-one

The simple believeth every word, but the prudent man looketh well to his going.

~Proverbs 14:15

Cat roused herself from her grief after the long night of tears and depression. Roderic demanded the reason for her collapse.

"I've had some grave news. My father is . . . dying."

"Dispense with this mystery, Catherine. Tell me the way to your home, and I shall take you to your father at once!"

"No, Roderic. You cannot. If I leave, and it will be soon . . . I can never return," she said.

His expression clouded in anger. "You will not leave me! Let your clan come for you! Lay siege if they must, but take you they will not. You stood before the priest with me and took vows, in spite of your lies! You could carry my child even now. King Alexander will understand Mackay's trickery. When I speak to him of this, he will sanction our union. If your family has cast you out, how did you know of your father's sickness?"

Cat sighed, shook her head, and was silent. She was weak and tired in spirit from her night of grief. Her father's illness had been an almighty blow. Howard must have been ill long before she went to work on the film in Scotland; he said nothing.

She felt not only profound grief, but despair born of betrayal. The decision to stay or leave Roderic was made more difficult in the knowledge that she could never say good-bye to her father, though he was ill. Her mind was tired from the frantic thoughts that plagued her. Merlin was adamant in his command, and there would be no changing her mind once the decision was made.

Roderic walked to her and with a graceful movement took her in his arms to sit on the bed. The lethargy she felt, coupled with her depression, made her numb. Sitting in his arms like a broken doll, she pressed her cheek to his collar bone, and sank gratefully into his warmth, his embrace.

"My love. You will not leave me. My life, my heart will be barren without you. You are tired and overwrought. Do not be afraid of the future with the loss of your loved one. I took you as my wife for all time, and honor has this pledge from me to care for you in your father's place from the day we wed. Don't cry, for I will be your shield and shelter."

Embracing him, she kissed his cheek, and sighed. "Roderic. Let's not speak of the future, and enjoy our time together."

He kissed her passionately, his tongue sweeping past her lips to caress the inside of her mouth.

Cat wrapped her arms around his neck and pushed her fingers in his hair, determined to enjoy every precious second she had left with Roderic, her husband, her heart. She only hoped she would have the strength to leave him.

The next two days were a trial for Cat. She tried to be with Roderic and Hope every second, knowing she would return to her time when Merlin came. Roderic continued to have her guarded, but she knew Cameron would be no match for Merlin's powers.

She found herself hoping that she would have a child for her comfort. She wanted to stay with Roderic. She wanted to go home. Determined to stand by one decision, only hours later she would relent and change her mind.

On the third day she dressed in the green gown in which she was married. Cat felt an unbridled anxiety when Roderic watched her intently at the evening meal. She ate little, far too emotional to feel any real hunger. There was to be a minstrel to entertain them all at the close of the meal, but she rose to leave after the first song.

"You wish to beg my leave, lady?" Roderic said.

Through the riot of emotions Cat was suddenly exasperated. "Nay! It is not my custom to beg permission, yours or anyone else's, to come or go!"

"Catherine." The word was spoken as if his sword was drawn in challenge, and it was a clear warning. "Tread lightly."

Gazing into his warm brown eyes, she thought of their countless nights of pleasure, then glanced up to see the evening sunlight low on the walls of the castle. This would be their last few moments together, and she did not want this memory marred by a careless word.

"Forgive me. May I take my leave, sir?"

"Aye," he said.

Cat turned and made her way quickly to the east landing of the castle. Cameron, of course, followed. She turned to him when she began to see the lavender mist through the door by the landing.

"You mustn't come any closer, Cameron."

"Catherine! Wait!"

The hoarse shout was Roderic's. He moved around Cameron to stand before her, tall and angry. Kenneth drew him forward by the hand. The lad was frightened as he ran to her, sliding to Cat's feet and wrapping his arms tightly around her legs. Whimpering and moaning, Kenneth shook his head despairingly.

"Kenneth, what have you done to me?" she whispered to the boy as she looked into the angry face of her husband.

Kenneth stood and tugged at her arms, trying to pull her away from the mist. How did the boy know she was leaving? Embracing him, she kissed his forehead and tried to calm him. Cat had been unable to bear saying goodbye to the baby girl. Was she leaving her family forever? Who would care for Hope in her absence? Would Roderic one day take another woman as his wife? The very thought battered her with an envious wrath.

"What is this fog, Catherine? Come away from here," Roderic ordered.

Cameron drew his sword. "Think ye the fog is of this world, Roderic?" It was a frightened rasp of a whisper.

"There is nothing to fear. It is just that I must go now," she said.

"Kenneth, come here!" Roderic barked, his tone commanding.

The boy tore himself from her arms in tears and ran past Cameron.

"Take him away, and leave us," Roderic said.

Cameron backed away slowly, sword drawn, staring at the mist. Extremely pale, he trotted away from them in an attempt to catch up with Kenneth.

"Tell me now you are no witch!"

"I am not, Roderic. I love God just as you do! I serve no evil entity, but I must go back where I belong. It is best this way."

"No!" Catching her in an embrace, he moved much more quickly than she could have ever imagined possible. "Stay with me! I will protect you from this evil!"

"There is no evil! Please believe me! Roderic, don't make

it harder. I don't wish to leave you, but you don't know what you ask of me." She made a futile attempt to push his arms from around her waist. They felt as bands of steel, and she fought to break away.

"I ask that you honor the vow taken in truth and trust. A pledge before God! Was it meaningless? Was it all born of deception? Are these senseless tales more of your lies?" He spoke harshly.

"I never meant to hurt or deceive you!" Cat blurted, knowing full well how weak it sounded.

Roderic went on, his eyes conveying the fury within him. "I ask no more from you than you promised to do! I ask that you stay my wife, be a mother to my children, forsaking all others for all time!"

"For all time. Your time, not mine," she said.

He kissed her then, and their passion flared between them, born of desperation and fear. His mouth slanted over hers again and again.

Cat pulled away to frantically whisper, "I can't do this! I can't stand this pain! I must go!"

Bending down, he threw her over his shoulder, and she fought him, kicking and squirming.

Cat was horribly afraid. Her last chance to see home, her father, her time, was disappearing before her eyes. "No, Roderic! Put me down!"

Turning her in his arms, he cradled her there. Holding her with a possessive determination, he nuzzled her cheek to his and spoke hoarsely. "I need you."

Cat suddenly felt the comforting touch of her mother's hands long ago. In the caress was tenderness and reassurance, but she also felt the plea of his spirit. The child abandoned, the man never truly accepted by other Scotsmen, reached out to her for solace, for love.

Feeling the tension drain from her body, she knew in that second she could never leave him. Roderic set Cat on her feet. Whirling to look for the mist, he saw it was no longer there. The sun had set, and the decision had been made.

"I told you I would not allow you to leave me," he said.

"Roderic!" Cameron shouted as he ran to them.

"Arm yourself! Gavin has returned with our sentinel guard, and the two clans have circled the perimeter beyond the castle. He was near captured, and has seen the enemy!"

"The enemy?" Roderic demanded.

"Aye!" Cameron said.

" 'Tis the Kincaid Laird with his warriors. They are seven-hundred strong, and have joined the Mackay rogues. Gavin has seen them! The warriors be near to our gates, and we are under siege!"

Chapter Twenty-two

The desire of the righteous is only good; But the expectation of the wicked is wrath.

~Proverbs 11:23

Roderic found Gavin stretched out on the long table in the great hall. Stripped to the waist with a bloody wound under his left arm, he grimaced while Glyniss stood over him washing the blood away. Edna stood by to help, and there were several men clustered around the table. Roderic shouldered through them, and placed his hand on his friend's heart.

Gavin's eyes opened to peer intently, sharp and alert. "Nay, ye blackguard, no need to dig a hole, for 'tis a wee nuisance, no more!"

"Thank all that is holy, my friend," Roderic said, tugging mightily on Gavin's long hair.

"Be still!" Glyniss barked at them both. "Nuisance or not it could become full of infection! I'll cover it with salve if ye stop thrashin' about."

"How did you escape through them? How many do they number?" Roderic questioned.

"I ken they were to capture me, so I couldnae warn ye. 'Tis Kincaid, and he has seven-hundred men with him, but that is not the worst of it! Mackay has joined them. I saw one of his men. But, 'tis Kincaid we need to fear. Why would the Laird want ye dead? It must be more than the fact ye be a bloody Englishmon," Gavin said.

"Aye. It seems the woman I married is not the real Brianna Mackay. She escaped to marry Kincaid's brother. Angus captured this lady, and forced the deception so the clemency wouldn't be lost."

Gavin looked at Roderic's wife with a spark of humorous admiration in his eyes. Gavin looked at all women with a bold lustiness. Roderic was accustomed to it, still it rankled.

"So, lass, ye fooled us one and all," Gavin said.

"She had no choice; Mackay forced her! Still, if his daughter is now the wife of a Kincaid, maybe loyalty for the marriage has brought them together to seek the return of Mackay's holding," Roderic said.

"Best ye speak to Kincaid through a courier. His men ready themselves for war, though they are encamped. Why would they wait? When I passed through, they were not on the offense. It was an afterthought to capture me, but I was more determined to escape. We must wait for news from Kincaid. Tell me, ye mean to keep this red-headed wench as your own?"

"Aye," Roderic said. His brown eyes rested on her, then winked at Cat in amusement. Smiling back at him, she spoke to Glyniss. "Can I help?"

"Nay. This will be enough if he will lay still," she said. Glyniss had finished with the salve and pulled Gavin's arm down to lie on the table. Paling visibly, he appeared to fall asleep.

"He will awaken soon. 'Tis best to leave him be for now."

"Cameron," Roderic said.

"Aye, Sir Roderic."

"Invite the women with no one to defend them to bring their children, leave their cottages and come to the safety of the castle. How far is the enemy camp?"

"Gavin said they were only a mile from our gates. Gavin is right, the enemy has made no move to attack."

"Be that I could speak with Kincaid alone, I could undo the lies of Mackay. However, I will not risk death by trusting a man bent on vengeance. We will prepare for battle and wait," Roderic said.

"This keep will be impregnable. Mackay's own defenses were many. We can stand off a long siege. I vow they will tire of it before we are in danger of starving," Cameron said.

Calum Mackay challenged Roderic daily. On the fifth day, Cat walked to the tower to be with her husband. Roderic watched the burly Scot vent his rage. Calum cursed not only Roderic but every Englishman ever born. The vitriolic speeches were meant to spur a man's temper to lose his head. Cat felt a surge of respect for Roderic when she viewed how little emotion he invested in the whole affair.

"He should be with a troubadour in a play, the way he loves to hear himself shout," she said.

"Aye. Courtly love and devotions to women are the virtues those men speak of. Their songs and poetry readings are full of such. Mackay has no regard for women other than to abuse them. He could not properly cloak his brutality to agree with them, I fear," Roderic said.

"Very true. Roderic, will they cease . . . blustering, and attack us soon?"

"I will hope they do not until I can scheme to speak to Kincaid alone. I would defuse a fight if possible, until the King reaches our borders," he said.

"He comes? It is a certainty?"

"Aye. Though once it was a thought that brought only peace, I am now far from at ease with his visit. I may be facing a fight to keep you at my side, wife."

"He will put an end to our marriage?"

"He can. 'Tis in his power," Roderic said.

Gasping at the thought, a troubled frown worried her brow. He took her in his arms and Cat rested her head on his chest. Roderic took her chin to look into her eyes.

"Don't trouble yourself, lady. I've grown accustomed to

having you with me."

She smiled, her green eyes sparking as she playfully nipped his finger.

"Sinking your sharp teeth into your master, now? Is that what you are about?"

Firmly pinning her arms to her sides, he smiled at her.

"Nay, for no master do I have, laddie! I have a husband that I seek to honor, but I bend my knee to no man!"

"Ah, my Catherine, you are a trial to me. You will not be haughty to our King when he arrives, or you will learn better at my hand!" The sting of the arrogant words was soothed by his manner. His voice was warm and sexy, eyes soft and alight with humor.

"I won't shame you. I am your wife, and if God is merciful . . . that will not change." She ended her last thought in a longing whisper.

Cat felt anxious at the concern in his brown eyes. Wrapping her arms around him, she sighed and prayed for God's mercy to motivate King Alexander of Scotland to show them the same.

Four hours later it was not God's mercy and patience she found lacking. It was her own. Coming upon Roderic in a council with Gavin and five other men in the great hall, she joined them. They had been speaking of a plan to devise a private meeting with Kincaid, but the men immediately stopped all conversation when she sat down.

"Please, go on. I had no wish to interrupt you," she said.

Roderic turned to her. "Have you need of me, Catherine?"

"No. I had hoped to be a help," she said.

The men sat silently, staring at her as if she were an intruder.

"This is a private council, Catherine. It does not concern you," Roderic said.

She took immediate exception to both his words and his manner. "You speak of the siege we face, do you not?"

"Aye," Roderic said.

Her eyes snapped green fire. "And is my life not also in danger if the walls of this castle are breached?"

Roderic glared at her, frowning when he answered. "It is not your concern. We speak of matters of war, and your presence is not needed. You must trust me. Leave us now, wife."

Her blatant stare seemed to be accusing him coldly. Standing up, she looked each of them in the eye, and reading their impatience and irritation, felt her fists bunching at her sides.

Cat was furious by the time she had got to her chamber. Stomping about, she was unable to vent her fury until a sudden thought came to her.

Strolling over to the large chest that belonged to Roderic, she opened it to find her sword. Edna had placed her old clothes in the chest as well. Cat sat and held them, remembering the day the wardrobe department had issued them to her. The job she loved was now like a far away dream.

Rising, she undressed, flinging the gown from her body

as if it were filthy. Cat dressed in her own clothes, picked up her sword, and began practicing, her body moving in tune with old routines, slipping into the movements with ease.

Imagining David there as her partner, she executed each and every move with precision. To start, she stretched her memory to perform the first sword routine she had ever learned. When it was completed she moved on to others, practicing the fencing and sword choreography she had, in the past, perfected. Her anger dissipated as her body and mind strained to accomplish her old stunts, and it was a comfort to her spirit.

Cat pondered the threat that the enemies could attack at any time, and hoped she could fight long and hard, if need be, defending the people of the keep.

She whirled when Roderic entered the chamber.

He studied her momentarily, taking note of her appearance. "Why are you dressed this way, wife?"

"They are my clothes! Why should I not wear them?" Her response was biting, and she stood before him trembling with indignation, ready to do battle.

Giving an impatient shrug, his stern expression belied his indifference. "Wear what you wish, Catherine, but the sword is not a weapon for a lady."

"It's mine! I am no lady, Roderic, and maybe that is a fantasy I should relieve you of at last. These are my own clothes! This is my weapon! If I could return to my world at this moment, I would. I should have left! But, that chance is dead! That window of escape is closed, and I have no one to berate but myself! I allowed a pretty haze of lust to cloud my reason!"

"Your world? This is the world you spoke of on the landing?" he asked with a puzzled frown.

"Aye, sir. My world. A world you could never understand. Women fight for the battles they choose, and they fight in armies! They have struggled for these rights! It is a world... lost to me now." She sighed despondently.

"Catherine. Put the sword down."

Speaking slowly, he enunciated as if speaking to a child, and stepped closer. "You are tired and overwrought." Roderic's brows gathered at the sight of the sweat on her brow.

Angered even more that he thought he should humor her as he would Kenneth, Cat raised her sword in a mock salute. "Fear not, noble husband. It would suit my desire at this moment to do you harm maybe, but I do not intend to hurt myself." She snorted derisively.

"You are angry with me?"

"Quite clueless aren't you, laddie? A bit slow to catch on?"

"Give me the sword, Catherine. You are upset, not yourself, and if you lie down and rest, you will think clearer," he said.

"You want the sword? Then take it!"

It was a challenge, thrown down with no lack of aggression.

"This is foolish, Catherine."

"Are you afraid, Roderic? Are you afraid you might find

I am capable of fighting to defend this keep? Shall we wager? If I hold my own with you, I keep my sword and use it when I please! If not, I do as you wish."

He smiled. "My wish shall be for your forgiveness this night, and an end to your anger. Will you give it to me and come to bed?"

"Aye," she said.

"How shall we determine 'holding your own', as you say?"

Cat wanted to wipe that smug expression from his face. He approached this as if it were a game.

"If you do not manage to take my sword from me before the candle is gone?"

Roderic glanced at the candle. The wick would not last more than ten minutes. "Done."

It was the longest ten minutes of her life. Cat fought using her speed more than her skill, and twice he nearly forced her sword from her grip. She dealt with the blows by using a move she had perfected in one of her films. It called for her to toss the sword in the air, catch it with her left hand, and continue her attack. Fighting with a crude but accurate thrust, she returned her sword to her right hand.

Roderic was amused at her first recovery. "The wager is done, wife. You have lost your weapon."

"Only for a moment. The wager was you take it from me!"

Continuing to fight with few aggressive moves, he chuckled.

Cat fought on, desperate to prove something to herself,

she had spent her life being strong, fighting. As the battle raged within her, she realized she was fighting her own emotions. Caring for this man so deeply, she would gladly give up all convenience, all comforts of the future. Roderic was the one she hoped to be the father of her children. Still, her life as a wife and mother here would mean a surrender, an acceptance of her role as Lady Montwain. Merlin knew this and urged her to surrender to her heart.

The feminine feelings of being protected were unfamiliar and uncomfortable to Cat. She took exception to Roderic's dismissal; she could react no other way.

But, as they fought she could read his confusion. He gave no validation to such injured feelings; in in his world they should not exist. Women were not welcome at a war council, and his wife was no exception. His men would have been insulted.

As she came to the conclusion, Cat became less aggressive in her attack. She wavered when the strange, disquieting thoughts raced through her mind.

Roderic studied her with curious intensity. "Catherine, stop this, now! You have had enough!"

She was exhausted, and the chamber suddenly fell to darkness. The candle had burned out. Backing away, she turned from him, and dropped to her knees. Behind her she heard his efforts to light another candle.

He stared at her in amazement. "You are truly skilled with your weapon. But, I knew this from the moment I saw you defend Kenneth. What more did you need to prove to me?"

"I had to prove something to myself. Roderic, no matter how much loyalty you have from me, I will not be owned! I know how to fight, and I want to carry my sword."

"If I allow you to use it in battle, it could mean your death!"

She breathed deeply, dragging the air into her lungs. "It could also mean my life! If they attack, I will fight! I must!"

"Why do you feel you must do this? I will protect you!"

"For a very good reason! No one has over protected me, I've stood alone! I'll go on alone! I don't want to need you!"

Cat was stunned by her outburst. Roderic knelt down to put his own weapon aside, then carefully took her in his arms.

Disheartened, she held him tightly. Cat had begun to trust him more than she had ever trusted anyone in her own time, even her family.

All the longing for her place in the future began to dissipate. Her life was here, now, with Roderic, and in spite of her independent nature, there was a deep abiding desire to lay down her struggle, to allow someone else the power to care for her. Cat wanted a partner, someone she could, at times, lean on. In her own time, it would be considered silly, feminine, and weak. In this time, it was not only permissible, it was a way of life.

"Fear not your need of me, my love. For I, too . . . have need of you."

He spoke tenderly as he kissed her brow, and carried her to bed.

It was her whimper, a soft, yet desperate cry in the night that warned him. Roderic moved with lightening quickness to avoid the blow of the sword. It was imbedded with a heavy force near his ear when Cat screamed his name. His attacker next tried to pierce him with a knife. He was not accurate in the darkness because Catherine had risen to cover Roderic's side, to protect him. Screaming out, this time in pain, she continued to fight courageously, and it was then Roderic realized the enemy was dragging her from their bed. Catherine was the true prey, not himself, and the rage that any man would hurt his wife surged up inside him, a deadly bile.

Letting out a roar of anger, Roderic grabbed his sword and attacked, lunging with a sword thrust, but uncertain if he had truly wounded his opponent. The enemy let out a brief grunt of pain and fought with all his considerable strength. After a mighty blow, Roderic felt the bone in his right arm come close to breaking when the intruder struck. His enemy broke his hold on the sword and flung it from them to slide across the stone floor.

Suddenly the big man was pulled off of him and a flash of brilliant light blinded them both for seconds. In the center of the light stood a lone figure, calling out.

"Catherine!"

Roderic heard the sound of the enemy fleeing the room. His own fear was at war with the recognition of the familiar voice. Once heard in kindness, it was now an angry, vicious hiss.

"This is not to be born!"

Arms outstretched, the fire flew from the old one's fingertips. Darkness enveloped them for a heartbeat, then a beaming lavender light as a cold wind swirled around them. Roderic covered his eyes to save them, and came to his knees.

"Roderic!"

The cry was from Catherine, weak and breathless. Frantic to find her, to help her, he opened his eyes while he struggled to his feet. What he saw took his breath as he staggered in shock and disbelief.

The old one stood, the smoky light behind him, lavender in color, beautiful. Under his arm he held Catherine close to support her. Bleeding from her shoulder, her face was white and drawn. Her green eyes spoke to him of tenderness, and she spoke the next words as if they were her last. "Roderic . . . I love you."

Roderic knew then. He would lose her. The word came up from his belly in a frantic shout. "No!"

The old one closed his robe around her, and the brilliant light, bright as many suns, flashed again. Roderic slipped to the floor, and felt the cold stone to his cheek as he reached out to be engulfed in blessed darkness.

Chapter Twenty-three

Honour thy father and mother . . . That it may be well with thee, and thou mayest live long on the earth.

~Ephesians 6: 2, 3

"Catherine. You mustn't sleep any longer. Open your eyes. Wake up."

Cat felt the enticing pull of the deep sleep once again. Still, the nagging voice persisted. "Catherine."

"Merlin . . . help me," she murmured. Struggling against the disturbing visions dancing about her brain, she moaned. Someone pursued her and she tried to back away. The pain in her shoulder suddenly brought her to full consciousness.

"That I have, child. Look about you," said Merlin.

Doing as he asked, she blinked her eyes to focus. She was in a hospital room, very modern. Obviously, she was in her own time.

Merlin was dressed in blue scrubs and a white coat. His long hair was pulled back behind him, and he could have passed for any surgeon making rounds.

"Where am I?"

"Saint Luke's Memorial, near the medical center," he said.

"Saint Luke's! In Houston? You've brought me to Texas?" she gasped weakly.

He lowered his voice while he glanced furtively at the door. "Aye. The portal is not a door that only opens and closes in Scotland, miss. Think of it as a road, a means of travel that is open to but a few. Would you not have sought to find your father had I brought you to Scotland?"

"Yes. You're right, of course. I would have come here to find my father because I must. But, you told me I would have to forever stay if I decided not to meet you. So . . . why?"

He reached out to take her hand. "It was never my purpose to bring you back in time to be murdered in your bed! You must also make a reconciliation with your past, a peace with your father. Then and only then can true harmony be found with Roderic. You must return to him with no regrets, no wavering goals, but with a new strength and purpose. I did not wish for him a corpse as a wife."

"Bluster all you like, Merlin. You could not abandon me to primitive medicine, and that is the truth of it," she said with a feeble smile.

"I will not see you again, Catherine, until I come for you. You will be properly healed here, then you may visit your father. I will return for you," he said.

"Thank you, old friend," she whispered. Touching her lips with her fingertips, she blew a kiss to Merlin as he left the room. Once again she fell into a deep sleep.

"Cat? Catherine Terril?"

Opening her eyes, she saw a nurse standing over her. The woman had long, blond, curly hair. She wore a crystal around her neck, and had on brightly colored scrubs.

Cat frowned. "Sierra? Sierra Casslin? Is it really you?"

The woman smiled. "The one and only. I haven't seen you since high school. Your family has been told you're missing, and from all accounts they thought you were dead! You've been in the news a lot. There was foul play on that movie set, according to the paper. The article said it would give the film a lot of negative publicity because one of their stunt people disappeared. What happened to you?"

"It's a long story," she whispered.

"No doubt. But it's not as if you're going anywhere," Sierra said.

"I don't want to talk about it now."

"Well, it's understandable. Being stabbed is not a great memory. You should speak to the police and file a report about who did this to you, but I know you're weak. For now, just concentrate on getting well."

"Thank you," Cat said.

"I'll bet you didn't expect me to go into nursing." She grinned.

"No. Too establishment. Too PC. Now, if you ran the first hippie commune since the sixties . . . that would make sense," Cat said.

"True. I've always gone my own way, but I love this job! There's nothing like caring for people; watching them get well and walk out of here."

Cat smiled and nodded.

"Cat, they have you listed as a Jane Doe. We found no identification, and we need to let people know you're alive and well, especially your family."

"Sierra, hold off on that a bit, please? Can you give me a chance to face everyone? I'm not up to the press."

"How about your father?"

"I don't want him to see me like this. My head is so sick and cloudy," Cat said.

"You have a bit of a concussion. It can be that way for a while. If you think it's best, and the doctor agrees, I'll do it your way for now. But eventually, we'll have to let them know who you really are," Sierra said.

"I know, but allow me a little time. If you must speak to the authorities, can you tell them I can't remember, that I have amnesia?"

"I suppose it's as good a story as any," Sierra said.

The pain in Cat's shoulder eased after three days. Both relieved and full of dread to be back in her own time, she was still confused.

There were times she didn't answer to her own name.

She had become Catherine Montwain and had immersed herself body and soul in the role of being Roderic's wife.

Time and again the events of her rescue came to her and she was thankful to Merlin. Time travel was a huge mystery that he had been unwilling to share, but he saved her life when it was in danger. Cat took comfort in the modern hospital, and the care she was receiving. Glyniss could have wrapped and cared for her shoulder with skill, but here she was also given antibiotics. Thankful for the drugs, she was confident they would speed her recovery.

She missed them all, especially Roderic, and felt an overwhelming desire to return to the excitement of the life she had left behind, in spite of all the modern conveniences she would miss. Cat would stay long enough to arrange her affairs and see her father. When Merlin came for her, she would leave it all behind.

Regardless of the outcome of the siege, she wanted to be with her husband. Roderic was the only man she had ever loved, and she would rather spend a small bit of time with him, than a lifetime with one who could only be a poor substitute. Merlin would have his way after all. She would follow her heart.

On the fifth day she was sitting up in a chair when Sierra bustled into her room. She fetched Cat some water to swallow her medication, then tidied the area.

"I don't feel I need this any more," Cat said.

Sierra shrugged. "It's for pain. I'll leave it here by the bed in case you change your mind. Did you call your father today? If all goes well, the doctor will release you in the morning."

"I know. Sierra, sit down for a moment. I must talk to you, as a professional, and as a friend," Cat said.

"Sure," Sierra replied. Glancing at her watch, she sat down. "I have a few minutes."

Cat opened her mouth to begin, then closed it. Taking a deep breath, she swallowed hard.

"What would you say to someone if they told you they had experienced something phenomenal? Something they could not explain?"

"You mean like a UFO?"

"Similar. Oh, this is going to be more difficult than I imagined. You know the theories about traveling through time and space? What would you say to someone who said they had traveled back in time?"

Sierra smiled and folded her arms. "My first thought would be that we have a whole wing of this hospital for people who have those kind of notions."

Cat's expression was not one of amusement.

"You're serious," Sierra said. Studying her patient, her demeanor changed to one of curiosity. Cat nodded.

"Then, I'd like to hear all about it. So much of life is a mystery. Many things can't be explained. I've witnessed medical miracles."

"This isn't one of those. You see, I . . . traveled back in time. I lived in the early thirteenth century in Scotland."

Sierra's expression was concerned and curious. "When you were missing?"

Cat understood the skepticism, still, she went on. "Yes. I was in Scotland working on that film. I traveled back in time through one of the castle doors. I married there, Sierra. I fell in love with my husband, and we even adopted a child together. I'll go back there when I'm well, but I want you to do some things for me. I'll pay you with money in a savings account. My father is ill with cancer, and I want you to take care of him at home when he's finished with his cancer treatments."

"That's where I've seen him! He gets his treatments at the cancer center, doesn't he?"

Cat nodded. "I'm sure. You see, we've never discussed his disease. I found out through other means."

Sierra stood. "And what with starring in movies, and going back in time to fall in love with 'Braveheart', you haven't had the time?"

"I didn't star in movies! I was a stunt-woman, and my husband was an English knight, not a Scotsman," Cat said.

"Even better! A knight in shining armor," Sierra said, barely containing her laughter.

"I know how it sounds! Far fetched?"

"It sounds worse than that, sweetcakes. It sounds like

you've gone over the hill from far fetched right into the valley of 'Wacky USA'."

"Listen , I want you to go with me to the bank when I'm well. I want you to have everything. All the money in exchange for taking care of my father. Why would I give everything away if I could use it where I'm going? Think about it. I need to go home to the ranch when I'm released tomorrow. Come and see me, and we'll talk about it again."

Sierra helped Cat lie down. "You poor thing. You really believe this happened to you."

"I'm very serious, Sierra, and I need your help. Please, say you'll come to the ranch as soon as you can! Promise me!"

"All right, all right, calm down. Take this pill now," she said. Sierra handed it to Cat, then tried to bring the glass to her lips.

"I promise. Just swallow this and rest," Sierra said.

Cat heaved a sigh of relief as she took the pill, and allowed Sierra to bundle her back to her bed. She would trust her to come.

Cat's return home was much more complicated than she anticipated. Her shoulder was much better, she felt capable of driving, so she rented a car and made the trip herself. It was a long, tedious journey, and she was relieved to see the house.

Her father looked thin. He moved slowly down the

steps from the porch, exhibiting an unexpected anger as he watched her exit the car.

"Where in goddamn hell have you been? A nurse from Saint Luke's called. She said you've been there a week and didn't call me! How the hell did you get stabbed?" He glanced at the sling she wore.

The hurt little girl inside responded in kind. "Welcome home to you, too, Dad. It was an accident with one of the stunts."

She hated lying to her father, but there was no way she could explain to him that she had traveled through time. Howard was pragmatic in nature, not given to an open mind about things he did not understand.

"That's not what your boss told me. He said you disappeared two months ago, and he hasn't seen hide nor hair of you! You care to stop lying to me, Cat?"

Cat knew his bark had little bite. "What does it matter now? I'm home. You've been keeping secrets yourself lately, haven't you, Dad? If you don't mind, I'd like to continue this conversation when I'm not so tired. The Houston traffic hasn't improved, I should take a pill for my shoulder, and I'm hot, sweaty, and tired. I need a shower and some rest before you light into me."

Her father, once a robust man, seemed to shrink visibly. Thin, pale, and haggard, his body gave evidence of the disease. Putting his arms around Cat, he held her close.

"Thank the good Lord you're all right. I thought you

might be kidnapped or worse, baby girl."

"Oh, Daddy." She held on tightly, and cried. Traveling back with Merlin had been worth it. The pain she had suffered from her injuries paled in the joy of seeing her father again.

Cat lay in her bed, having slept several hours of the afternoon away. She wanted to be with her dad as much as possible, although she planned to give as little information as possible concerning her disappearance.

Sierra was an efficient nurse, had done hospice work, and she trusted her. Sierra was also feisty, and would take none of Howard's guff. Cat wanted to make arrangements for her father to have the best health care available. Merlin had implied that she must go back with a new purpose, and therefore she must first be here for her father until the end.

That evening Cat strolled out to the barn to find her father with the horses. Acknowledging her with a nod, he went on with his work, slipping a bridle on the horse.

"Dad, why didn't you tell me about the cancer?"

Sighing heavily, he stood silent for a moment, staring off at nothing.

"I would have come right home. You know that," she said.

"You had your job. It made you happy. What was I suppose to do? Ask you to come home to listen to me whine, and sit by my bedside?" He spoke angrily.

"You've never whined in your life! What's wrong with family taking care of one another? That's what I'm here for! I can hire a nurse. There are treatments . . ."

"I've had all I can stand! I'm not going back. I won't spend my last days on this earth puking with my hair falling out when it won't do any good anyway!"

Cat turned away, tears running down her cheeks. Her father patted her shoulder awkwardly. Tears and emotions embarrassed him, still he offered comfort.

"Don't cry, baby. I've lived my life just as I pleased. Hell, they even give me the pain pills I need close to the end. I've known it was terminal for months since they told me it had spread to the liver and kidneys. You're going to think I'm crazy, but I feel a peace inside, especially now I know you're home safe. I read once that when Gary Cooper was dying of cancer, he spoke of it to a friend who was in the same boat. 'Bet I beat you to the barn' he said. Now I know how he felt. It won't be long until I'll be joining your mother."

Cat threw her arms around him.

"One thing I've always appreciated about you was I never had to baby you. Even when I wanted to, you would have none of it. You were as tough as an Appaloosa pony. Well, I'm glad for it now. I need you to be strong."

Cat stepped back and swiped the tears from her face.

"I know, Dad. I know."

Chapter Twenty-four

*For I was my father's son, tender and only beloved
in the sight of my mother.*

~Proverbs 4:3

Sierra came to the ranch three days later. Cat's shoulder still gave her minor pain, but she was already on horseback. "Take a ride with me. We need to talk, but in private."

"Sorry. I don't do horses." Sierra smiled.

"How about pick-up trucks? Do you 'do' them?"

"Sure," Sierra said.

As they walked to the flat-bed pick-up truck, Sierra, always mindful of Cat's injury, offered to drive. "Won't your father need his truck?"

"He sticks close to the house these days," Cat said, her eyes taking on a sadness as she glanced forward.

Sierra drove as Cat directed, and they stopped after twenty minutes by a cluster of trees. Parking the truck in the shade, Sierra waited patiently. Cat sat silently drinking in the beauty of her surroundings. She had ridden here by the pond countless times as a child.

Sierra broke the silence. "Your lawyer called me. He said he wants me to sign some papers about my being the recipient of quite a bit of money. What's that about?"

"I told you. I want you to take care of my father."

"I've done hospice work before, but the amount is a lot more than my salary. Besides, why don't you take care of him?"

"I plan to be here as long as needed. But then I'll be leaving, and I can't use the money where I'm going. Someone might as well have use of it."

Sierra folded her hands in her lap, and smiled. "Oh, that's right, Scotty may beam you up at any moment."

Cat did not take the bait. "Something like that. After your fee is paid, plus a bonus, I want the remaining funds and the swords in my collection to be given to David Sellinger. He's my old boss. See he gets it, would you, Sierra? But don't contact him until I've disappeared again."

"Catherine Terril, may I ask why you decided to pick me to tell this outrageous, cock and bull . . . ?"

Cat interrupted. "It's not a lie. This is not a story. I will be leaving, and I want my affairs arranged. Have you asked yourself why I would do this if I could use the money where I'm going?"

Sierra sat and studied Cat for a full minute. "Oh my God, you're leaving all right. You're giving up on life. Cat, don't even think this way. Other people lose a parent. You go on. You can handle it."

"Sierra, calm down. I am not suicidal. I'm going back to my husband."

Sierra quirked an eyebrow. "You never did answer. Why me?"

"You aren't the average nurse. You have a good sense of humor, but you're tough. You'd be good for Dad, especially at the end."

"I understand about your father. Why am I the only one you've told about the time traveling?"

"Let's just say you have an eccentric reputation." Cat smiled.

"True. If I ever told anyone this, they'd think I'd finally flipped and dropped acid. I'll do the hospice job for your dad. If you want to arrange a payment now, that's up to you. It'll be impossible to know at this point how much care your father will need, so I'll do as you ask. Privately, I think you'll need to keep your money. For mental health care."

Cat said no more on the drive back to the house. Her lawyer could handle the rest.

Sierra began her job of home care slowly and carefully. Howard was not one to accept the arrangement gracefully. He raged at Cat, in particular, for wasting her money.

Sierra stood patiently listening to the exchange, then put her hands on her hips.

"Listen, old man, I am not your daughter! I will not put up with being bullied! So, bluster all you want, you aren't ruining this job for me!"

Howard stared her down with cold blue eyes. "Is that what you call a 'bedside manner'?"

"It's the best you're going to get until you stop being rude!"

He stalked out of the house. Sierra smiled at Cat.

"Round one to me," Sierra said with a wink.

Cat continued to pace her recovery by taking more time to rest. She rode with Howard in the mornings, and her heart wrenched when she saw him climb on a horse in spite of the pain. He spoke of many things: the past, his love for her mother. Just as often he said nothing, but Cat savored every moment with him.

Evenings were hard for Howard; the pain medication made him drowsy. If she were with him, he wouldn't take the pills unless Sierra bullied him.

"He doesn't want you to see him in this weakened state. He's always been the strong one, and it's also this macho creed he's believed in. That's why he suffers it in the mornings, to be with you. If you absent yourself for a while after supper every night, I know I can wear him down and get him to take the meds."

As a result of that conversation, Cat kept to herself every night after supper. She checked out books at the library, and looked up information on the Internet. Sitting in front of

Howard's computer one evening, she patiently waited to download an article about natural healing. Her father's computer was old, and the modem was slow. Intent on her work, she didn't hear Sierra enter the den.

"How's the shoulder?"

Cat jumped. "You startled me! It's not giving me too much trouble. I've gone all day with only a couple of aspirin."

Sierra sat down in a chair by Howard's desk. "Cat, have you ever heard of post traumatic stress syndrome?"

"Yes. I have. Why?"

"You may have a misconception about it. It can affect not only war veterans. It also can be a problem for those who have experienced a severe trauma, such as being attacked, raped, or stabbed."

Cat stopped reading. Her black lashes fluttered as she stared at Sierra, contemplating her friend's statement. "You think I have a post traumatic stress disorder?"

"It's possible. Our mind and memory can block out harsh experiences. Children do it when they're abused. They transport themselves to another world."

The compassion in the other woman's eyes moved Cat. Sierra was professional as a nurse, yet there was nothing clinical or cold in her emotions. She cared deeply about her patients.

"I understand you're concerned, Sierra, but . . ."

"You have never spoken to anyone about your attack, not even the police. Is it because you can't face what really happened?"

"No, it's because this happened in the year 1230. If you think the Houston PD wouldn't find that strange, may I remind you of your own reaction when I tried to tell you the truth? One particular remark about my being 'beamed up' comes to mind."

Sierra smiled wickedly. "Sorry, it slipped out."

Her expression all at once became professionally somber. "I'm worried about you."

"I know," Cat said.

"If you want to start seeing a shrink, I know a couple. They're not boring, I promise. They have open minds."

"That's not necessary," Cat said.

"One of the doctors was raised by a couple of hippies just like me who rebelled by going 'establishment' and becoming a psychologist. You'd like him. He may even swallow the Medieval thing without laughing out loud."

"Sierra, no."

Sighing, Sierra stood. "You're as stubborn as your old man. By the way, your boss, the stunt coordinator, called. He's coming to see you."

"What! When did he call?"

"Yesterday."

"And you're just now telling me?"

"I'm a hospice home care nurse. I get paid to cook meals for your father and see to his medication. I am not your personal secretary, Lady MacBraveheart."

Cat narrowed her eyes at the ridiculous title.

"Well, what did he say? Did you tell him I was fine and there's no need for him to come?"

"You can't hide from your friends, Cat. He's going to want some answers, and I don't blame him. His entire company was questioned by the authorities because they were some of the last few people to see you unharmed."

"Oh, no," Cat said, closing her eyes.

"Of course, if you want to call him yourself, you can. The number's on that yellow pad in the desk drawer."

Cat retrieved the pad and walked to the door. "I'll call him from my room."

Sierra watched as Cat left the room and mounted the stairs. She ambled around the desk and sat down, listening intently to the sound of Cat's footsteps climbing. Not wanting to get caught snooping, Sierra waited a bit, then began to read the information Cat had downloaded from the net, and shook her head. It seemed Cat was increasingly unable to recognize fantasies as delusions.

Picking up the sheet, she studied it. It was research materials about Medieval history concerning the Scottish clans, herbal remedies, and healing plants indigenous to the Scottish Highlands.

Chapter Twenty-five

The heart of him that hath understanding,
seeketh knowledge.

~Proverbs 15:14

S ierra returned to her apartment and went to bed
early. Needing to move a few more of her things to
Mr. Terril's ranch in the morning, she set her alarm
for five-thirty. She'd been sleeping for a half an hour when
she suddenly felt a movement on the bed as if someone sat on
it. Thinking it might be her cat, she turned on the lamp, then
pulled up her black satin sleep mask.

"Holy shit!"

"Be at ease, lass. I mean you no harm," he said.

Sierra bumped her funny bone when she scrambled off
the bed, moving away from the man on her bed. Sitting on
the floor, she breathed deeply, agitated, and rubbed her eyes,
staring hard at the intruder.

The man was dressed as a Medieval knight, in deep blue
and gold. The costume was regal, as if he just stepped off a

film set. He had long, white, flowing hair and blue eyes.

Sierra stood up, holding the blanket in front of her, trembling with fear. "I'll tell you right now, if you mean to rob me, my rings are all cubic zirconia!"

Shuffling over to the phone by the nightstand, she stepped away from it when he rose.

"I do not mean to harm you; do not fear me."

"Then what the hell are you doing in my bedroom?"

"I must speak with you, Lady Casslin," he said.

"I'm suppose to be impressed you know my name? You can find that information on the Internet! What are you? Some kind of stalker?"

"Nay, lady. I seek not to harm you, or to rob you."

"That's right you're not! Because I'm calling the police!" Trotting over to the phone, she picked it up.

"I shall be gone before they arrive," he said. He spoke calmly, as if certain of an escape plan. When he came toward her, she saw that he held a sword.

She brandished the phone receiver, shaking it in his direction. "You say you mean no harm, but you brought a weapon?"

"I beg of you, lady, but a moment of your time and I will be on my way."

"In some kind of hurry? Have to make the supper show at one of those restaurant stunt shows where they make you eat with your fingers?"

"Nay, I wish to speak with you about Catherine," he said.

"Cat! Oh, Lord, she paid you. That's it, right? You're an actor!"

"Nay, lady, this is no jest. And you will listen!" He stalked toward Sierra, and she decided very quickly to humor him before she started to scream the rafters down. Dropping the phone, she put out her hand as if to keep a distance between them. "That's far enough, Grandpa! Just say your little piece at a safe distance!"

Sierra was already regretting that she had not called 911 when she had the chance. He came closer, and she reached out to touch his chest, testing to see if she was seeing things.

He smiled. "Do you think I am your mind's fabrication?"

She shrugged. "I've had some pretty crazy dreams in my time, but they were after too much tequila. I was sober when I went to bed, and I'll give Cat hell for this. How did you get in here? At the very least, this is breaking and entering."

"I have my ways, and you will find nothing disturbed. Do not berate Catherine. She knows nothing about my coming here. Catherine will have need of your assistance. I wish to beseech you to give it."

"In what way?"

"Your knowledge as a healer is vast, indeed. Catherine must find answers, and will seek out tools for her journey. I ask that you help her find them."

"Okay, okay. I'll do what you ask. Just leave. If Cat needs my help, she has it anyway. You didn't have to scare me like this."

"Your fears, lady, are your own crop, planted and watered by a falsely assumed threat. I have no need to frighten you. You would be wise to remember that Catherine tells you no lies, and she needs your help." He pulled something small from beneath his robes.

"This, I believe, belongs to you," he said.

He put the object in her hand, and when Sierra bent down briefly to examine it, he walked toward the wall.

"Wait, you can't go out that way."

Blinking, she saw the mist, and he literally disappeared before her eyes. Running to the other room, she checked to see that both doors were locked. Her heart pounded when she came back to bed and sat down. How did he leave the building?

Snatching up the phone, she dialed Cat. It was late and the machine picked up.

"Cat, this is Sierra. Meet me first thing in the morning at that fifties-style diner off the freeway by Mullins. We have to talk."

Cat was a few minutes late, and Sierra was already seated when she arrived. She sat down and gave her order, then looked across at Sierra. Her face was pale, and she sat holding a snow globe.

"What did you need to talk about? You sounded upset

on the phone."

"And you have no idea why I would be upset?"

"Of course not, why would I?"

"You're in trouble with me, lady. Sending that crazy knight to scare the hell out of me in the middle of the night?"

"Sierra, I don't know what you're talking about. Tell me what happened."

Sierra reached out and put a pretty Victorian snow globe on the table. "Do you know what this is?"

"It's a snow globe. It's beautiful," Cat said.

"No, that's not what I mean. He gave this to me last night, Cat. This is a unique snow globe. It's part of my collection. Most of them have unicorns and such in them. But this one was given to me by my grandmother. I dropped it accidentally while I was cleaning the cabinet two weeks ago, and broke it. Look, it still has the initials my grandmother let me paint on it with pink nail polish. It's the same globe."

She turned the musical snow globe upside down, and there by the wind-up key was an 's c'. Cat's eyes began to gleam.

"Sir Raven came to you, then?"

"If that's what he calls himself," Sierra hissed angrily. "I thought he'd broken in to rob me, and it scared a few years off my life!"

"I'm sorry, Sierra. But please believe me, I did not set this up." Cat shook her head. "I haven't seen Sir Raven in weeks."

"He told me that you would need my help." Turning the snow globe over, she set it down carefully. Cat looked at

Sierra with a triumphant spark in her stare.

"I have no explanation for this, Cat."

"Of course you don't, because your mind doesn't want to accept that time travel is possible. I understand, Sierra. I went through the same thing when he first took me back in time. He's the one that told me Dad was ill. He brought me a newspaper clipping about his death, *from the future*."

"So, this really happened to you. And you got married while you were in Scotland?"

"Yes, I did. We adopted a baby girl. Her mother died. She was so beautiful, Sierra. So, you see, I left a family behind." Keeping her voice in a low whisper, she explained how she married Roderic, and how she was injured.

"Did you see who attacked you?"

"No, it was too dark, and I was fighting to stay alive. But Sir Raven knows his identity, and we'll go back to expose him when we can. I needed this time to heal, and to see Dad again. But I miss Roderic desperately. I want to be with him, Sierra."

"Do you love him?"

Cat met her friend's questioning gaze with conviction. "Yes, I do. I've decided to go back when Sir Raven comes for me. That's why I needed your help with Dad. You believe me?"

Sierra took a deep breath, and exhaled slowly. "It's too detailed for it to be a story, or an illusion. Let's just say, I'm more willing to accept that this could have happened to you. What do you need of me? He said something about the fact that I'm a healer?"

Cat nodded. "You know how primitive the healing methods were in Medieval times?"

"Yes, I do. I wouldn't even call what they did to people medicine. A better word would be torture."

"True, up to a point. I've been researching on the net, and there are some methods of healing that I could perhaps adjust, and incorporate the right medications if I had them with me. I need to get some antique bottles, and crush up some basic drugs to take back with me."

Sierra shrugged. "That's easy. I know a drug salesman that is positively hot for me, and asks me out every time he visits. He comes every month on the twelfth. I'll tell you which drugs can work best on the bacteria that frequently cause infections. If you meet me at the hospital, I'll figure something out so you can get the drugs."

"That's next week! That's good. I love the way your devious mind works."

"It's not as if they don't give the drugs away every day to doctors. I have a lot I can tell you about some home remedies that work. For instance, I know it sounds awful and it burns like hell, but cayenne pepper will work great for clotting the blood on a minor wound."

"Speaking of that, what can be done for a woman in childbirth who has a complication of severe bleeding?"

"That depends on the severity of the blood loss. You should talk to Michael Oltmanns. He's in obstetrics, on staff at St. Lukes and one other hospital. You can also speak to an anesthesiologist. Most people don't realize that it's the anesthesiologist who makes a lot of decisions in the surgery. They see a lot of severe bleeding and complications, and are instrumental in giving orders for drugs, or a transfusion."

"Can you set up a meeting with him? I'll work around his schedule," Cat said.

Sierra nodded. "As long as it's not in the morning when he has surgery, it shouldn't be a problem. Cat, there is only so much you can learn to take back with you. In light of the fact this is such a primitive time for medical care, you still want to go back?"

"Oh, yes. I love Roderic, and I want to go back to be with him. I'm willing to accept life on those terms."

Sierra nodded. "I'll do whatever I can to help you, just say the word. I'll try to respect your decision. I know your dad is your only family, and, well, I might as well say it. He doesn't have that long."

Cat nodded. "I appreciate your help. It's a relief to know someone believes me."

"One more thing, Cat." Sierra picked up the snow globe, holding it gently, enjoying the light and iridescent colors.

"Your mystery knight with the white hair? The one who gave me this?"

"Yes? You mean Sir Raven?"

"Tell him I appreciate the gift. But if he ever shows up uninvited like that again, I am going to kick his ass!"

Chapter Twenty-six

Who can find a virtuous woman? She seeketh wool, and flax, and worketh willingly with her hands.

~Proverbs 31:13

David flew in from Los Angeles and called Cat from the Houston airport.

"You don't know how wonderful it is to hear your voice, Cat. The explanations can wait. How do you get to the homestead? I want to see you face to face. This airport is a nightmare," he said.

"You should have flown into Hobby. Houston International is always a nightmare." She gave him directions and he interrupted occasionally to double check her instructions.

After she hung up she was looking forward to seeing David again, and hoped he could forgive her for the trouble her disappearance had caused him. She still wore the sling for her shoulder, but it was improving daily. It was, however, the first thing David noticed when he stepped inside the house.

"You've been hurt!" He put his arms around her immediately. "I was afraid you were dead. Thank God, Cat. Thank God." He frowned while considering her injury. "Did I hurt you?"

"No, David, it's nothing. Come in. Let's go to my dad's office. We can have some privacy there."

Closing the door behind them, David wasted no time in venting his feelings. "You had better have a good excuse, Cat. Where the hell have you been?"

Cat had thought long and hard for an explanation that he would accept. She'd done her best to come up with a plausible lie.

"I was attacked, and they stabbed me. I fought them and we ran off the road. I came through the accident, but I had some memory problems. But, I knew I had lived in Houston, in Texas. I came home and still had severe headaches, and some complications with my arm, so I was hospitalized at St. Luke's while they ran tests. A few weeks went by, and I remembered more and more."

"But why didn't you just call me! Pick up the goddamn phone and let me know what happened! That was a closed set. How did they get past security?"

"David, I told you, I couldn't remember. It doesn't matter now."

"Well, the authorities would argue that, and so would the studio. It was bad publicity for the film. It took them two weeks of interrogation to clear me of all charges."

"You!"

He nodded grimly. "I was the last one to see you that afternoon."

"David, I'm sorry. I never meant to cause you trouble. You see, there's something else I'm dealing with right now. My father has cancer. He's dying."

David frowned, his expression compassionate. "Oh, Lord, Cat, I am so sorry."

"Thank you, but I need to spend as much time as I can with him. Do you understand?"

"Of course I do. Later, when you can, would you want to join the company again?"

"Not for a while. I need to be here."

He nodded gravely. "Is any treatment available? Chemotherapy?"

She shook her head. "He's done it all. You know the medical community here in Houston has no rival, even in LA. He's made the decision that he wants no more treatment, no more drugs. I respect his wishes. I'm just trying to savor every moment I have left with him."

David folded his arms and studied her. "You understand why I had to come and see that you were alive and well? I needed to see you, have proof. We had imagined the worst."

"Yes, I'm sure you did. But David, I can't go back to work. My place is here with Dad."

"I understand. And if you're ready by the next production date scheduled, you can always call me. We've optioned two more films from Miramax. One is a pirate film, and you're the best."

She smiled. "Thank you, David. Why don't I show you to your room upstairs? Supper is in an hour, and Dad ... well, he usually retires early because he takes pain pills. You'll have my undivided attention."

"That's great, because I need to get back to LA tomorrow." He paused. "There's something different about you, Cat. Whatever has happened has changed you."

"What do you mean?"

"In spite of this sad news about your father and the attack, you seem ... content?"

She smiled. "What would you say if I told you I've met someone?"

"You were kidnapped, and managed to meet a man? Is he a cop?"

Shaking her head, she smiled. "Not exactly, but he certainly has the authority of one. He protected me. I love him."

Chuckling, he took her hand. "It's about time. Tell me about him. When can I meet him?"

"You won't get to meet him, but he's good for me. He is the fairy tale."

David flew back to Los Angeles the following morning, and Cat had an appointment with Dr. Oltmanns, the specialist in obstetrics. They met at five o'clock in the afternoon at the hospital cafeteria.

Oltmanns was tall, very tan and fit, with friendly brown eyes. He shook her hand.

"Hello, Catherine. Sierra said you had some questions?"

"Yes, I promise not to take much of your time."

"As long as you don't mind if I eat while I talk. I may not get another chance."

"No, of course not." Cat ordered coffee; they sat down, and he began eating.

"Sierra tells me you're a stuntwoman. I assume that's how you got the injury?"

Cat wanted to avoid an explanation. "Yes."

"I'm sure that's interesting work, but why do you need to interview me?"

"Actually, I am thinking of writing a screenplay, a medical thriller, and I had some questions about complications during childbirth."

Cat took out her pen and notebook, and sipped her coffee. "What can cause severe bleeding after a delivery?"

"Well, any number of things can cause hemorrhaging. One is *abruptio placenta*, which is when the placenta tears away from the wall of the womb. Then there could also be a tear in the vagina, or the cervix. Sometimes, too, the uterus doesn't contract the way it should. That also can cause bleeding. What sort of scenario did you have in mind?"

Cat went on to describe what Meggie had experienced

before her death. "What could have been done to save her life at that point?"

The doctor took a sip of water and frowned. "In some cases a woman can lose about one pint of blood during delivery. But from what you're describing, with the severity of the bleeding, the doctor's options would be few. The body cannot handle the trauma of losing that much blood that quickly. It would be rare for a patient to bleed out like that, similar to what you're describing, but it happens."

"So, there was nothing that could have been done? Women still die in childbirth in spite of all the medical technology at our fingertips?"

"Oh, yes, and that can be the most difficult thing to accept. The more we learn, the more we realize how helpless we are." The doctor's pager went off, and he reached down to his waist to read it.

"I've got to go, I'm sorry, it's the ER."

Cat stood and shook his hand. "That's fine. Thank you for your help. I appreciate the information."

Cat walked out of the hospital and, for the first time, felt a sense of acceptance about Meggie's death. She understood that there was a strong possibility that even if Meggie had been in a modern hospital, she most likely could not have been saved.

The following week she met with the anesthesiologist Dr. Moore. He was puzzled when she asked him what was usually done for severe hemorrhaging.

"That depends. Would the patient have a reason, personal or religious, for refusing a blood transfusion?"

"No," she said.

"Then we'd give the blood, of course, but sadly, there can be complications. Sometimes the body rejects it. Sometimes, and I really hate to say it, but the blood supply can be tainted. We test for AIDS, but the test is not 100% accurate. Then there's the possibility of hepatitis."

"And if a transfusion is not possible?"

"Well, there are nonblood volume expanders, such as dextran, saline, Ringer's solution, or hetastarch. It's a way to build up the patient's strength without blood."

Cat wrote the names of the treatments in her notebook. "Have you seen this treatment used?"

He nodded. "Often. It's our only option when someone's beliefs don't allow transfusions. Interestingly, we have had good results with that treatment when we've had to use it."

Cat sat in his office at the hospital and talked to Dr. Moore for another fifteen minutes, then rose to leave. "Thank you so much, you've been a big help."

"Put in a good word for me with Sierra, and we'll call it even."

Cat smiled and winked as she shook his hand. "I'll do my best."

Cat set about acquiring antique bottles to put the drugs in, and a leather satchel to store them. On the twelfth, Sierra set up the meeting at the hospital with the drug salesman. Once Cat came home with antibiotics and drugs for pain, she spent some time with Howard. After he had retired, she went to the kitchen and crushed up the pills with a mortar and pestle.

Sierra came into the kitchen with her hand full of papers, and held them up.

"What is all this, Cat? I found your notes by the computer. And these diagrams? What is this contraption? And who are Marillier and John Harrington?"

Cat smiled and glanced up from her work. "Marillier was one of the first inventors of water closets. The diagram is a prototype, though I don't know if it can be used in a castle. John Harrington was the godson of Queen Elizabeth, and he set about making a 'necessary', for her in 1596, which was what they called them. He also made one for himself. He was an accomplished inventor, but was so ridiculed by his peers for the device, he never built another one. But the Queen is said to have used hers until her death."

Sierra chuckled. "You're going to build yourself a toilet?"

Cat shrugged. "I don't know if it's even possible with the tools in the thirteenth century, but don't knock it. It seems a fairly simple design."

"Didn't like running outside in the cold? I understand. That sounds a bit too primitive for me."

"I was much more concerned with disease. There are

some interesting suggestions on the net. An oil-based compound, or a paraffin wax will kill the insects that can spread nasty bacteria."

"I suppose you never once had a decent bath when you were there?"

"I beg your pardon! I most certainly did. It was a very large wooden tub."

"And you lugged buckets of water?"

"Nay, for Roderic's soldiers did it for me, lassie," Cat said.

"Well, excuse me, Lady of the Manor. By the way, when you use that Medieval speech, it is a bit unnerving."

Cat grinned. "I know. Why don't you help instead of harassing me. I'm making labels for these bottles."

Sierra examined them. "Where did you get these? They look as if they came out of an ancient pharmacy."

"That's because they did. I got them from one of those online auctions, and paid extra for next-day shipping. But they're perfect to transport the drugs. What do you think of calling penicillin 'healers mold'?"

Sierra picked up one of the labels. "As long as you remember which is which. So many of these pills are white. On which one of these do you want me to put 'eye of newt' and 'gnat's eyelashes'?"

"Very funny. Try to help with a little less sarcasm," Cat said.

Sierra grinned. "Sorry, I've watched one too many episodes of 'Charmed'."

"What did you think of the midwife information I downloaded?"

"It looked as if it were put there by an expert. Birthing at home is very popular. I loved it when the hospital finally got with it and started decorating their birthing rooms to look a bit more like home. Childbirth is less stressful to the mother if she doesn't feel she's in such a clinical environment."

"I also want you to show me how I could mix up a good cough medicine," Cat said.

"Don't make it too hard. Your classic hot toddy of whiskey, lemon juice, and honey will work."

"And if I can't find lemons?"

"How about apples? Were they in supply at the castle?"

"Yes! Apple juice is sweet, too, and it would cut the taste of that homemade brew. It's so strong, even the honey can't overpower it."

"You're doing your best, Cat. But you can't take the present time back with you."

"I don't plan to. Maybe Sir Raven will veto my taking anything, I don't know, but it won't hurt to try. Do you mind answering some more of my questions about nursing before you go to bed tonight?"

Sierra shook her head. "No, not at all. So, you don't have any idea when this dude will show up again? Doesn't that make you anxious? He scared me so much I was babbling."

"Not really. I'm ready to return with him. It gets harder every day to watch Dad . . . "

"Die," Sierra said. "It's just a word, Cat."

"I know, but maybe I am not ready to let go of him."

"You have to. He's ready. He told me he wants it over." Sierra spoke with a hint of compassion in her tone.

"What he wants over is his own weakness. He can't abide it. Dad's always had to have life on his terms, or none! Never mind what it does to the others who love him."

"I don't want to hurt your feelings, Cat, but it's not about you. It's about Howard, and what he wants."

"Oh, well, go ahead, don't pull any punches," Cat said, eyes narrowing.

"I never do when it concerns my patients. I believe wholeheartedly it's his call."

Cat shook her head and sighed. "I know. Your right, I'm sorry, and I'm doing my best to accept what he wants in the way of treatment. He's just so stubborn."

Sierra smiled slowly. "No, he's just an old cowboy. You love him, or you leave him alone, but you're not going to change him."

"Amen to that," Cat said.

Chapter Twenty-seven

Greater love hath no man than this, that a man may lay down his life for his friends.

~John 15:13

Roderic awakened from sleep bone weary. Though he knew it hopeless, he had spurred a search for Catherine.

"The castle held no trace of her, merely her blood in the chamber. The women have washed the stone," Nigel said.

The thought of her injury gave birth to a new rage in Roderic. Nigel bent down to whisper, his words for Roderic alone.

"The traitor was not found. We cannae go a fathom beyond the border of the castle grounds with the armies encamped so near."

Though Roderic considered his injuries minor, Glyniss hovered about him, concerned for his head. Vision blurring, he again fought nausea as Nigel went on.

"Ye may have killed him. He was wounded when he ran."

"Nay, it was not a mortal wound. Tell me where the trail of blood leads."

"As if he disappeared into the wall. A secret door?"

"Aye. Mackay would have such to provide an escape with so many enemies." His voice was a hoarse whisper. "Hold fast now, Nigel. It seems I must sleep."

A fortnight later Glyniss snapped a curt reply to Edna while they prepared the meal to break last eve's fast. Sir Roderic would not be present to eat it. The English knight, thought to be a bane, had been a blessing to the people, and Glyniss was peevish to see his state. Speaking to no one, he isolated himself in his chamber though the pain in his head had abated. It was not merely the wound.

He was forlorn in spirit and heart. His grief over the disappearance of his wife was no surprise to Glyniss, though she suspected it was a shock to the knight. A man's pride would deny the power of a mere woman to dictate their lives. Yet dictate she did, this mysterious wench who had become Lady Montwain. Glyniss did not fear her. She had tossed their lives about like a caber. One loved her or despised her, but could not ignore her.

Roderic saw that Glyniss was watching him when he awakened. Her presence gave him an odd comfort and he pondered what he had seen the night Catherine was taken from him. The old one would know. The answers he so desperately sought would lie with Sir Raven, the old knight. After saving his life, he had brought Roderic to Alexander. But when Roderic had asked his identity long ago, the old one would only answer "Sir Raven." After his childhood home had burned, Roderic had clung to him, in despair over the loss of his family. He had begged Sir Raven to stay. The man had comforted him, but was adamant about leaving him with Alexander.

"There, young warrior. Be brave, and learn to stand alone, for I, like the raven, must fly away. But fear not your destiny. I will come to you as the autumn winds, and do as I must to protect you."

Roderic knew well the debt he bore the old one. His life, his very breath would have been torn from him in the blaze of the fire that destroyed his home. Sir Raven had brought him hope. He brought him to Scotland, and a life far from the murdering Saxons.

Still, Roderic felt a deep and abiding anger. Sir Raven had taken Catherine away in a flash of unearthly light.

Roderic vowed to find her. Sir Raven came to him no less than every two summers. Be it two summers or forty, he would wait, and he would find her.

Roderic moved about with more ease the following morning.

He could not allow the army he had trained so well to be without purpose. Arranging to send a message to Kincaid, he stood ready to fight.

Gavin, his arm still bound, joined him in his chamber. "Ye gave Cameron the command," he accused.

Roderic smiled wearily, his face gray. "Your shoulder has not healed. Someone must command lest they attack before I take counsel with Kincaid, and the pain in my head is still a nuisance."

"Pain of body, or pain of spirit? Ye are beset with melancholy for the loss of that wench!"

"That wench is my wife, Gavin. I will find her."

Gavin sighed. "Alas, it may be best ye leave her from whence she came! She be a contrary, strange lass, no matter how pleasant she be to bed. Never forget, my friend. Take your comfort in a woman. Sink into their blessed softness, take the gift of their beauty, and their carnal joy, but dinnae ever give them your heart, laddie. For that is the folly of a weak mon."

As her father's illness progressed, Cat spent every day with him. The date on the newspaper Merlin had given her told her his death was imminent. He could no longer ride, and this in itself brought a harsh realization for Cat.

Howard was a man that had spent a lifetime on horseback, and it was hard to watch the disease ravage his body. The last three days Sierra put him on an intravenous drip of morphine. He was able to press a button to inject the medication if the pain was severe. Cat was grateful that at least, in this small way, he was in control.

She sat in a chair near his bed. Sierra woke her at three o'clock in the morning to say he was having trouble breathing. Cat did her best to endure the devastating last talk with her father. Gripping his hand, she struggled hard not to break down in tears. His hands had always been so strong. Now they were thin and weak.

"I love you, Dad. You know that, don't you?"

"Yes, and I love you, too. Be strong when I'm gone. I'm ready."

Cat broke down and, knowing how emotions embarrassed him, was thankful that he went to sleep. Slipping into a coma, Howard died later that night.

The funeral was not as she had expected. Howard had made all arrangements months before. Cat felt numb with pain, but was relieved his suffering was over. Sierra stayed with her for several days after the funeral.

Three weeks later, Merlin appeared. Preparing her for their departure, he gave her two days to get ready to leave. She was allowed to bring the drugs in the satchel, and Cat longed for the moment when she would once again see Roderic and the baby.

She thanked Sierra profusely for all her help, and as she

did so, Sir Raven appeared before them. It was time. He led them outside the house. It was near twilight.

"You take care of yourself, Lady Montwain," Sierra said. She turned to the old man.

"Sir Raven, visit me and tell me news of this one. But be sure and knock first, so I don't call the cops!"

"Farewell, Lady Casslin," he said.

Sierra stood and watched them disappear in a stiff wind of mist and light.

Sir Raven brought her back in the forest west of the castle. They stepped lightly, hearing the army encamped nearby. It was twilight, and the evening sun danced through the trees. He bid her to stay across a small stream while he threw up the dark hood of his robe, and seemed to disappear into the mist.

Cat lost track of time as she waited, her sword in her hand. Small sounds of the forest were a comfort. Then a tall black form appeared at her left side.

Cat pulled herself up short to silence a scream, patting her chest. "Where were you?"

"I brought you proper clothing, a gown and a robe. Be silent, for there is a council inside the Kincaid tent. Roderic speaks with the Laird, and yet . . ."

Cat interrupted. "I know. I mustn't be discovered, not yet."

Darkness had fallen; Cat stayed close to Merlin as they made their way to the meeting tent. She set the heavy satchel down. Listening to the sounds of the Kincaid army, the soft laughter and the clank of weapons in practice for war, they settled on the grass near a tall tree behind the structure. Cat hurriedly dressed in the gown, her sword hidden inside the black robe.

She drew a hasty breath when they heard the familiar tone of Roderic's voice.

"Kincaid, I know nothing of your brother's death."

"Nay, you lie. Ye killed them because she favored Alastair. The priest sent word to me from Melrose Abbey when they returned his body to rest on our land. The Mackay lass has disappeared, and is also thought dead. They upset your plans. Ye lost face with the King, so ye ordered one of your own to murder them. If it cost the death of every mon that stands with me, I will avenge my brother."

Mackay was not allowed at the council, and had wisely commissioned Kincaid to speak for them all.

"I was betrayed by Mackay. He gave me a young woman as my wife, an imposter. I was just informed of the truth not long ago. Do you think I knew of the trickery? I laud your desire for justice, and hold my own as dear. If 'tis my death you seek, so be it. But, let there be no war. The noble Scots that follow me will not die for vengeance brought against me. I lay my soul down willingly . . ."

"Ahh! No!" The harsh words came from Gavin.

"Be silent!" Roderic said. He spoke once again to Kincaid. "I'll lay my soul down willingly, if I have your word no other blood will be spilled."

"Ye speak with no authority! Ye must make this known to our council to sanction," Gavin said.

Roderic's voice, though quiet, had an ominous quality. "My warriors will obey my command."

Cat made the attempt to rise, and Merlin reached out to hold her back.

"No," she whispered. "He can't do this, Merlin, he can't."

The older man put his thin hand on her mouth. "Be silent, lady, lest you forever bury the hope of setting a trap for the traitor. The one who betrayed Roderic is not merely free, but in his council. You must not make yourself known. The man would have to kill you."

Cat knew he was right, but it did little to quell the panic she felt inside. She must get to Roderic before he turned himself over to Mackay and Kincaid. They would not hesitate to kill him. Roderic would give his life for the loyal men that followed him. Cat must sway him from being martyred.

Once again she heard her husband's voice. "Do I have your word?"

Cat held her breath as she waited for Kincaid to answer.

"Ye speak to your council. I will speak to mine. War may come with the tide of this hatred, no matter we wish it naught," Kincaid said.

Merlin pushed her aside out of sight behind the tree as

Roderic and Gavin came out of the tent. Cat raised the black cloth and peeked through the small space to gaze at Roderic. How she missed him! She longed to go to him, but Merlin was right.

"It is imperative we expose the traitor at the proper time. Maybe Roderic and I can set a trap for him. When does the King arrive?"

"Soon. 'Twas my hope he and his army had even now joined Roderic."

"What about the abandoned cottage? Can I stay there until you bring Roderic to me?"

" 'Tis no longer cast aside. Glyniss was given the cottage. I will take you there. Glyniss is a true healer and will not cause suffering. You can trust her, Catherine."

"I agree. Glyniss would sooner die herself than hurt another."

"She can be an ally to you in this conflict. Lest ye forget, you furthermore face one with your husband."

"I do not forget. I am hoping his regard for me can withstand our obstacles. The main one has been conquered. I'll never leave him again. You could help by telling him it was your decision to intervene."

"Aye, so I shall. But you, lady, should make use of the charm at a woman's hand to cool his anger."

She smiled. "Aye, I will. If I have the time before he throttles me."

Glyniss greeted Merlin with suspicion. He called himself "Sir Raven" and asked that she take a message to Roderic. Her sharp eyes went to Cat's bandage on her shoulder, and she pulled her inside, beckoning Sir Raven to follow. Shutting the door abruptly behind them, she twisted to face them, and her silver eyes pinned Cat relentlessly.

"Ye be on the mend, I see. Could ye not send a message that ye be breathin'? Sir Roderic kens ye be a corpse! Half mad himself with worry, he has torn the castle apart in a search for ye, in spite of the siege we face!"

"I know, Glyniss! I could send no message and I can trust no one at the keep." She glanced at Merlin. "Sir Raven saved my life, but the traitor is very close to Roderic. I must see him alone before he gives himself to Kincaid in ransom for the clan! We have just heard his plans."

"Aye, I have no doubt of it. The mon's spirit is crippled since he thinks ye dead! His own treasure of life be spoiled. Tell me now. Does he hold any power over your heart?"

Cat fought the tears that welled in her eyes. "Aye, Glyniss. I love him so much I have left all that I know to be with him always. If he will have me."

Glyniss let out a very unladylike snort. "Have ye he will, lass, for though ye be imposter, he would have fought Mackay, Kincaid, and verily the King himself to keep ye. He be a good mon for the clan, and he has my fealty which be no small feat, so if ye hurt him again, I'll beat ye myself!"

Cat chuckled softly. "I am certain you would, Glyniss. Maybe you would relish the deed. My husband inspires loyalty in those around him. But, we must see him alone, Sir Raven and I. He must know who the traitor is, so that we may set a trap for him. Only then can he be prepared to fight him."

"Best ye be quick, lady."

Glyniss picked up her heavy cloak. "I'll do as ye bid, and bring him back alone."

Chapter Twenty-eight

*Let him kiss me with the kisses of his mouth: for thy
love is better than wine.*

~Song of Solomon 1:2

Roderic was annoyed as Glyniss beckoned him to follow her to the buttery behind the kitchens, but he
tolerated her insistence.

"Your wife has returned, Sir Roderic. She awaits at my
cottage," she whispered fervently.

Roderic clutched her forearms, lifting her as he studied the sober expression in her gray eyes. "She is alive?" His
heart surged with joy and hope.

Glyniss nodded. "Please, she trusts no one, and bids ye
come to her alone. She knows the mon that attacked ye both
in your bed, and wants to warn ye."

Roderic thrust away from her without an answer, making his way to run through the trees. He teemed with desire
to see Catherine, touch her, secure his own belief that she
was truly unharmed. But his ardent longing was coupled

with rage for both the man that hurt her, and the one that had taken her away.

Roderic burst into the cottage, and drank in the wondrous sight of his wife sitting by the hearth. Shutting the door and approaching her in a rush, he pulled her up from the stool with such violence it tipped over. He held her in a fierce grip bringing his mouth down on hers. Cat held his cheek, wincing.

"Mind ye her injury!"

Roderic immediately stilled, gently caressing her bandage as he turned to the older man.

"Sir Raven." A virulent anger flared in his eyes before he let out a roar and attacked, grasping the man's throat.

"You! You took her from me!"

"No! Roderic, stop! He helped me!"

Roderic felt Catherine holding him, pressing herself to his back.

"Aye, I took her, puppy. Do not raise your hand to me! I fear not your rage!" Sir Raven's eyes were a piercing blue, his outrage evident.

"You best do so, old man. Did I not owe you my life, you would feel the very blade of my sword. You come into my life as you please! You take my wife!"

"As I give her to you! She would not be yours at all were it not for me!"

Roderic sucked in his breath in shock. "What say you?"

"Roderic, please, it's true. Sir Raven sent me to take

315

Brianna's place and be your bride. Don't be angry."

Roderic dropped his hand, but continued to stare into the older man's blue eyes. "Then why did you take her from me?"

"To save her life from your enemy!"

"Who?" He turned to face her. "Give me the name of the one that hurt you!"

"Roderic, I will tell you soon. We can set a trap of our own. But please, you must not despise Sir Raven."

"Hush! I need no mediator when I am the reason this one lives!" The older man faced Roderic. "Seek not your own haughty squabble with me, when there be vipers in your own keep! My loyalty need never be in question! I have fought for your shelter and peace — then, and now!"

Roderic's brown eyes were piercing, those of a warrior. "Then never take her from me! I want your vow on all you deem holy! Now and forever!"

Sir Raven, Merlin, the man of enigmatic power to travel over time, did not answer at once. He glanced at Cat. She nodded.

His blue eyes twinkled. "Aye, ye have it. If you gift this lady with respect for her strength and courage. Ye fathom not what she has given up for you. All she loves she has put aside and her spirit has no joy without you. Best you know this in grateful supplication."

Roderic circled Cat. "I thought I would never again hear you speak those words. You love me, then, little warrior?"

Cat smiled at his salutation. They made no move to stop

Sir Raven when he slipped away, going outside and closing the door.

"Aye, my lord, I love you. You are my breath, my light . . ." Her voice broke and she got no further.

Roderic kissed her with an ardent aggression, his tongue plunging into her mouth. Lifting her, he pushed her up against the wall.

Cat put her arms around his neck and met his desire with the heat of her own. He pulled at her gown, moving it up, and she wrapped her hands in his long hair and whimpered when she felt the warmth of his hands on her bare thighs.

Roderic kissed her breasts and teased the sensitive tips; the cloth of her gown became wet as he suckled. His tender thoroughness sent a flick of sensation from her belly to the wet heat between her legs, and Roderic stroked her there, then reached down to adjust his clothing only enough to free his erection.

"I want to be inside you," he said hoarsely.

She lifted her legs, and held onto his shoulders. He teased her, entering her only an inch, then licked her bottom lip slowly as if she were not desperate for him.

"Roderic, please," she gasped.

He slipped in another inch. "Is this what you want?"

She squirmed like a fish on a hook, her back moving on the wall behind her. Reaching down to grasp his hips in an attempt to pull him forward, her nails scratched his skin.

"Aye, scratch me, Catherine. It will gain you naught in

spite of your begging. Tell me you will never leave me!"

She understood then the depth of his longing, his vulnerability. He was angry still for her leaving. Her body was on fire for him, but the affection she felt was stronger than her body's need. Cat would do anything to appease him.

"Forgive me," she whispered. "I never meant to hurt you. I'll never leave you." She caressed his face, his hair. "Never."

Staring deeply into her eyes, he plunged inside her. Then he was still, buried to the hilt.

"Oh, God, you feel so good inside me," she moaned.

He kept her impaled a long moment. His eyes narrowed as he breathed deeply and rapidly.

"I wish I could beat you!"

"I know," she said.

He began to move then, no longer able to deny them both the paradise within their reach, and Cat welcomed his every thrust. She was soon plunged into a lake of fire, a physical boon to the senses that touched her soul. Her love was stronger than time, than death.

Roderic found his own release with a loud groan of possession, and he rested his forehead on the wall, his cheek next to hers.

When she had recovered enough to speak, he felt her smile. "I think you have gotten your wish to beat me, my lord. Next time, love, can you take the time to remove your breastplate?"

Roderic burst out in a rumble of laughter that shook

them both.

God above, how I love her.

Chapter Twenty-nine

For the Lord loveth judgement, and forsaketh not his saints; they are preserved forever: but the seed of the wicked shall be cut off.

~Psalms 37:28

Roderic made his way back to the castle alone. He longed to bring his wife back with him, but agreed with Sir Raven's plan to trap the traitor. The man Roderic thought to be friend, ally, and loyal to the King had betrayed them all.

Roderic was flayed by his conscience, he felt in a large way at fault for the attack on Catherine. Had Sir Raven not stolen her away, she would have been killed. Still, there were questions in his mind.

If the traitor was who Sir Raven had said, why was Catherine his prey instead of Roderic himself? Roderic would be loath to see and face the betrayer when he longed to kill him. But he agreed with Sir Raven's decree that to expose him now would be folly. He had to deal with Kincaid, and his charges, and must confront the threat in a way that would quell the possibility of war until the King arrived. Catherine had given him her pledge of love, and he was now infused with a new purpose. No longer apprehensive of Alexander's view of his marriage, he would take her away from Scotland if he must; she was truly his mate, his destiny. They would be together in spite of all hardship, for Sir Raven had chosen well.

The old time traveler paced outside the tiny cottage, unable to abide the confinement of the dwelling. Cat fretted inwardly about Glyniss, she should have returned from the keep. Roderic had been gone for over an hour. Sir Raven suddenly entered the cottage, and spoke rapidly to Cat.

"There is an army moving in the distance. 'Tis large. I must go and assess the threat. Stay inside and open this door to no one save your husband."

With that he was gone, briskly and silently. Cat barred the door in the cottage, and picked up her sword. Long minutes passed while she paced back and forth. The waiting was maddening, yet she knew she must stay. Roderic would come to her when he could.

With no warning she saw a broadax burst through the door. It plunged down again and again. Cat gripped her sword more tightly. The enemy made a hole in the heavy door, and splintered through. She watched with dread as someone reached in to lift the bar from the door.

There was no other way out of the cottage. The door opened with a loud crash and Cameron stood before her but a second before he attacked.

Cat tried to duck the blow, and though his fist missed her cheek, it landed heavily on her shoulder. Falling down to her knees, she scrambled away, and he clutched her skirt to pull her toward him. She kicked his chest, and struck him on the temple with the flat of her sword, and Cameron lunged up to grip the handle, pulling it away. Cat felt as if he had torn her arm from its socket. He wrapped his fist in her hair, dragging her closer.

Cat's mind raced as she planned a defensive move at his groin, aimed her foot, and kicked out. Cameron moved quickly, and the blow fell on his thigh instead. Suddenly, she saw Glyniss, charging Cameron like a lion, snatching his hair to rear him back. He reached behind him, grabbed her gown and shoved her to the floor.

"Sir Roderic will kill ye for this, ye viper," Glyniss hissed. Like an angry cat, she spit in his face while he lay his entire weight on her body to hold her down. He grabbed two rawhide strips hanging from his belt and tied her hands together. She tried to bite him.

Cat saw her chance and attacked from behind. She kicked him hard near his kidneys, and he groaned, but did not release Glyniss. Turning, he held Glyniss before him, her face white, his hand clutching her throat. She struggled, yanking at his meaty wrist, trying to break his hold to breathe.

"Leave her be! It's me you want, isn't it? You can't face Roderic, so you seek to hurt his woman!"

"Aye," he shouted. Standing, he threw Glyniss to the floor the way a child would throw a rag doll, then stepped over her.

Glyniss groaned when her head hit the stone. Her body went limp and very still. Cat hoped it was an effort to trick Cameron, rather than a true injury.

"Why? Why do you want to kill me?"

"Not only kill, but savor it, make it slow, watch ye suffer, all the more will he feel it! Because he loves ye, lass. And I dinnae seek merely to kill him, I want to destroy him. He cares for ye, so that be his failing; no wise mon will show his weakness to an enemy! And, aye, despise him I do. Alexander would put him above us! Above me!" He slashed his arm to his chest.

Cat backed away, trying to circle him, holding her gown out of her way with one hand. He picked up his sword, and she took a defensive stance.

"You're like a spoiled little boy! You hate him because he's everything you're not!"

Amused by her efforts to keep him at bay, he smiled. "Ah, so now ye fear me. 'Twas not so long ago ye begged so prettily to save me a beating. Ye pleaded with him, your lovely eyes full of compassion for his mercy. Yet ye see, lass, he has none."

"He does! He lessened the punishment!"

"Aye, and is thought benevolent by all these Scots who serve him. The renegades who seek a pat on the head from the King who put an English traitor above us. I prefer Mackay, one who kills or pillages with no self righteous cloak of integrity!"

He brought down his heavy sword, and Cat dodged it gracefully, turning a full circle around the small table. Then Cameron lunged, and she ducked under his arm. He knocked her to her knees, and she saw a chance to do him damage. She doubled up the fist of her right hand and hit him in the crotch with all her strength.

The big man roared in rage, and buckled, falling down hard, clutching his genitals. Cat scrambled to get away from him, but he reached out and grabbed a handful of her long hair. She screamed when he slammed her face down on the floor. Wrapping his hand tightly in her hair, he pulled her head back and rested all his weight on her.

"Get off me, you bastard!" Cat reached behind her with one hand, and grabbed for his face. She raked her nails down his forehead, and aimed for his eyes.

Panting, he strove to catch his breath, and caught her hand. He grunted when she elbowed him. "Ah, what a fighter ye be!"

He rolled off Cat when her movement again punished his groin, and she scrambled up. Using several self-defense moves, she kicked him in the leg and chest, and pushed a wooden chair on top of him, then ran for the door.

"I'll kill her!"

As she turned to look at him, she stilled completely, for he stood over Glyniss, his sword to her throat. She lay silent, her eyes closed, yet Cat could see she was still breathing.

"Don't run, or I will kill her!"

"No! I will do as you say! Just leave her be!"

Holding the sword in place, he smiled, and beckoned Cat with a brief gesture of his free hand.

"Come to me!"

Roderic spoke to Gavin as soon as he arrived at the keep. "Bring Cameron to me. I must speak with him."

Gavin left to do as Roderic bid. The King's messenger, a warrior named Robert had arrived, and arranged to speak with Roderic alone. They talked at length about the meeting with Kincaid.

"King Alexander knows of the threat ye face. He sends his greetings, Sir Roderic."

"When shall he and his men arrive?"

"Soon, but he has been delayed. He must travel first to Melrose Abbey. Sir Alec was murdered weeks ago."

"I feared as much. I sent him to the King, and had no word."

"King Alexander bid me say little of the matter. He wants to inform ye himself, and share his proof. I fear there is more amiss. The colors I wear gave me quarter as I rode through the armies of Mackay and Kincaid, but there is another army moving strong to the west."

"Did you see the colors?"

"Nay, I saw no one, but I have been in many battles. I know the sounds of many warriors when they move in a distance."

Roderic once again wrestled with an abiding fear for Catherine's safety. Sir Raven waited at the cottage with her. He had proven well his skill at taking her from harm's way and had promised fervently to move them to a safer position if anyone approached the cottage. Even so, it was with foreboding Roderic viewed the coming confrontation. Kincaid was not one to attack without proof of the wrong. But Mackay had a powerful ally in the traitor in Roderic's own camp.

"The Kincaid Laird has the respect of the King. Alexander bids you hold fast and do naught until he arrives," Robert said.

"Aye. I will do as he commands. But, there may be no time. If the armies of Mackay and Kincaid attack, will you see to the safety of the women here?"

"Sir Roderic, I fear not the wrath of these men. Kincaid is an honorable mon, a Laird well known for his integrity in matters of war. Though he is blinded by grief and Mackay's lies, he willnae be a part of a slaughter of women and children. Mayhap he will render Mackay bound until the King arrives. 'Tis his own army, his warriors that pose the threat.

They have no allegiance to Mackay. They ken the King is eager for peace with England, as his own wife is the sister of Henry. Alexander knows well the hatred many Scots bear him for that alone. He took you as his own, Sir Roderic. That, I fear, bred a hatred that has festered until the King wants an end to it."

"As do I," Roderic said.

"As do we all!" It was a gruff shout.

Roderic looked up, the sound of Cameron's voice had come from the ceiling. There, on the landing stood Cameron, Catherine at his side.

"Did ye ken to keep her from me?"

His wife was gagged, and he saw evidence of their struggle. His little warrior had fought. There was a purple bruise above her eye. Cameron held her tightly by her braid, his dagger at her throat, forcing her to walk along the landing, then down the stairs to the great hall. The King's emissary drew his sword.

"Nay, he is mine!" Roderic turned to Cameron. "I will send you to purgatory this day." His rage erupted in a hot mist before his eyes. The man in whom he had placed his trust stood before him, once again trying to hurt his wife.

"Coward!"

Cameron pushed Catherine to the floor and faced Roderic, sword drawn.

Roderic stared at the bloody scratches on Cameron's face and glared at his enemy with burning, reproachful eyes. "So, you did not take her with ease, and she a mere lass."

Cameron advanced toward him, stepping over Catherine.

"The bitch will pay for that slight. Alas, though, that pleasure will have to wait. I have longed for this day, English dog."

The man's eyes were a reflection of his hatred, stripped bare, no cloak of deceit to hide it.

" 'Tis the way of one lacking courage to nip at the heels of an enemy rather than challenge, as men of honor favor," Roderic said.

Their heavy swords came together as they circled each other. The serenity Roderic displayed while he fought for his life incensed Cameron, for he himself had never mastered the warrior's calm in the face of death.

"You did your best to bring war, in spite of my orders," Roderic said.

"Aye. Think we would lay down and have a Norman rule us like children? Able-bodied Scots, all warriors true, should be set aside while ye reap all the lands? Ye have no right to the woman, or such reward!"

"But had he bestowed the same to you, you would have had my fealty," Roderic said.

"I'll have it now, stained in your blood and braced by your bones!"

Catherine moved, moaning. Sir Robert, the King's emissary, made as if to go to her.

"Nay! Dinnae go to her. You, Sir Robert, must die with

this one. Alexander will believe it the work of the Mackay."

"The King is no fool, Cameron. Ye understand him so little, though he be part of your own blood," said Robert.

"Aye! The mon has no justice or integrity! Alexander ignored us to show pity for his pet and pay homage to Henry!" His gaze rested on Catherine. "She will pay, indeed, when ye both are dead. Think of me, English. Ponder me havin' her with your body only steps away."

Roderic strove hard to stamp down the anger the image evoked. "You wanted her dead! Why not come at me?"

"I wanted to destroy her first, for ye care for the witch. Blind to all save her charm, ye dinnae let them burn her as a heretic."

Roderic parried another thrust meant to disable him as he continued to speak.

"Tell me, Judas, why did you not try to kill her all the times you were alone with her? When you guarded her?"

"We were never alone! That cursed half-wit boy was forever underfoot. I ken he couldnae hide his fear of me did he see me kill her, no matter he cannae speak. Ye would have known."

Cat closed her eyes, trembling as she thanked God for Kenneth. His constant presence had saved her life.

On and on they struggled, muscles straining as their swords came together. Cat kept still lest Roderic be distracted. Cameron seemed to be tireless, although he went on to further inflame Roderic.

"No doubt ye ken I killed your messenger. Alec interfered, so he felt my dagger in his chest."

Roderic let out a roar and finished it. Cat was shaking inside when she watched her husband. The warrior, the knight capable of a fury born by a deep sense of justice, was a fearful sight.

Roderic saw his opening when Cameron once again stepped back, and sliced his opponent above the elbow. Cameron howled in pain, and moved in an attempt to remove the head from Roderic's shoulders. Roderic's movements were swift, full of grace and power. Ducking, he surged forward, and his sword pierced Cameron at his ribs. Roderic stood over him and stared into Cameron's eyes.

"For Alec," he whispered fiercely. Roderic placed his foot on Cameron's belly, and pulled the sword from him. Cameron slumped forward and died, eyes open, staring at nothing.

Robert removed the leather strips and gag to free the lady, helping her stand. Roderic caught Catherine in his arms when she rushed forward.

"Glyniss made her way to the cottage, and she tried to help. We must send someone to help her. She could be badly hurt."

Roderic set Sir Robert to the task, and the man left the keep immediately.

In less than an hour, Cat had Glyniss safely tucked into bed. Cat struggled, but managed to mix medicine to the healer's instructions, and Edna was especially tender and kind as she helped. Glyniss was peevish when Edna insisted she take a bit of soup, but swallowed a few sips with the potion. Finally she slept, and Cat walked downstairs to be with Roderic.

He sat on the bench across from Robert. Cat sat next to him, and tucked her head under his jaw, sighing.

"Sir Raven gave me his word he wouldn't leave you." Roderic was irritated.

"He had no choice. He went to assess the threat of the new army."

Kenneth sat down on the other side of Cat. She caressed the boy's cheek.

Gavin entered the hall. "May ye have peace, Lady Montwain. I vow this one be content to have ye back with us."

"Aye, Gavin. As am I," she said.

"I disposed of the traitor's remains," he said, glancing at Roderic.

"Aye," Roderic said.

"I would share in your joy, but we have another messenger. I think you, too, should see him, Lady Montwain."

"Bid him enter," Roderic said. They stood.

The tall man had a touch of gray sprinkled in his black hair. He had a full beard and wore the blue and yellow plaid of the Maitland colors.

"Lord and Lady Montwain. I offer ye greetings from my Laird, Robert Maitland. He commands me to speak thus. 'May ye have peace. It seems ye have a bit of trouble. I stand at your west flank; my armies number nine-hundred strong.

331

May I offer my assistance'?"

Roderic was amused by his wife's cry of joy. Cat jumped up to wrap her arms about his neck. He, too, smiled as he held her. Roderic silently thanked God, for they were granted a short reprieve from the siege. It would buy them time.

Chapter Thirty

He that covereth his sins shall not prosper: but whoso confesseth and forsaketh them shall have mercy.

~Proverbs 28:13

The King and his party arrived eleven days after Sir Robert. They came late in the evening, and were so exhausted they had retired immediately. The King had a secluded council with Roderic for an hour. Roderic did his best to reassure Cat that his trust in the King was not misplaced when he returned to their chamber.

"He commands that I go with him to meet with Kincaid at first light. He has evidence as to who killed Alastair Kincaid. The witness is one beyond reproach."

"Who is it?"

"The King would not divulge that for fear of the man's safety. His warriors surround the witness at all times. But he has assured me he wishes an end to this conflict with peace for all."

"And our marriage?"

"He has decreed his wish to speak with you. The King knows Mackay forced you to marry me, and why, and he is concerned that you were forced. He will speak to us both when this is settled with Kincaid."

The King sent his messenger to both Kincaid and Mackay, and commanded an audience. He and Roderic were gone the entire day, and into the night.

Roderic returned and wasted no time to inform Cat of Alexander's decree.

"Mackay is in exile. He has been sent from Scotland, escorted by the King's guard, and Kincaid is no longer a threat. We will meet the witness on the morrow, and you will understand."

"But, Roderic," she protested.

"Nay, fear not. All will be well, my love. You must trust Alexander."

Cat was so nervous about meeting the King, she rose early, being unable to sleep. Dressed in her best gown, a deep blue brocade, she stood with Roderic as the King came downstairs. Roderic grasped her hand.

The King was not alone. He walked into the great hall with a young woman at his side. Dressed in a brown tunic, and scapular, she also wore a black cappa and a novice's white veil.

King Alexander was a handsome man, much younger than Cat had expected. She made and awkward curtsy, and smiled at them both.

"Come, sit down, Lady Montwain; we must talk," he said.

Cat looked at Roderic apprehensively. Her husband winked at her, and he was so relaxed in his demeanor, she breathed easier. They all sat at the table in the great hall.

"Lady Montwain, I would like to present my ward, Brianna Mackay," Alexander said.

Cat gasped in shock.

The young woman had lovely green eyes, and pale skin. She shook her head slightly and raised her hand. "Nay, Brianna Mackay is dead. I will be Sister Michael once I return to Melrose Abbey, and in time I will take my vows. I dedicate my life to the Lord and take the name of Michael the Archangel. He protected me, and kept me alive when others perished."

Tears spilling from her eyes, she turned to Roderic. "I tried to warn Sir Alec, Sir Montwain. The good mon . . . he tried to help me, and he died upon my chest."

Cat reached out and took her hand.

"Are ye certain the one called Cameron is dead?" the novice asked.

"Aye, lady, he will never kill again," Roderic said.

The young woman crossed herself. "Amen," she whispered.

"I will respect your wishes in this if you are certain it is what you want, Brianna," the King said.

"Aye, I have no wish to stay here, sire."

"You needn't go to the Church. Kincaid has offered you a home with his clan, and he wishes you to return with him."

"Aye, he is very kind. But Alastair is dead, and I would-nae care to live with his memory made manifest every day. It would be a misery, and the holy sisters are gracious. I feel safe at Melrose."

"Very well. Therewith you need only send word to me if you wish to come to court. The Queen shall welcome you."

"I am very grateful, sire, but I will decline."

The King turned to Cat. "What is your name, young woman?"

"Catherine, of the house of Terrill."

"Roderic has explained that Mackay forced you to wed him. I have spoken to those of the clan. They feel you have made many sacrifices on their behalf, and wish me to pronounce no judgement upon your deception. I must therefore ask you now, do you wish to remain his wife?"

When Roderic began to speak the King silenced him with a wave of his hand.

Cat was filled with emotion as she gazed at Roderic.

"Aye, my King. It is my hope, with your blessing, I may remain Lady Montwain. Now and forever," she said, smiling.

A long moment passed while Roderic held his breath. Finally, Alexander spoke.

"So be it."

Epilogue

Roderic walked slowly through the apple orchard behind his son, and Hope. He smiled as he observed the two, one a pretty wee lass with hair the color of corn-silk, and the lad, a sturdy toddler with a bright shock of auburn hair. The two chortled, screaming in delight to run to Sir Raven.

The lass ran in circles around the older man. The old knight picked up the boy by the scruff of his neck and dangled him at arm's length. The boy burst into giggles and joyful noise. Roderic was fiendishly amused by the fact that, although Sir Raven thoroughly disregarded children, they invariably sought him out.

"If you mean to discourage him, you have not. It has been over a year, old one," Roderic said.

Sir Raven's blue eyes twinkled as he easily set the boy

337

on his feet. "I am back to bring more mischief. I fear you too content."

"Aye sir, I am that, but then you gifted me with this pleasure."

"That I did, for never will I forget the abject desolation in your young face. It was as if the fires of Gehenna had destroyed your world, and you were devoid of hope. I searched for an exceptional woman to be your mate. I wanted one cultivated in both strength and courage. I found her."

"You did, indeed. Catherine is the mother of my children, the guardian of my heart and joy, yet, still mysterious."

"Aye, give her my best wish for peace. I am but delivering a gift."

Roderic was intrigued. His brows came up as he spoke. "To whom?"

Sir Raven threw his head back and laughed. "Gavin MacLaurin. And your wife will be very interested in this parcel."

Roderic was curious as Sir Raven walked away and disappeared through the trees. Coming upon a bundle in black wool, he reached down to lift it, and stepped back on his heels, surprised. He untied the black cloth, and strands of light-colored hair confirmed his suspicions.

The lady was sleeping deeply, and she did not awaken when he held her up under her shoulders. She was lovely, a vision with soft curly hair, black lashes on her cheeks, and a full pink mouth. The children surrounded her, excited, and

Hope knelt down to touch her cheek. "Father, is she sick?"

He shook his head, and bent to hoist the lady over his shoulder. "Nay, merely sleeping. Shall we take her to Glyniss?"

"Oh, yes, she will make her well. Mama and I will help," Hope said. He smiled at his daughter. She had boasted to all to be a healer.

"She is to belong to our Gavin?"

Roderic did not miss the hint of disgruntlement. Hope was very jealous; Gavin had won her affection as a babe. Chuckling to himself, he made his way to the castle, taking the boy's hand.

He turned to Hope. "Aye."

They returned to the keep, Hope rushing to be the first to speak of the mysterious lass with the light hair.

Catherine allowed Hope to urge her forward, pulling her hand, so excited that she would see the stranger. Glyniss had been summoned, and she sat next to the young woman. Catherine let out a startled gasp when she gazed upon the woman's face.

"Sierra!"

Smiling at the old one's "gift," Roderic turned to leave the chamber and seek Gavin.

He was matchmaking again.

Author's note

The real Robert Maitland inherited not only his father's lands, but also received a charter to the lands of Lethington, near Haddington, from Sir John Gifford in the year 1354.

Miracle
in the Mist

Elizabeth Sinclair

Pediatric oncologist Dr. Steve Cameron has lost faith in himself and his professional skills. The possibility of miracles in his business seems nonexistent. Then a mysterious bag lady in Central Park talks him into taking a vacation at a cabin in the Hudson Highlands. But this isn't just any cabin. It's a gateway . . .

Village Healer Meghan Peese has been waiting for Steve, waiting to heal yet another broken spirit who has entered the magical, misty valley. This time, however, with this person, something goes terribly wrong. Meghan has fallen in love.

But Steve must leave to fulfill his destiny. And Meghan cannot leave the village with her memory intact. Besides, a destiny of her own awaits.

All they can cling to is love, faith, trust, and a . . .

Miracle In The Mist

ISBN#1932815651
Jewel Imprint: Amethyst
$6.99
December 2005

little big heart

dolores j. wilson

---

today . . .

Widowed neurologist Dr. Daniel Lucas has a comatose Jane Doe patient. The only thing he knows about her is that she was badly beaten by someone and left for dead. And that he is strangely, inexplicably drawn to her. So drawn, he allows his young son to sit by the woman's bedside and relate stories of the old west once told to him by his deceased mother.

yesterday . . .

The abandoned wife of an abusive husband, Cassie struggles to maintain the small Montana ranch she and her young son call home. When drifter Daniel Lucas comes by she hires him on, grateful for both his physical labor and the support he lends against a greedy neighbor who wants her land. And although she is still legally bound to the man who deserted her and her son, Cassie finds a   transcendent passion. A doomed passion.

today . . .

Dr. Lucas' skill finally brings his Jane Doe back into the world of the living, and her secrets are revealed. Along with a brutal ex-husband who is coming back to finish the job he started. Is Cassie doomed to suffer the same fate twice? Or is love indeed strong enough to transcend time?

ISBN#1932815414
Jewel Imprint: Amethyst
$6.99
Time-Travel
December 2005

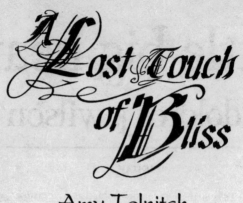

A Lost Touch of Bliss

Amy Tolnitch

Five years ago, Cain Veuxfort, Earl of Hawksdown, followed duty and broke Amice de Monceaux's heart. But now he needs her. Desperately.

For Amice has a very special talent. She is a Spirit Goddess, able to help restless souls move on. And Cain has a very restless ghost he wishes fervently would leave his castle. Anxious to regain order in his chaotic life, Cain offers Amice the one thing he's sure she can't resist; an Italian villa on the sea in exchange for her unique services.

Although Amice's wound is deep, and as fresh and painful as ever, she agrees to help her former lover. Life on the Italian coast will be the start of a new life for her. Perhaps then she will finally be able to put the past behind her as well as an importunate Highland lord who wants nothing less that her hand in marriage. But there is more going on at Castle Falcon's Craig than a simple haunting, and more than one tragic tale of unrequited love. Yet to set things right, for both the living and the dead, Cain must find the courage to shed his mask of indifference, Amice must move beyond her pain to forgive . . . and long dead, star-crossed lovers must lead them all on the path to . . . A Lost Touch of Bliss.

ISBN#1932815260
Jewel Imprint: Amethyst
$6.99
Available Now

R. GARLAND GRAY

PREDESTINED

IN AN ANCIENT REALM OF MAGIC, LOVE HAS A DESTINY OF ITS OWN

Abandoned at birth on the shores of a sacred loch, Bryna never knew her family or true heritage. She exists as a slave in the fortress of a Roman invader, her only friend an ancient, blind Druidess, Derina. Her life is bleak and without hope. And then Derina tells her she must rescue the prisoner in the dungeon.

Tynan lies naked, chained to a cold, stone slab, both body and mind tortured by the Sorcerer, evil ally of the Roman lord. The Sorcerer's purpose? To discover if this one, at last, might by the Dark Chieftain, the fulfiller of prophecy.

Even deeper in the dungeon, trapped by magical enchantment, are the faeries. They await their liberator, the one who has been prophesied.

And the Dark Chieftain awaits a destiny of his own . . . mating with the territorial goddess . . . a union that will set the land, and many lives, aright. First, however, he must gain his freedom and find her . And Bryna is on her way to the dungeon . . .

ISBN#193281552X
Jewel Imprint: Amethyst
$6.99
Available Now

CATHERINE KEAN

DANCE of DESIRE

Desperate to save her brother Rudd from being condemned as a traitor, Lady Rexana Villeaux must dance in disguise at a feast for the High Sheriff of Warringham. Her goal is to distract him so her servant can steal a damning missive from the sheriff's solar. Dressed in the gauzy costume of a desert courtesan, dancing with all the passion and sensuality in her soul, she succeeds in her mission. And, at the same time, condemns herself.

Fane Linford, the banished son of an English earl, joined Richard's crusade only to find himself a captive in a hellish eastern prison. He survived the years of torment, it's rumored, because of the love of a Saracen courtesan. The rumors are true. And when he sees Rexana dance . . .

Richard has promised Fane an English bride, yet he desires only one woman — the exotic dancer who tempted him. Then he discovers the dancer's identity. And learns her brother is in his dungeon, accused of plotting against the throne. It is more temptation than Fane can resist.

The last thing Rexana wants is marriage to the dark and brooding Sheriff of Warringham. But her brother is his prisoner, and there may be only one way to save him. Taking the greatest chance of her life, Rexana becomes the sheriff's bride. And learns that the Dance of Desire was only a beginning . . .

ISBN#193281535X
Jewel Imprint: Sapphire
$6.99
Available Now

LADY DRAGON

JEWELL MASON

2004 Romance Studio CAPA Award
Winner for Best Historical

What will a lady do to keep all she holds dear?
Lady Celeste Brystowe has very little left in the world; her
ancestral home, Ambellshire; a haunting remembrance
that threatens to destroy her life; and a dark secret she
will do anything to protect. The last thing she needs,
or wants, is a man in her life. Particularly the one man
who can unravel the fabric of deceit she has woven, and
leave her with nothing but a memory of betrayal.

What must a man do to take what is his?
Devon de Grenfeld has it all, and as liege lord of Ambellshire,
goes to accept the oath of fealty that is due him. He expected
it to be a matter easily taken care of. He did not expect to
become entangled in a web of intrigue, or to be attracted to a
young woman who, mysteriously, fights him at every turn.

Together . . .
Devon and Celeste might put the past to rest and salvage
the future. But they are caught, instead, in a clash between
love and lies that could destroy them both. And put an
end, forever, to the noble and courageous Lady Dragon.

ISBN#0974363952
Jewel Imprint: Sapphire
$6.99
Available Now

For more information

about other great titles from

Medallion Press, visit

www.medallionpress.com